Ordinary Patriots

Ordinary Patriots

Elsa Pendleton

ORDINARY PATRIOTS

Copyright © 2016 Elsa Pendleton

ISBN: 1523364394

ISBN-13: 978-1523364398

Published by COMOE Press, Livingston, Texas

As long as our planes fly overhead the skies of America are free and that's what all of us everywhere are fighting for. And that we, in a very small way, are being allowed to help keep that sky free is the most beautiful thing I have ever known.

I for one am profoundly grateful that my one talent, my only knowledge, flying, happens to be of use to my country when it is needed. That's all the luck I ever hope to have.

Cornelia Fort (1919 – 1943) first WASP pilot to die on duty

This is a work of fiction. However, some historical individuals are included, notably Father John J. Crowley, Toyo Miyatake and Ralph Palmer Merritt. They played important roles in the Owens Valley during the twentieth century. I respect them greatly and have done my best to describe them accurately.

These people made this book with me: Bob Pendleton, Laura Nathanson, and Ann Seider. Thank you for your hard work, your imagination and knowledge, your tactful critiques and your patience.

Descendants of Spencer Richardson and Molly Capshaw

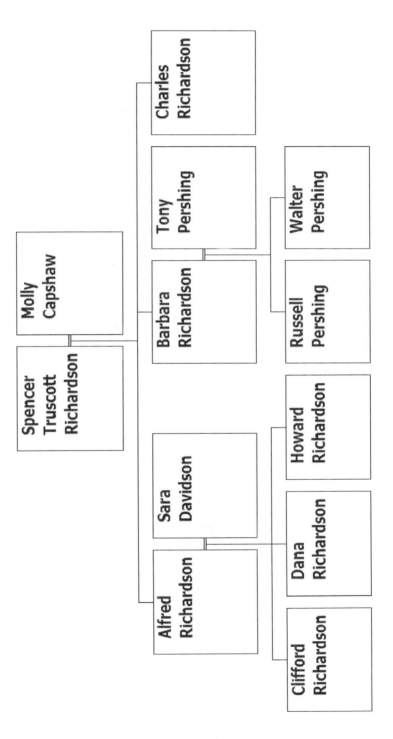

1

The Owens Valley of California lies between the Sierra Nevada to the West and the White Mountains to the East, about two hundred miles north of Los Angeles, watered by a couple of lakes and the Owens River which snakes down the valley, sometimes flooding, sometimes almost dry, its unpredictability a frequent source of despair to people in the valley. The population, mostly miners and herders and farmers, grew slowly over the years until, in 1913, the boomtown of Los Angeles acquired much of the Owens River water to irrigate its orchards and support its own population. Since then, the Owens River is little more than a scar on the ground, and the valley's population is dwindling.

Some people, though, have always relished the opportunity to live in open land. A small but dedicated number of prospectors and miners, artists and poets and dreamers, can be found running businesses in the tiny towns, or up the dirt roads and in the canyons. Those who stay a few decades probably will never leave, and their children will grow up seeing the entire bowl of the starry night sky, hearing the coyotes, smelling the sage.

Alf Richardson stood on the sidewalk in front of the Miners Cafe. *Well, times have certainly changed,* he told himself. *It used to be Molly's Place -- why'd they have to change it? And Mom would have fits about that missing apostrophe. I knew there'd be changes after all this time. I wonder what it's like inside.*

He straightened his shoulders and entered the cafe. In truth, it hadn't changed much since the days when his mother had run it. The flowered curtains at the front window were bright and freshly laundered, the menus still bore the drawings his mother's best friend had created. Probably the prices would be higher, but that was to be expected. It was, after all, 1938, almost a decade since his parents had sold the place. The Great Depression may have been less ruinous here in Owens Valley than elsewhere, but that was mostly because nobody had anything much to lose anyway.

The big table at the front was still the gathering table. Here in late morning most of the chairs were filled with men, most in jeans and flannel shirts but a few with jacket and tie. Just as Alf remembered, the conversation was lively and the volume rather high.

Alf moved over to one of the empty chairs. As he sat down, he looked across the table, seeing a familiar face. Its owner stared at Alf, then grinned.

"Am I right, You're the older Richardson son? Charles Richardson's brother? What brings you back here? Weren't you down in Pasadena?"

They shook hands. Conversation at the big table dwindled to silence. Looking around, Alf saw several more familiar faces, all turned to watch him.

"You're right. I'm Alf. I'm up here for a few days on a kind of prospecting trip a bit farther North. Thought I'd stop in and see what was going on up here. You're the man my brother Charles worked for, right? Owned the gas station?"

Joe Magnusen grinned. "I could see you try to figure out did you remember me," he said. "Yep, I taught Charles about cars, and look what it got me. I lost him when he found out about airplanes."

"Been a lot of changes here, everywhere. I remember most of you. At least your faces seem familiar. "

A low murmur ran around the table. Then Magnusen spoke up:

"I don't know, son. The last time somebody showed up here from out of town on a prospecting trip, we ended up losing our river."

Alf nodded. "I saw the Owens River, or what was left of it, as I was coming into town. Not much there. Looks like some of the farmers have left, too. "

Everyone began to speak at once, telling the stories of the failed farms, the lost savings. They talked about their unsuccessful efforts to take back some of the water rights lost when Los Angeles built its aqueduct. Finally, Alf stood up and reached into the small satchel he had carried with him.

"Just prospecting this time," he said mildly. Pulling a rock collector's bag from the satchel he spilled several handfuls of light-colored pebbles and dirt on to the remains of the morning sports pages.

"Anybody know what this is? "

They crowded around, picking up pieces, sniffing, crumbling them between their fingers, rolling them around on the paper. One man dropped a couple of rocks into the water in his glass, then poured them out onto some napkins.

"It's quartz," one man stated firmly. "Maybe not a rose quartz, but quartz just the same. Look at that shiny, glossy face."

"So what's the excitement? You can find quartz just about any place."

Alf smiled and shook his head.

"It's not quartz. It's scheelite. You probably know they're mining tungsten up on Mount Tom. It's this ore they are actually bringing up. My company, well, my boss anyway, thinks that there must be more ore bodies in this general area, so we're looking at ways to figure out how much there really might be."

"You sound just like Spence," somebody said.

"I know. I picked it up from him. Spence—my dad—and I could talk all afternoon about a piece of rock, wondering what it was good for, who would buy it, what other rocks would be in the same places. I think we were teaching ourselves some geology, except that most of the time we either didn't come up with any answers, or our answers were wrong."

Laughter.

"But now we know so much more," Alf continued. "There are tools that we can take with us into the field. And we can find traces of minerals that you wouldn't see unless you were looking for them. Take scheelite, for example. It comes from -- or actually with -- tungsten. And tungsten is just about the hardest metal we know. The Chinese knew it. Unfortunately, lots of other countries know it, like the Germans and the Russians."

"So is that why you're looking for it?" The speaker was a large, burly man wearing a battered fedora. His boots were caked with mud.

"Yep, pretty much. If we get into another war, we don't want our enemies to control our strategic minerals, and we may need all we can find to make war materials."

"So, you think there's going to be a war? What do they say down below? In the city?"

4

Alf shrugged. "Nobody knows. Or if anybody has a good guess, they're not telling. But we got a contract to go hunt, so that's what I'm doing. Anybody here a rock hound?"

Everyone knew about mines and mining along the Eastern Sierra. Grandparents would tell grandchildren about gold washing up in the creek after a storm, or about Burro Schmidt's tunnel. They talked about the men who found a thick vein of silver, carefully marked the location next to a cottonwood tree, set off to Bishop to register the claim but lost the paper with the details and their map on the way. And always the children would head out on a Spring afternoon after school and find a likely looking tree and dig and dig and dig. Sometimes they found something interesting, but mostly they came home with bug bites and sunburn.

Everybody who had grown up in the Eastern Sierra had tried prospecting like that. If they didn't want to dig, they took a pan to a creek and sloshed water around, looking for gold flecks. It was a pleasant way to spend a Spring or Autumn afternoon, when it wasn't so hot that the creek water itself felt warm against your legs. Nobody ever got rich prospecting locally, or even felt lucky enough to stake a claim, but everybody knew about a friend of a friend, or somebody's uncle or a cousin who claimed to have found a good vein of ore.

The men at the big table crowded around Alf, discussing the possibilities of locating new sites for tungsten mines. Scheelite, molybdenum and tungsten were major subjects of conversation. The relative merits of sinking exploratory mineshafts versus more major excavations of potential sites were reviewed; this had been a favorite conversation topic for many years running. The big mine at Pine Creek, so high up in the Sierra that it was next to impossible to reach in the winter, served as an example of mines that cost more to get the ore out than the ore was worth.

"Until the prices go up again, of course," somebody said.

"Which they won't," Magnusen responded gloomily. "With all this war talk, nobody wants to take any risks."

"Nobody's going to want to depend on China for war materials. Right, Alf?"

"That's what has brought me up here," Alf replied. He had a quick, vivid memory from childhood of crouching under the big table listening to the endless repetitions of opinions on politics and ranching and the weather.

He collected a few names and addresses. Everybody knew that mining was extraordinarily chancy. Guess wrong on the quality of the ore, or suffer a tunnel collapse, or simply fail to acquire enough money for buildings and equipment, and you were done for. Might as well go back to Minnesota or someplace. Only the possibility that a spectacular ore strike could bring great wealth -- life-changing wealth -- enticed men into the business.

Gold was easiest to bet on, if you were a gambler on minerals. All you had to do was make sure you had found a rich enough source of ore. The Eastern Sierra and the Owens Valley were rich in minerals; but while some were highly sought-after, some just weren't interesting. To make things complicated, some of the uninteresting minerals brought prices nearly as high as gold. And some of the well-known minerals just slogged along with buyers and prices which seemed not to change for any reason.

In the case of tungsten steel, Alf thought, the really interesting part was deciding what could be built with it. The most durable material known, it was an obvious choice for the hull of a ship, the chassis of a tank, maybe even the fuselage of a large airplane—unless it was too heavy. Was it too heavy? He followed the rest of the men out into the sunshine and headed for his truck.

Whenever Alf visited the Owens Valley, he stayed with his sister in Manzanar. Barbara had spent most of her working life in the apple orchards there. She had started as a teenager, helping out wherever she was needed, and had become expert in growing, processing and writing about the fruit which had a reputation as some of the tastiest and sturdiest apple varieties in the West.

Barbara and Tony and their boys lived in a small house with a large porch at the end of a somewhat rocky dirt road. The house was surrounded by apple trees. Now, at the end of summer, the trees were heavy with fruit and the air smelled faintly like applesauce. Just as Alf pulled up, Tony's pickup truck appeared behind him.

The back of the truck was piled with ladders, boxes and various kinds of long-handled tools. Alf recognized a couple of shovels and something that looked like giant shears.

"So are you gardening?" he asked.

"Not even a movie company tries to garden in this desert," Tony smiled. "But I guess it's kind of like that. Every now and then we have to cut down a plant, or part of a plant because it's blocking part of what they want to film. Crazy. What are you doing up here?"

"Looking around for tungsten ore. Ever seen any?" Alf pulled out his rock hound bag and tipped some scheelite into Tony's palm. "That's scheelite. When you find that, you generally find tungsten. And vice versa."

"Well. Tungsten. Did you know Len is working at the Pine Creek mine? If you ask him nicely, maybe he'll show you around. If you find him. He's up there most of the time. "

Barbara came bustling out to them, wiping her hands on her apron. "Last of the summer squash, I think. We're having squash pie for supper, and trout, of course. Hi, Alf. Good to see you."

After supper, the three sat on the front porch, enjoying the breeze, watching the buzzards circle over the foothills. Alf stretched and took a swallow of his iced tea. It was always good, he thought, to come home to Owens Valley, to find family and friends, to relax a bit far away from the city. He only wished he weren't so aware of the way everything was becoming shabby, worn, used.

"I'm probably just getting old," he murmured.

"What do you mean?" Barbara asked rather sharply.

Alf, embarrassed, replied, "I must be getting old because I didn't realize I'd talked out loud."

Barbara set her glass down with a thump.

"Alf, you're just being goofy. What were you thinking about? You'd better tell us now."

"Oh, Barbara -- I was just thinking that it's been such a long time, and nothing has changed up here. Sure we have children, and all, but here in the Valley the buildings are the same, many of the people I saw today in Pinyon Creek are people I remember from when I was a kid myself. You and Tony are doing the same work you've always done. What do you think?"

"Ah, Alf, the same people are here because where else would we go? I haven't heard of any big pots of jobs lying around, have you? And don't you see some of the same things down in the city?" She shook her head sadly, then stood up. "Well, it doesn't do any good to sit around and brood about things. I want to send some apples home with you. Come and help me pack them up."

Leaving Tony who was dozing in his chair, Alf followed his sister to the back of the house. He could smell the light sweet fragrance of the apples before he could see them. The porch was filled with boxes of fruit -- apples and pears, the latter packed in straw -- large and heavy with juice, their skins rosy.

"What are you doing with them?" he asked, already greedy for some of each.

"You must have room in your truck. Take a box of each. It's the height of the season, you know, and we are drowning in them. It's been a really good year, especially for the apples. We had a couple of hard windy times, but not as bad as last year. We've taken some to the Mission, and to the churches, and we're selling them as fast as we can pick them!"

"Who is doing all this ?"

"Just about everybody up here, I think. Of course, the orchards are officially dead and most of the old farmers are long gone. People who know about them come, from time to time, and pick some fruit to take home. Somebody who had money, they could make a pretty good business packing and shipping fruit -- you remember, that was the big selling point of Manzanar apples from the very beginning. They just didn't get bruised like other fruit. "

She selected an apple and sliced it. Alf took the first piece, then grabbed two more.

"But nobody seems to want to take it on, so we go along, picking them and selling them here in town and in our little stand out front. As long as Tony's working, it's something that keeps me busy. When the boys come back—if they want to come back here-- it might be different. "

"What do you hear from them?"

"I get letters from the boys when they send their checks home, or when something goes wrong. And then there's Charles, well, who knows what he's doing? Sometimes when I'm outdoors and I hear an airplane, I look up and wonder if maybe he's coming back. But of course, he never does—yet. I hope someday."

She began to set plates on the kitchen table. No point in talking about Charles, she knew. At least, not yet.

2

Alf had forgotten how difficult it was to reach the higher elevations of the Sierra. Standing at the bottom of the mountain where the Pine Creek road made its final connection to the valley road, he scanned the mountain wall, gray and rocky with a jagged summit line. With no trails or buildings, or even many trees, it was hard to judge the height. Only when you could see a tiny speck which turned out to be a truck, or a dot that was pointed out as a smokestack, you would become aware of how very much altitude lay between you and the mine. To make it even more daunting, the mine works themselves were virtually hidden behind a series of twists and turns of a path originally made by mule trains, and still reserved almost entirely for mules and their drivers.

Fortunately for Alf's schedule, the mine offices themselves were easily reached. He drove slowly and carefully up the gravel road. While the entrances to the tunnels lay two miles high, the offices were halfway between the mine entrance and the highway, placed so that the processes for handling ore could be monitored. His destination was just where the gravel road turned up and became dirt. He turned into the small parking lot and entered the office.

The continual traffic raised clouds of dust and he still had to shout to make himself heard. It took only a few minutes for him to explain his proposal to the smiling young man who greeted him, thrusting out a set of ear protectors and explaining in gestures how to fit them over his head. The sudden diminution of sound was a great relief.

"Do all your visitors get this good treatment?" he asked.

"For obvious reasons, we don't get many visitors -- in fact, hardly any at all. But when we heard somebody from Bishop Metalworks wanted to come, we decided to give you whatever we can provide. What would you like to see?"

It was a question Alf always hoped to hear on his travels but seldom experienced, because the culture of secrecy surrounding mines and mining was universal, ever since the first claims were entered. He explained that his company was interested in the minerals found near scheelite in this location.

"So I would like to take back some sample rock from various locations, if you'll allow me. We'll study them and maybe find some way that you can get something out of them as well. There's all kinds of new alloys being developed these days and we're getting better at using new tools."

The young man nodded.

"And while I'm up here, since it's not exactly on my route..." Alf grinned "...if I can arrange to say Hi to an old friend who I hear is working here, I'd appreciate that. Len Reyes?"

"Well, sure. In fact, he should be around here right now. He's supervising part of the road they're building. You can almost see it from here." He pulled his jacket on and led Alf outdoors.

Great clouds of dust were rolling up from the roadbed under construction. A tractor, its driver almost invisible through the mud caked on its frame, rolled back and forth pushing rocks from the path.

But most of the work was being done by mules. Alf had to smile as he watched a mule drag a thick log along a new stretch of roadway, smoothing out the surface. Other mule teams pulled wagons filled with rocks and branches cleared from the path, while one team of four waited by the side of the road. They were hitched to a double set of wagons.

"Len! Len Reyes!" the mining camp man's voice was loud, echoing off the canyon wall.

A sturdy man, his face shadowed by his wide-brimmed hat, stepped from behind a nearby building.

"Somebody to see you, Len. "

Alf grinned and shook hands. "It's been a long time, Len. Alf Richardson. Charles's older brother. Haven't seen you since we were all kids, I think."

Len moved with the same slow grace that Alf remembered, and his voice was the same -- deep and thoughtful. He was tall and sturdy, his skin dark brown, his long black hair covered by a print band.

"I guess I'm not that surprised to see you, Alf. I've been hearing that you're working with minerals. Kind of like your dad, I guess. Spence, right? What brings you up here?"

"Learning about tungsten. My boss thinks it's a good time to get smart on how to find it, how to mine it and how not to give it to possible enemy nations."

The mine representative who had been carefully listening stepped closer.

"I think," he said, "that the most important part is the last thing you just mentioned. You remember, Len, those visitors we had about a month back? There were these three men, drove up in a big sedan..."

"They were scared to death they'd get a flat or worse, and that was on the highway," Len added, grinning.

"They were all dressed up. Suits, city hats, shoes all shined up. City shoes, not boots. Neckties. We could tell they didn't have the least idea what the desert is all about."

"I take it they weren't here to make movies," Alf said.

"Nope, not at all. They wanted to know all about the mine. About our capacity, our output, the quality of the ore, the flotation process to release the tungsten. They had done their homework, that's for sure."

Len shrugged. "They want to buy tungsten. And they want to buy tungsten mines as well."

"But we didn't feel like we wanted to tell them anything. They had these really strong accents, and they kept looking at each other instead of us when we would say something. We were polite and all, and usually we like visitors, but these were different."

Alf said, "My boss said that there are German—not spies exactly, but business people who are trying to get information. Was it like that?"

"Yep, exactly. So we told our boss and he called somebody at the FBI. I didn't even know there were any FBI agents any place around, but he knows a lot of people. Pretty soon a couple of more men in suits came by, and they showed us their badges, and they were FBI agents and they were pretty interested in those guys."

Len sighed. "But you know they left when they figured out that we weren't going to tell them anything useful. So, I think the

FBI is still trying to catch up with them. They said we should call in case they ever come back. But I don't think they will." He grinned. "They hate these roads too much to want to drive on them if they don't have to."

Behind them, the mules stirred restlessly. Len shrugged into his backpack. "Want to have a muleback ride, Alf? We're headed up to our new mine head."

Alf happily climbed aboard the indicated mule named Sweetheart. It was a long pack train, perhaps twenty or more mules, some in pairs, some with large packs, others unburdened. The most unusual was a team of two each wearing special saddles. They shared the job of carrying a long iron beam destined to be added to timbers and braces which would shore up the new tunnel.

"It's something I bet you haven't ever seen before," Len called back from his place on the lead mule. "They're swivel saddles. Just wait—you'll see."

The mules were clearly familiar with the track up the side of the mountain, moving steadily along the straight paths but occasionally balking at difficult areas. At one point, Len's helper Gus came up from his place toward the rear and walked next to one of the mules, talking softly and stroking its nose, until they had passed an area where a small rock slide had deposited piles of stones and dried mud. Then he returned to his place and the procession began to pick up its pace.

The path to the mine was not only steep and rocky; it was so narrow in places that the packs carried by the mules scraped against the cliff wall.

"Next time we do this, I'm taking time to re-pack, put everything on top. Can't have nervous animals here. I keep telling them...."

"How long have you been wrangling mules, Len?"

"Maybe about six, seven years. No work back at home but this is good work for me. I like working for Pete. He's a stand-up guy. And I like the mules. He has some Indian in his family, too."

They had been climbing for almost an hour when Len called, "we've got a rest stop coming up."

The path had reached a small meadow, just large enough to safely bring the mules to a stop where they could graze on alpine plants mixed with grass. Len, Alf, and the other two packers quickly hobbled the animals, who were well accustomed to this break.

"I want you to see the swivel saddles," Len told Alf, "so for the next bit you and Sweetheart take your place behind them. Every time we use these, I think about the story your dad would tell about the dancing mules."

As quickly as they had settled, they re-assembled the pack train and started off again. Before long they had reached one of the many switchbacks. Gus came to the mule pair, leading his own mule. It was an intricately choreographed maneuver, with the mules as performers. Gus simply watched in case of trouble.

The heavy beam was balanced between the two mules. Each saddle held an end of the beam with a swivel clamp about a foot from the end.

Just before the sharp turn of the switchback, at Gus's signal, the rear mule walked past the front mule who was standing still with legs braced. The beam began to move on the mules' backs, as one passed the other. Gus chanted a string of nonsense words, his voice a calming reminder to the animals of their roles. After a few moments, the rear mule had passed the front mule and both moved forward, completing their turn around the switchback.

The procession resumed.

As they reached higher and higher into the mountains, the path itself smoothed out, with fewer hair-raising twists. Finally, after another two hours, they could see the roofs of the mine shacks, their destination.

Alf looked up at the mountain peaks still high above him. Even now, at the end of September, he could see patches of snow in protected spots of the cliffs.

"I've never been up this high," he admitted to Len.

"I used to go hunting pretty high up, but not here," Len answered. "And not often, and I never did bag anything. It's just too tough to get here."

The mine crew made short work of unpacking the mules, turning them loose in the small pasture area where a creek provided cool water and the meadow grass grew in abundance. The two men entered the mine works where Len explained to Alf how the scheelite ore was processed and transported to the main works below.

"Soon we should have the tram finished," Len said, gesturing at the scaffolding all around them. "We never could have built it before the price of ore got as high as it has. And that's why those men were here, huh? They wanted it for—what? Germany?"

"That's what they say. They say war is coming, that we'll be in it before long." Len was silent for several minutes. Then, "Heard from Charles at all?"

"No, not for several months now."

"Oh."

3

Back home in Pasadena, Alf waited until the evening, when the remains of supper had been put away and the children were in their rooms doing homework. Then he poured two cups of coffee and joined Sara at the kitchen table.

"Alf, you look exhausted," Sara said. "I knew it would be a long trip, but there was more to it than that, wasn't there?"

"It was all the people," he said. "I couldn't stay away from Molly's Place and there were all these men I remembered from when I was a kid."

"You'll have to tell your folks all about that part." Sara smiled. "But what else?"

"Oh, lots.. Barbara and Tony are still scratching a living. Their boys have joined the CCC. She is still ridiculously cheerful, picking those apples and selling them, apple by apple. He's working for the movies but that probably won't last much longer, if the movie companies decide to relocate back to Los Angeles."

"We should go see them."

"And remember Len Reyes? The Paiute? He was Charles's friend. We went to that Fandango, that Indian celebration, one time, remember? He's working for the tungsten mine. Driving mules, if you can believe that? In fact, he took me on mule back up the side of the scariest mountain I've ever seen."

He told his wife about the conversations at the mine, the German visitors and the plans for expanding the tungsten and scheelite production.

"I can see that I'll be there a lot. Not only at the mine --"

"--and no more mule rides--" Sara said.

"Well, maybe. They're about the only way to travel up there. But there are other mines in the area, and I know I'm going to have to visit all of them, and often."

Sara sighed. "We'll have to work something out. Can you stay with Barbara when you are there? Maybe this weekend we can go see them and maybe they'll have some ideas."

She brought the coffee pot to the table, poured two more cups.

"Has anybody heard anything from Charles?

"No. And everybody asks. On the other hand, *everybody* has heard from Russ and Walt. They're not shy about telling about their jobs. They are enlarging the fish hatchery and consider it too hard. Lots of rocks to carry. Buckets of water to move. Carrying large stones here and there. Not enough food. Not enough movies at night. I swear, Sara, they're as bad as our own boys with their carryings-on."

"I worry about them, Alf. Everything you're telling me makes me more sure that we're going to be in a war sooner or later, and the boys -- at least Cliff and maybe Howard too -- are going to be called up. I can't...

She blew her nose. "And now you're telling me that you're going to be traveling more. I need you at home, Alf. The children need their father to talk to them, to guide them--"

"To tell them to do their homework," Alf said. He flourished a workbook he had been examining. "If Howard can't write more clearly than this, he'll never amount to anything."

Giving her a quick pat on the shoulder, he left the room in search of Howard. Sara was well aware that he could never handle emotions.

One very good thing about living in the Eastern Sierra, Alf reflected, was that you were in your own little world. People in larger cities were already preparing for war. Draft registration was a subject on everybody's mind, so lunchtime conversations always seemed to include the draft, or draft versus enlistment, or what was going to happen, and tended to veer wildly into speculations and worries. But up in the mountains nobody seemed to think about it much.

Of course, without all the big city news, nobody even knew what was going on in Los Angeles, let alone London or Paris or even New York. He smiled to himself as he remembered Len's story about the German visitors. They might have been spies, he thought, probably were spies in fact, but he liked the way Len and his boss brought them down to size, made them just ordinary men from far away. He'd have to tell his own boss, he decided.

Spence and Molly had reluctantly moved into a small house closer to the center of Independence, where Spence could take his morning walk past the stables where some of his mules still lived. Molly, on the other hand, never visited Molly's Place; the changes to her former café simply made her sad.

"Alf says he spent a morning at Molly's Place," Molly said as she and Spence shared afternoon cookies on the front porch. "He says they call it The Miners Café now. He said he was

20

surprised to see so many familiar faces, even though he knew hardly any names. He did mention Joe Magnusen."

"And I'll bet Joe made some kind of comment about Charles. He always asks about him," Spence responded.

"Mostly I think they talked about rocks. Alf still tells everybody about going rock hounding with you and my dad." Molly picked up her watering can and dampened the vines at the edge of the porch.

"Molly, when you wet the jasmine, it starts to smell. Did you know it would do that? It's wonderful."

"It's almost too intense for me. I'm hoping that the lilacs we planted will hurry up and bloom. That's a smell I remember from when I was a wee child."

"I miss the mules, Molly. And I miss the mountains. If I ever get over this whateveritis and the doc lets me, I'd go back there. At least part-time."

"And then you'd faint again, or a mule would step on your foot. And then what would we do? Ah, Spence, we are too old for mountains. How about some ice cream?"

Their small bungalow sat at the end of a street where trees had been left to grow as they wished. The result was a canopy of branches stretching down the street past four small dwellings. Molly believed the summers were cooler under the branches, but she admitted when pressed that she was probably imagining things.

They both heard Alf's car as he approached the house, and were ready on the porch to receive the baskets of apples and the boxes of Barbara's good cooking, including soups and casseroles.

Quickly, they settled him on the porch with a bowl of Molly's ice cream and a stack of Barbara's cookies and listened to his report.

"It's nice to know that so many of our friends are still around up there," Molly said after he had finished. "But how are they doing? Are there any jobs? Any new folks moving in?

"I know people always say this about mining," Alf smiled, "but I think that if we continue to find tungsten deposits, there will be work for just about everybody for quite a while."

Spence was more interested in the mules. Alf and his father were soon side by side at the kitchen table, studying the drawings Alf made of the custom swivel saddles.

4

The boys were home! Barbara and Tony woke early, hearing the unaccustomed noises from their sons' bedrooms, thumps and yelps and the slap of pillows hitting flesh. The dogs were going crazy, scratching at doors. The cats had disappeared under the house.

At breakfast, they found themselves regarding these strangely large young men sitting across the table

"It can't be only six months ago that we saw you last," Barbara said, sliding another set of pancakes onto Russell's plate.

"And if we had food like this at the camp, we'd be even bigger," Walt said.

But the conversation sputtered and died. Clearly the boys had something serious to say. Tony, who ordinarily would do his best to avoid anything that looked as though it would become emotional, finally pushed his chair back and stood, his latest cup of coffee in his hand

"So is this something you want to tell just me, or will your mother be in on this conversation as well?"

As always, the boys were surprised that their father could sense their unease.

"It's just...we were talking...we think...." Walt stopped.

"We don't want to re-enlist, now that our first term is over."

Tony sat back down.

"You haven't been there that long, actually." he said slowly. "What's the problem? You were both so excited to join up."

"Did something happen?" Barbara asked. "What made you change your minds? And do you both feel this way?"

"The CCC's a good program," Russell said. "And we've got no big complaints about any of it. We think we're doing useful work, we have what we need, and it's great that we can send some money back home."

"The guys are great," Walt added. "In fact, that's part of the problem. It's just not us."

Tony and Barbara sat silently for a few minutes. Russell continued,

"See, when we joined up, it just sounded like a great adventure. Camp outdoors, work hard, build muscles, make useful things. We didn't really understand that for some people -- for a lot of people there—this was a lifesaver. We think we're taking places that other men could have, who need it a lot more."

"But..." Barbara said.

"It was a couple of weeks ago we started thinking and talking about this. Because they just got in a whole new group, men from down below, I think around Los Angeles or Fresno maybe. Anyway. They were so, so...raggedy."

Walt added, "One of them was saying that he hadn't slept in a real house for over a year. They were talking about sending money home, and it was money they really, really had to send. It was food money for their parents."

The brothers were stumbling over each other to tell the story.

"They were so grateful for blankets. They wondered did they have to have their own tools because they didn't have any. Sometimes in those first days you'd see them just standing there gazing around, like they didn't even know where they were."

"So we talked, Walt and I, about how we think we can get jobs right here. Can't we, dad? Maybe up in Lone Pine, or in one of the mines, or maybe helping with construction or something?"

"Because," Walt concluded, "if we leave, there will be two places for two more men and they need this work more than we do. We think."

After a moment, Barbara said, "I know you boys well. I need to ask you whether you can tell me honestly that this is the main reason you want to leave. Because I can think of several others. You always complain bitterly about getting up in the morning. And the last time we talked, you were saying that the work was hard and also boring. And I know there was at least one officer that you felt didn't like you. If you want to leave because you think it's too hard, or maybe you don't like your companions, then I think you should stay one more term. Sure, it's six months, but you can survive that."

The boys both spoke at once. "No, really," Walt protested. "We actually like—well—most of it. We know we're getting stronger. We know how to do some things we didn't know how to do before."

"Like, do your own laundry," Russell muttered, and they all chuckled.

"We are very proud that we can send money home to you each month. And that would be part of whatever job we get here, too. But at least as far as we know, you aren't going without food in between our checks."

"No," Tony told them. "We're never rich, but we have a house and wood for the winter and my truck and food to feed us all. I'd say you've made a fairly convincing case. But you would have to work just as hard here, or wherever you go."

The boys looked at each other, relieved by their father's words. Barbara found it difficult to raise the final question.

"What happens when the war starts?" she asked. "Have you thought about that? I think there really will be a war, and they are talking about a draft. You are both old enough now. How does this change things?

"I don't think anybody knows," Russell answered. "So we can't make plans that depend on how we deal with the war. We'll just have to wait and see."

"We already talked to our boss, and told him what we had been thinking. We made sure that if we leave, they'll accept two more men in our places. We explained that we know there are many men who need the money and the job more than we do. So he said, all we have to do is, when it comes time to re-enlist next week, we don't sign up, but instead we apply for discharge."

They hoped to find new jobs before Thanksgiving. Walt was able to talk Joe Magnusen into recommending him for a job in the new gas station to be opened along the highway. Russell had a much harder time deciding what he wanted to do.

Remembering Alf's previous visit, Tony had an idea.

"Russ, I think you met Len Reyes one time. He's the Paiute, friend of Charles and Alf, right? Took us up into the hills that time hunting grouse?"

"Yeah. We never did find any, and we were all pretty happy about that, I remember. Too pretty to kill."

Tony smiled. "Don't tell Len that. He was really disappointed he couldn't produce any. But I was just thinking. He is working up at the tungsten mine, at Pine Creek. He might have some ideas for you. What do you say we ride up there tomorrow, see him?"

"Can you get away?"

"There's nothing much going on right now. I might even want to pick up some work if he's got some. We should leave really early, maybe before sunup. OK?"

By the time the morning light reached the highway, Tony and Russell were well on their way. Tony's elderly truck took its time navigating the switchbacks and dodging rocks, so it was midmorning by the time they reached the office.

As Tony introduced Russell, Len stared hard at him for a few moments then nodded.

"Sure, I remember you. It's been awhile. Don't like leaving the Sierra, is that it?"

Russell reddened, realizing that Len had already heard about his experiences with the CCC.

"It's not that so much, sir," he replied. "But they didn't need me, and I wasn't learning anything new, and I need to figure out what to do with my life."

"And you think you'll figure this out in our tungsten mine?" Len shook his head.

"Well, I don't know anything about mining. Or mines. Or tungsten, except that it seems to be an important mineral. High-priced right now, anyway. So there's a lot to learn about all of this. And it is so beautiful up here."

"You didn't give the CCC much of a chance, seems to me." Len frowned. "I know you finished your required term. But most men stay on after. I wonder whether you really have a good reason for leaving. You and your brother. I wonder whether there's something you're not telling me."

"No, sir. Honestly. In fact, our Captain said we could re-enroll if we change our minds, and he would be happy to have us. But there are other men who need the jobs at the CCC more than we do."

Len stood silently for several minutes, occasionally looking carefully at Russell, then pacing a few steps. Finally he spoke.

"Lucky for you we have work you can do for us right now. I understand that you did some record keeping for the CCC at the fish hatchery."

"Yes I did. And that was really interesting. I kept lists of the different kinds of trout, and when we stocked the lakes, and which ways of carrying them were best, and how did the weather affect them—it was always surprising. I'd wonder what would be the results, and then I was almost always wrong."

"OK. I think I can convince my boss to try you out for a while, see if you are worth paying for. I've been telling him I've been running flat out, trying to keep on top of things, and I could use some help, but we hadn't come up with any good ideas. And now..."

Russell grinned. "Whatever I can do, I'll try my best, sir."

Len smiled. " Can you drive a truck?"

Russell pulled out his driver's license. He was relieved to have something to show Len.

"Dad made both of us get licenses after he found us driving up and down the roads around Kennedy Meadows."

"Then I have a job for you. If you get this done right, it might lead to more work. There's a man, Mr. Ralph Merritt. He's supposed to come up here, either get some information or tell us what information he needs. He works for the company that's thinking about buying this mine. So, we're looking for somebody to help him—drive him around, run errands, figure out what'll make him happy. I think you'll do just fine, because you don't know anything about what goes on up here, so you can't..."

"Anyway, here's the keys to Truck Three, outside. Take this truck and get to know it. If I know Tony, he's already taught you how to take care of the minor stuff. Spend the day today driving around up here. Then I want you to drive down and back up the road to town, before you take on any passengers. OK?"

Russell was quivering with excitement. "Yes, sir!"

He shot out of the office. Len and Tony watched from Len's office as Russell walked around the mine truck slowly, occasionally squatting on the dirt to peer underneath. Climbing into the cab, he readied the vehicle for his first drive.

"You did well, Tony," Len grinned as Russell honked the horn, lit the headlights and signaled left, then right. The truck bounced a bit as he found first gear. Before long, Russell was checking every likely road and path in the mine area. After several hours, including a long wait for the truck to return up the switchbacks from its first trip down to town, Len felt that he could let Russell relax.

"Russ," he called out, waving his arms to catch his attention. "Come into the office and sign some papers."

Len concluded with his first instructions.

"Tomorrow is your first full day of work. Up here, we start at seven-thirty so most men sleep up here, at least during the week."

He waved in the direction of the bunkhouses. "I expect you'll be doing the same, so wander over there before you go home tonight, check out what you want to bring up here. They'll show you a bed and all. But tomorrow the first thing I want you do is go to Bishop, so take the truck home with you.

"Mr. Merritt is coming in on the ten o'clock train. You go meet him at the railroad depot in Lone Pine. Bring him up here and then we'll see what's next."

Quick signatures to formalize employment status, a hasty good bye to Tony, and Russell was on his way.

When he got to the Lone Pine train depot the next morning the platform was empty except for one man who was sitting on a bench reading. Russell drove as close as he could and slammed on his brakes. A cloud of dust settled on the truck.

Russell ran across the platform.

"Mr. Merritt?" he called.

The man slid his reading into his travel case and stood waiting.

"I'm here to take you up to the Pine Creek mine," Russell said, slightly out of breath. "Do you have anything we should take with us? Luggage? Do you have a place to stay tonight? I'm sorry I don't know anything about your plans, but whatever I can do..."

Mr. Merritt smiled a small smile and indicated the case at his knee. "This is all, young man. I have reserved a room here for the rest of the week. I assume you can bring me down the mountain again this evening. Is it very far?"

"Not far, but pretty steep, so it takes longer than you'd think. I was surprised how well this old truck did it." He took a deep breath. "Sir."

"Well, it's an adventure. And what is your name?"

"I'm Russ Pershing, Mr. Merritt. I'm working at the mine. Actually, I just started yesterday."

"We'll be learning together, then." Was that a small sigh? Russ wondered. He liked this tall, long-legged man. It would be nice to work for him. In fact, everything connected to the Pine Creek Mine seemed interesting and appealing. But what was his job and what was he supposed to do?

"I've got to get some gas before we start up. Do you want to wait here?"

"No, no. Let me come with you. I want to see as much as possible while I'm here."

They set off. At the gas station, Russ introduced his guest to his brother and to Joe Magnusen.

Then they began the climb. By the time they reached the end of the paved road, Mr. Merritt had removed his coat and vest, substituting a lightweight jacket. They took a short break to wait off the dirt road half way up as a string of mules passed. A camera, dug from the travel case, recorded mules and their unconventional packs, as well as the increasing number of structures which lined the hillside -- braces for mine shafts, miners' housing, and, reaching tall into the sky, the reinforced pillars which would carry cable for the ore cars.

31

The two did not talk as Russ threaded his way up the switchbacks. Russ pointed to a mountain sheep much higher on the mountain side. Merritt nodded.

As they neared Pine Creek meadow, Russ eased the truck off onto the grass and pulled out two canteens, handing one to his guest.

"Fresh mountain water," Russ said. "Best there is."

Merritt took a small swallow, then a larger one, then wet his handkerchief and wiped some road dust from his face and hands.

"Good lord, son, this is amazing scenery—and an absolutely terrifying drive. You're pretty good. Did you spend a lot of time up here when you were growing up?"

"Some, but not a lot. My uncle Alf—he's a geologist—he'd bring us up here and make us go rock hounding with him. And my granddad was a mule wrangler till he got sick and had to retire. We all know mules, though."

"I see. I think. I know I have some busy times ahead of me."

5

When family and friends asked Barbara what news she had of Charles, she simply smiled. She was the only family member who knew where he was and what he was doing. He had asked her not to tell and Barbara, who had kept her younger brother's secrets ever since he had learned to speak, never wavered.

She received his occasional letters addressed to her at the address she had created for her apple orders. Even though the business was just barely alive, she had a list of faithful customers to whom she would ship fruit as it ripened. Since nobody believed that the Manzanar orchards had any kind of a future, nobody paid much attention to her activities, giving her the chance to spend her time, and the apple money, as she pleased. I could be a good spy if I wanted to be, she thought.

This morning's letter was postmarked from a town in New York State.

Dear Barbara and everybody,

I know you haven't heard from me for quite a while, but this may make up for the lack of letters. First, you must examine the envelope carefully. Can you tell that you are holding an AIR MAIL LETTER?

33

Now for the details. I had a bunch of barnstorming jobs, all very pleasant, as I moved East. Unfortunately, the work that is the most fun pays the least. I signed up with a flying club that stopped at County Fairs as we moved East. We had a chance to try new tricks, we had air races between two or three of us, sometimes we would give people rides. It was great, and we met some wonderful people. But by the time we paid our bills and divided the profits, we didn't end up with much money.

So, I got a job as an airmail pilot. They were just then figuring out how to develop their air mail service. They made some trial runs first, here in New York State, just to see what would happen. Luckily, everything seemed to work pretty well, so they kept expanding it. As you can imagine, they needed more and more pilots, more than they could just find locally.

That's when I heard about it. They liked the different kinds of work I have done, and they had a plane for me to use, so up I went -- as soon as I had passed their medical exam and showed them my licenses and all.

So, for the last couple of months I have been delivering big leather bags of mail to small post offices here and there. One of the best parts is flying in different weather, with different loads, to different cities.

The weather is different here in the East, I'm sure of it. The rain storms are different and you can feel them coming on by watching the clouds boiling up. Rain in the East, at least the parts I've seen, can sometimes be a shower as short as five minutes, or a steady all-day affair that makes puddles everywhere. I wasn't used to the rain at all. I had to buy boots.

We try to fly to a schedule. It's been hard to make schedules that are reasonable for the planes but that work out for the folks on the ground. It's still kind of chancy. Another thing is that a lot of the smaller airports have never had lights.

Do you remember when I was first working for Joe, driving his cars? The earliest cars didn't have lights or horns, so you just had to watch out for everything on the road. The good part was that there was almost never anybody else on the road, and that's the way it is with flying, still.

The other day I was heading West over some farmland that was just gorgeous – great pieces of ground were bright green, surrounded by sections of brown where crops either hadn't been sown or haven't sprouted yet.

In the middle of all this farmland there was a little village, with one street of stores and a church and a school. The children were out playing and when they heard the plane they all stopped and looked up. So, I dipped my wings to say hello. Boy, they loved it! They jumped up and down and waved – I couldn't hear them but I could see they were yelling to beat the band!

Some teachers came out so I dipped my wings again. More yelling and waving, and the teachers joined right in! As I left I could see them still watching, until they gradually turned away for other things. It was a sight I will long remember.

Love, Charles

6

Russell was pretty sure that nobody in the Owens Valley had a better job than he had, at least for the time being. Len had kept him busy for almost a month now, first escorting the company visitor, then, when Mr. Merritt returned to his San Francisco bank, working in Len's office. The office fascinated him from the very first moments he entered. At first glance, it appeared empty, with table and desk tops clear of everything except the occasional pen or perhaps a stapler or a telephone. But closer observation revealed the stacks of papers in trays on shelves hidden beneath the surface.

Even closer looks turned up photos, some framed and some curling, loose. Odd-looking rocks stacked on the floor in a corner turned out to contain fossils, and a windowpane was decorated with a colorful yarn weaving. The walls were empty of decoration except for the space above Len's desk chair, where Russell could see several framed certificates indicating Len's awards from mining engineering classes ("impresses visitors who don't believe an Indian can read," Len said).

His first major project was to create an address book. At first it seemed easy, because everybody knew everybody else, just about, in the Owens Valley. But Len wanted to list lots of people:

managers at other tungsten mines, managers at other, non-tungsten mines, store keepers and suppliers of construction equipment, mule wranglers, ministers and preachers and priests ("Father Crowley. Make sure we can reach Father Crowley if we need him."), schools the children attended, which reminded him that he didn't know who might have a list of all of the employees, their wives and children and the families' addresses.

Russell spent one exhausting day just going from house to house to house in Pine Creek, before somebody thought to tell him that the family homes were scattered through the canyons and sometimes in the surrounding communities. This encouraged him to make a map of the workers' homes, which took him another two days, with plenty of help from Len.

By the time the employee census was complete, Russell had spent his first month at the tungsten mine. Mr. Merritt was due back any day, so Russell and Len arranged a packet of papers for him to see. Most were in response to questions he had asked on his first visit.

"I like the way you have listed the really important subjects first," Len told Russell. "And I think we agree that the listing of employees and the maps are the most important things you've counted so far."

Russell grinned. "I have a lot more ideas. What do you think about a list of major pieces of equipment? If Mr. Merritt is working for a big company, and that company wants to know how much investment they have here in the mountains, they should know we have buildings and tractors and wagons and the buckets for hauling ore down --. But maybe we shouldn't tell him that. We were told not to tell any visitors things like that."

"We have to assume he has a right to know," Len answered. "His company is big enough and rich enough to operate even in the times when tungsten prices are really low. You haven't been here long enough to know, but we've seen ore prices hit rock bottom. When that happens, we have to lay off people who may not ever return. And if the rumors are true, that the Germans and the Chinese and the Japanese all want our ores, we can defend ourselves better if we're part of a good solid corporation. I think. Anyway, that's what I know about what is going on, and we might as well act as if that is true, because I hate to think of the alternatives."

They stood silently for several minutes, thinking about the possibilities. "So," Len concluded, "your job is to give Mr. Merritt whatever information he wants, because my boss told me to help him. I hope it's the right thing to do, because it's the only thing I can think of."

"And it's easier because Mr. Merritt seems like a really nice person," Russell said. "He's interested in Owens Valley and the people here, he likes to talk to them, he's not stuck-up even though he is rich."

"And he's paying your salary," Len added wryly. "At least, my boss thinks it's worthwhile for you to make reports, instead of, say, operating a tractor. Well, he'll be here today or tomorrow. We'll see what he thinks of your paperwork."

Waiting for their visitor, Russell continued to work on his latest report, a list of the different ores that had been identified and the locations of the first and best (not often the same) finds. Molybdenum and scheelite of course, but also bits of many other minerals were listed in logs from mine operations in the area. Russell thought about how his grandfather would talk about the mysteries of the ores, and how you didn't know anything near all the uses for them until you experimented. He thought he'd make a separate copy to show Grandpa Spence when he visited next.

On this visit, the driver for Mr. Merritt was Walt, to everyone's surprise. Russell was mildly disappointed; he had looked forward to driving down the mountain and maybe spending some time at the garage while he waited for the train, but he was nevertheless happy to see his brother.

Shortly before noon, the Magnusen Garage truck rumbled up the road, pulling to a stop in front of Len's office. Walt hopped out and helped his passenger unload several cases and bags. Merritt smiled at Russ, waved at Walt, and disappeared into the building, leaving the two young men together.

"Are you going to stop growing ever?" Russell asked.

Walt, now a full head taller than his older brother, grinned happily. "It's mom's good food. Much better than camp ever was. I'll be sorry when I move out."

"Where are you going? I thought you had a good job."

Walt shrugged. "It's pretty good. I'm getting lots of chances to drive all kinds of different cars, and I can take an engine apart now in just about no time. But you know it's getting kind of -- not boring, exactly, but there's nothing really exciting going on."

"You're not going back to camp, are you?"

"Oh Lord No. Talk about boring. No, actually, I'm not going to leave any time soon, not until I find a job I like better, or a place I want to go to. I'm kind of thinking about one thing though. Have you heard about the recruiters?"

"Up here, if it's not related to mining it doesn't exist. So, tell me."

"We've been getting visits from military people -- the Army and the Navy. They go to Bishop and Lone Pine because they're the largest places around here. They talk to men-- well, anybody from high school up to I think maybe as old as twenty-five or thirty, I don't know. They tell you about what it would be like to join and what you would get from it. They've got some good arguments. I'm thinking about joining the Army, because you know and I know that before long there'll be a war and I don't want to get drafted and just sent somewhere and I don't have a choice."

"What are you thinking? The Army? You think that would be better than anything you can do right now? Do you really think you would have a choice if you enlisted? Choice of what? A chance to kill people, that's what!" He began to shout. "We aren't a family that's filled with soldiers. Tell me anybody in our family that's been in a war. We don't do that."

From the corner of his eye he could see Len moving toward them looking grim.

"You can't do this, Walt! You can't even shoot a coyote! FI know that. How are you going to learn to kill people? How would you ever think you could do that? Anyway, it would kill Ma if she knew you were thinking about that. Does she know you're thinking about joining the Army?"

He started shaking his brother. Len took Russell's arm and pulled him away. "Get into my office. Now."

Len occupied himself with greeting Ralph Merritt, taking him on a quick tour of the mine works to show him the construction underway and the big new floater equipment designed to separate the scheelite from the tungsten.

Russell waited in the office, first sitting at his desk, then pacing the office floor, then standing by the window to see whether either of the men might be coming. He saw Walt talking quietly to Len, then unloading gear and luggage from his truck. Then he drove away. Watching his brother begin the descent, Russell began to feel a great sadness. What had they started, by leaving the CCC camp?

Russell was adding to his list of Owens Valley minerals as Len entered the office and closed the door softly behind him.

"You embarrassed me today, Russell," he said. "You embarrassed yourself also. You're not a child anymore and neither is your brother. You gave him no chance to explain his ideas or his desires. That's no way to communicate."

He sat down behind his big desk and gathered a stack of papers. Russell could see that they were the reports he had been creating. Looking out, he saw Ralph Merritt moving his packages into the small office that had been assigned to him.

Len said, "You know that you were originally hired to work in the mines. It was my idea to have you learn parts of our business and organize some of the material we work with. My own boss was reluctant to release you to me. It's very expensive to have a person earning wages from work that was never in the budget. He expects me to tell him soon whether this, this experiment, will continue, or whether we'll be sending you down below."

Russell had trouble breathing.

"Mr. Merritt will be coming in, any second now. I expect you to take each of these reports and explain to him how you decided what to report, how you built each, and what you think the results will show."

Just then the door opened again and Ralph Merritt entered. The three sat at Len's big conference table.

"Shall I ask questions, Russell, or would you like to begin by showing me what you have prepared to report?" Ralph Merritt's voice, calm and slow, made Russell feel less nervous.

He stood and distributed copies of the first report.

"When I was in the CCC Camp, we had to count just about everything," he began. "The government wants to know how many chairs, how many socks, how much gasoline there is. At first I thought I would go crazy, because I wanted to just go out and move fish around—we were working at the fish hatchery—but then I began to understand that it was really important to keep track of all of the different parts of the project. I'd see guys just sitting around, maybe whittling or reading, and I'd think, why don't they have some work to do. Then a couple of days later somebody would come up and say, the money came in for the new tanks, or something, and everybody would get up and get busy.

"So later, working for Len, I was thinking about what it had been like at camp, and I thought, if we keep track of all the different parts of the mine, then they could plan better and keep more workers working."

"That's about it." Suddenly shy, he lifted the first page.

"See, this is a list of how much tungsten ore is sent down the mountain each week. I was going to make it each day, but it was just too much work, and anyway we keep the daily numbers in case we need them. We just don't report them out."

Merritt nodded. Russell took each report in turn, describing its topic and the results he had listed.

Len and Ralph Merritt examined the list closely.

"If people had any idea how complicated the process is, they'd wonder if it's all worth it," Merritt said.

"It's true that this is a tricky run here," Len answered. "Not only are we ridiculously high, at the end of a road with—how many switchbacks?"

"Thirteen," from Russell. "Although that'll get better when the new road is done. If we don't do it up here or near here, we'll have trucks carrying tons of ore and we'll end up with a cupful of tungsten for our trouble. To tell you the truth, Mr. Merritt, if anybody asked me if it's worth it, I don't know what I'd say."

Merritt frowned. "We're in it now, for better or for worse. My bosses are determined to make a go of this tungsten business before anybody else thinks about it. It's bad enough the Chinese are interested. Now the Germans are sniffing around. Are they still coming here?"

Both Russell and Len shook their heads. "No visitors have come up here for maybe a month now. It's just too hard to get here, and nobody knows about us anyway."

Len added, "I forgot to tell you, Russell, your uncle Alf is coming up in a few days. His shop in Bishop wants to see how we run the floaters."

"You have a whole mining family," Merritt joked. "How about your brother, the young man I just met? Is he interested in mines also?"

Russell sighed. "Right now, all he wants to do is join the Army. When we were at the CCC Camp, all he wanted to do was breed fish. But they didn't want us to breed fish. What they wanted us to do was carry them from one place to another. Walt doesn't handle routine jobs very well."

"He'd best understand that the Army will be mostly tedious jobs designed by other people. And the uniform will be just as hot and scratchy as you had in the camp," Len said. "He's better off at the gas station."

Russell quickly picked up the next sheet.

"Now, here's the map I made of where the employees live. You can see that even though we have workers' dorms up here, they're not full. Lots of people live down below, maybe as far away as Lone Pine, and they hitch a ride up one way or another. And then stay up here for a week or a month at a time, but it's not their official home."

Soon the three men were deeply involved in the reports, trading papers and making notes, happily building proposals to explore in the weeks to come.

7

There was snow on the ground at Manzanar, as usual for February -- just enough to show white on the ground, and to paint the branches of the apple trees which still lived in the bedraggled orchards.

Tony was busier than ever with the film crews, as California businesses began to pull themselves out of the Great Depression. Four films were being made in the Alabama Hills or nearby. Barbara had been an extra in one of them, as had Walt, who had received permission from the owner of the gas station to take a couple of days of unpaid leave. He thought that maybe his future lay in movie-making and spent his spare time answering calls for extras or talking with the Los Angeles men about how to get started in the business.

When Alf made his next visit to Pine Creek Mine, he brought his family with him to Independence. He would be spending most of his time in the area for the next year or more as he scouted for sources of tungsten and other valuable minerals, and it made sense, he thought, to move closer. The family was less sure.

Sara would have to give up her teaching job in Bishop and face an unknown school and students in Independence. However, there was a shortage of school teachers just about everywhere, now that the Depression seemed to be over and there were more jobs available in many fields. Teachers who had lost their jobs as the Depression cut school budgets were now finding that there were plenty of jobs that paid more money than teaching. She was offered an English class in the high school.

Howard worried that he would have to face his mother in class, but she promised he would be placed in a different English class, one with a male teacher, to Howard's vast relief.

Cliff was the farthest from home, a student at Caltech in Pasadena. The location of the family home was of small interest to him, if he had a place to visit during school breaks.

But the happiest was Dana. She had almost finished high school and had made many plans for her future, most of them not shared with her parents. Her immediate goal was to learn to fly.

Dana thought that her Uncle Charles had the best job in the world—rather, a series of Best Jobs as he moved from place to place. Ever since she had been tall enough to climb into his plane, he spent part of each visit flying with her. They would spend an afternoon exploring the scenery in different directions near Independence. Dana had become expert at spotting changes in the landscape of Owens Valley as the seasons passed; pastures became farmland or farmland dried and stood vacant before returning as pastures. They saw sheep on the mountainsides and coyotes trailing jackrabbits. Catching sight of a horseman or a mule wrangler, Charles would dip his wings, usually receiving a wave in return.

Sometimes Charles would do a roll or another stunt maneuver to see whether Dana would be frightened. She never was—at least not that he could see.

No one else in the family wanted to fly. As far as they were concerned, flying was what Charles did. Dana, however, remained fascinated by the idea of flight. She read what she could find, she built model planes from paper, filling her bedroom with small aircraft suspended by strings from the ceiling. She saved her allowance and found occasional jobs to build her "flying fund" which she kept in a small purse her mother had discarded. When her high school graduation was approaching, Dana began to receive mysterious letters and post cards from her uncle Charles. She would read them, then tuck them away, thinking that even if he didn't follow through, she would have evidence that at least he was thinking about her.

But she never had to worry. In late May, she received a letter from Charles saying, "Watch the skies during the first week of June. Love, Uncle Charles".

Shortly after her graduation, he followed through, with one more post card specifying date and time.

Charles flew into the small airstrip in Inyokern. Dana was there to meet him, standing by the family car, proudly displaying her driver's license.

For the first few days of his visit, she was his chauffeur as he made several stops. He visited friends, replaced clothing and supplies, and, most of all, worked on his own plane, with Dana's help.

"You're really interested in the motor, aren't you?" he asked one afternoon, as, sweaty and grimy, they worked on the seating of the propeller.

"I am. It's so important. And it's something I can understand. I'm learning the names of all the parts of the motor. Can you find me an old one, that I can take apart?"

Charles wondered briefly what Dana's mother would think about having an airplane in the house, maybe even in Dana's bedroom, but he knew that Alf would be intrigued and happy. "I'll see what I can do."

Several days later the family gathered at Tony's and Barbara's house for a party. Alf and his family were preparing to move into the house in Independence which they had just found; Dana had graduated from high school; and Charles was here.

And as Charles carefully explained to each of them, they were part of a big secret.

They had brought chairs out onto the back lawn. Tables all along the back porch held food: ham slices, a green bean casserole, scalloped potatoes, sliced tomatoes and cucumbers, pickles, squash pie, mushroom and onion gravy next to a big pot of mashed potatoes. The corn on the cob would come last, steaming, from the stove. Breads and butters and apple butter came next, and then the desserts, pies and cakes and cookies. Each dish was protected against flies, in its covered pot or topped with a clean dish towel. Pitchers of lemonade and cool water stood ready.

Russell and Tony wrestled sawhorses and planks into tables here and there, pushing them into place on the ground which was almost bare of grass.

The rest of the family arrived almost together. Alf and Sara (carrying a covered dish of lasagne) were immediately questioned about their successes or problems settling into their new home.

"Jack-the-dog hates it," Alf laughed, answering Molly's bewildered look, "He's not used to seeing all the animals. He was chased by a jackrabbit the other day. It was embarrassing for him—and for me!"

"I'm already feeling at home in my schoolroom," Sara added. She had been decorating walls and assembling supplies.

Soon everybody had served themselves and had found seats, the younger people at the far end of the yard where they could become better acquainted with each other. There were enough cousins to fill a picnic table: Russell and Walt, Cliff, Dana and Howard. The boys started talking about sports. For a few minutes, Dana stood uncertainly on the porch, not eager to join them. Charles waved her over to where he sat with Alf and Barbara, near his parents.

"Dana, I think this is a good time for me to give you a graduation present, and I have just the right one, I'm pretty sure." He motioned to his brother and the two men, smiling broadly, left the back yard, leaving Dana to take his chair.

They soon returned, pulling one of Barbara's gardening carts. Resting on it was a strange object, obviously heavy, with a red bow on its top.

"Happy graduation, Dana, and may this be just the beginning of your next education." With a flourish, Charles drew her over. She looked at the object for just a moment and then gave her uncle a big hug.

"It's an airplane motor! A real airplane motor!"

The rest of the family gathered around. For almost everyone the object was not appealing at all – greasy and knobby, with unexplained parts sticking out of it all over. But they were eager to be part of the big secret about to be unfolded.

Charles smiled a big smile, including all the family in a wave of his arm.

"Yes, Dana. Better than that, it's YOUR airplane engine. I've been talking to people and here is the plan. My flying buddy here in Owens Valley, Tuck Watkins, is selling me a new plane. That's one of the reasons I've planned to be here longer than usual, because I'll be checking it out. Now, the plane I flew here from

New York is perfectly good but it needs a new engine. Everybody here in the yard pitched in, so we've bought it. For you.

"This is the engine that will replace the one that is right now in that plane. When you get this engine taken apart and overhauled and back together again, Tuck and you will put it in the plane, and do any other repairs you need. Because that is now your plane!"

It was the most exciting family party anybody could remember. Dana stood perfectly still, tears pouring down her face, while the cheers and laughter and applause surrounded her.

Charles continued, "Now you'll need flying lessons, and Tuck will help with that – he's got just about every license there is, and he has promised to teach you enough to get your pilot's license. And he wants to start tomorrow!"

The noise, already loud, got louder. Dana had to sit down.

Barbara brought plates for dessert and started passing food, which gradually calmed the group. Dana disappeared for a few minutes, returning with a freshly washed face, and sat down on a rock next to her engine.

Charles poured himself a big glass of lemonade and took some brownies to his chair, where his sister joined him.

"You got it all done, Charles," she said. "Good for you."

"Nobody could afford anything like that, but together we came up with enough to make Tuck happy. He remembers seeing Dana come flying with me during the past years. He's always hoped we'd have a woman pilot, or more than one, in the Valley. He's been very generous here, too."

"And Barbara," Charles continued, "you should know that both of your boys chipped in. I didn't even ask them directly, just described what I wanted to do. I think they loved the idea of their cousin up in the sky. Walt says he can wait another year for new boots."

Barbara sniffed a bit and found a handkerchief in her apron pocket. "Thanks."

8

At the highest point of the Tungsten mine works, almost two miles higher than sea level, the snow in early Spring mounded to more than six feet. The few workers who had volunteered for the Winter skeleton force at the mine head began to feel that their currently-unemployed former companions, now safe and warm in Bishop, had the best of it. It had been a long winter, with snow starting back in late October.

It would not be possible to do any actual mining until the snows melted, but there was plenty of work for everyone. The mine was so busy during its active periods that any unnecessary jobs had been put off until now. Even repairing the engines of the trucks was a winter job, along with mending hoses, stringing cables, replacing truck tires. The positive side was that because everybody was busy from morning till night, there was no time or energy to worry about family or friends down below, so homesickness was also postponed till Spring.

And it looked as though the food supplies, which had been hauled up on mule-back in early October, would last until somebody could make a trip to re-stock. Apart from wishing there were more cookies and pies, and wondering how all that coffee could disappear, all was reasonably well.

Many of the mines in the Eastern Sierra began as tunnels into mountains or nearby outcroppings. Pine Creek Mine was different. The vein of tungsten ore seemed to flow down from the top of Mount Tom through the rocks, to disappear from time to time and then reappear hundreds of feet below. Considering the difficulty of finding it, and the state of mining equipment in general, miners believed it was just plain luck that allowed any of the material to be removed.

Early Pine Creek operators had tried to shorten the journey from ore bed to transport and finally settled on the permanent solution: a tram carried the ore from the top of the mountain to the major mineworks. To those who began as miners at the top, the new works seemed like a major improvement.

Much of the work was done at mid-level, around 6,000 feet from the valley floor. Here were the milling and sorting machines and the offices, and just beyond were the dorms for the employees and the few families which had accompanied them up from town. School, of course, was out of the question, but some enterprising teachers managed to get some classes together to keep the students moving toward their next grade levels.

On a bright and windless day, Len and Russell had begun transcribing numbers of mineral samples to one of Russell's reports. Concentrating carefully, neither man noticed the sounds coming from outdoors until suddenly, Len lifted his head.

"That cracking noise. You hear it?"

They grabbed their jackets and hard hats and raced outdoors.

It was more than cracking. Outside, the ground seemed to be vibrating. The air was filled with groaning and knocking and thunder-like snapping noises. The sky was a cloudless blue, but up toward the summit of Mount Tom the snow rose in clouds.

"Do we have anybody up there?" Len called to Russell.

"It should be deserted. Nobody is working anywhere higher than this. If there's anybody, it would be skiers or stupid Los Angeles tourists. Should be empty."

They watched, entranced, as the snow clouds lifted and billowed. For a moment, there was silence.

Then a wall of snow broke away from the mountainside. Like a giant's bed sheet, it hung in the air for a second, then splintered, crashing down, filling the spaces in the canyons, gaining speed, hurtling down toward them and the mine works. The creaking and groaning began again, became louder, seemed to come from everywhere. Workers popped out of buildings, stared up at the mountain and the avalanche, ran for their trucks, loaded friends into the cab or the truck bed, started down the road. A couple of bulldozer drivers scrambled into their machines, and joined the procession.

Russell watched Len. What would he do? Russell knew about avalanches but had never seen one. Should he run into the building or down the hill? Then Len waved him toward the office.

"I'm staying. You go if you want, but I'll bet that road will kill somebody, if the avalanche doesn't. Too slippery, too crowded."

He disappeared into the office, and Russell could hear him calling down to the police station in Lone Pine, telling them what was happening. He set the phone down and crawled under the worktable, motioning to Russell to do the same.

"Now we wait," Len said.

The snow noises kept increasing, and now included thuds and crashes as rocks and parts of trees were thrown through the air. Russell thought he could hear sounds of metal pieces crashing together as though the trucks left outside were being tossed around.

Now the avalanche had reached them. The room grew dark as the snow covered the windows. The noise was so loud and so constant that Russell and Len could not hear each other screaming. Something hit the corner of the building. The metal roof buckled and screeched.

If it breaks, we'll be buried, Russell thought. But the roof held.

Finally, after minutes that seemed like hours, they began to realize that the avalanche noises seemed to be lessening. They stood and stretched, then began to work on the effort to dig themselves out. They could not see anything outdoors because of the snow blocking all the windows.

"It feels like night time," Russell murmured.

"It's been one hour and twenty minutes since it started," Len said. "Not even lunch time."

He found a half-dozen flashlights in a closet and handed one to Russell. The thin beams were reassuring. He removed the batteries from the others, sliding them into his jacket pocket. Rummaging in his desk drawers, he found a few more batteries, a paring knife, some other odds and ends. He picked up the telephone receiver and listened for a few moments.

"Of course, the line's down. I'm sure somebody will be coming up—but I wish I knew what's happening down below."

They checked each window, hoping to find a corner or a protected area which might be less thickly walled in. As far as they could tell, the building was buried.

"I've never seen snow this deep," Russell said.

"I'm older than you, and I haven't, either."

Russell thumped one of the windows, hoping to dislodge the snow. There was no apparent result.

"Is there a way to get to the roof? From inside?" he asked.

"Not that I know of. We never needed to get to the roof. At least, not till now."

They looked anyway, using the flashlights to expose all the ceilings in all the rooms. Nothing, no trapdoors or oddly colored spots or banners tacked up, or even posters, could be found. It was a disappointingly well-built ugly building.

It was also remarkably neat for a workspace ordinarily occupied by a dozen men working steadily through the week. Even the wastebaskets had been emptied just a few days before.

"I don't suppose we have any food here," Russell murmured. "I hate to say it, but I'm getting hungry."

That started them on another quest, resulting in half a loaf of rather stale bread, several apples, a box of crackers, and a jar of peanut butter.

"What's this for?" Russell asked, pulling out a large piece of cloth from a box at the back of a closet. It was a scarlet banner, with large white letters reading MUSTANGS.

Len smiled. "It was one of our really bad ideas. A couple of years ago, we were going great guns because the price for tungsten had hit the roof. So, we thought we'd have a baseball team. This would have been our banner."

"What happened?"

"Just about everything. The ore prices dropped, people wanted to play football instead of baseball and Lone Pine already has a couple of football teams, and almost nobody knew what a mustang is. We're not horse people here."

"Should have named the team Mules." He tossed the banner back into the box and they continued to inspect their work space.

A half hour later, he stopped again. "Look at the stove."

"And?"

"I'm thinking that if we can get to the roof someway, we can stick that mustang flag up there, and somebody will see it."

Len wrinkled his forehead. "And if the stove has a stovepipe, and if it's not buried, we can use that. Not a bad idea."

While Len disconnected the wood stove's pipe from the stove, Russell found several sticks, mostly brooms and somebody's ski poles and parts of a broken ladder. They poked a broomstick into the hole in the wall and pushed it up as high as they could. It moved so easily that they felt almost giddy.

It took less than twenty minutes to extend their flagpole by several additional broomsticks. Russell hammered the banner along the top part of their new flagstaff, then they wrapped it around the pole and sent it up one more time.

They could feel the banner coming loose from the pole. With luck, it would unfurl.

"Do you play chess?" Len asked.

"Sure. Uncle Charles taught me when I was just a kid."

Len set up his board and men.

Down at the foot of the mountain, people were gathering. Whenever there was a major flood or snowfall or rockslide, the people of the Eastern Sierra put their ordinary lives aside and came to help. Because so much of the work was simply the hard, tiring, tedious job of probing snow or rocks or mud, the important thing was to get as many helpers as possible.

The road from Pine Creek mine was now filled with stalled or broken vehicles; only a small number had managed to reach safety ahead of the avalanche. The avalanche had missed the road, spending itself on the steep mountain sides. Down near the highway, occasional puffs of snow showed how it was settling.

Mule wranglers appeared with their teams and set to work to pull the trucks and cars away to clear the road. Luckily, only the machines were damaged, although their drivers, shaken and sore and frightened, needed comfort.

The Sheriff organized work teams and equipped each team with a radio phone and flashlights, then sent them up the Pine Creek road past the jammed cars. Almost at once he received a radio message: the snow had pushed a bulldozer off the road and down the mountain. The next message reported that the driver and passenger had jumped out of the 'dozer's cab just in time and had been retrieved from a snowbank near the road.

The next call was from a searcher who had seen a hand sticking up from a snowbank. "His fingers were waving! I'm blinking my flashlight! Send help!" They frantically scraped snow from the top of a pickup's cab. "It's Red! Red Conover! I'd know his truck anywhere!" from the radio.

As soon as the road was cleared enough to allow it, the biggest Pine Creek Mine truck made its way slowly and carefully up the road to the mine works. The avalanche had plowed down the mountain on one side of the road, first knocking down the unfinished towers at the mine's top level, sliding faster as it hit the mountainside, clipping the mine works building, burying the workers' dorms and much of the office building.

The truck had not gone far before the driver realized he'd soon be stuck deep in drifts. The workers at the bottom heard his radio message -- expected news, but nothing they wanted to hear.

"We need the snow plows back up here, and more if you've got them. We need men on snowshoes—as many as you can raise. We know there are at least two people in the office building, maybe more, and who knows how many under the drifts."

Before he finished speaking, men were moving. The miners wore snowshoes almost every day during the winter months so the men outside were already wearing them. Soon a scraggly line of men began the climb, carrying lanterns, poles, and whistles. Each mound of snow was tapped and poked, dogs who followed their masters were allowed to explore and perhaps find traces unseen by humans.

Two snow plows appeared, diverted from clearing Route 395. They moved steadily up hill, just ahead of the men on foot, and occasionally turned to clear a suspicious spot.

The first discovery was near the snow-buried road. Tom Goodman, driving the first snow plow, stopped his machine and blew his whistle, waving at a snow mound nearby.

"I'm sure I saw movement here," he called to the first searcher. "I think it might be a truck."

Just then, loose snow at the top of the mound slid away. The watchers saw a gloved hand emerge from the snow pile, fingers waving. They ran over and grabbed handfuls of snow, throwing it from the vehicle. When the window was cleared, the driver opened it carefully and helped his rescuers pull him from his truck.

A man with a mule came up, prepared to carry the driver back down the hill.

"Anybody with you?" he asked the just-rescued driver.

"No, and I think I was maybe the last one out. Close to the last one on the road, anyway." He took the thermos of coffee from the wrangler and held it tightly between his gloved hands, then took a swallow. "There were lights on in the office when I went by. I reckon Len and the kid are still in there."

"He's not a kid!" the wrangler sputtered.

"If you say so. Anyway, they're up there."

"Wait. It's my brother up there. I'll find somebody to bring you down, but I'm staying here."

"Oh. You must be Tony's kid—son. Sorry. Are you Russell or Walt?"

"Walt." He twisted about, looking for someone he might know. The nearest man said, "I can lead a mule, son. I'll take over now. Here. Take my gear."

"Thanks." And Walt was off, moving as quickly as snowshoes allowed in the direction he thought would take him to the mine office.

By now the hillside was speckled with rescue workers. Men were calling to each other, and occasionally the shrill blast of a whistle stopped everybody momentarily. Walt trudged up the hills, poking his pole into each nearby snow mound no matter how small. As he crested one mound, he saw a group of men clumped together and shoveling snow. Near them lay a large red cloth. By the time he reached them, they had broken a window and had pulled Len and Russell through the opening. Walt snowshoed over to join them.

"How'd you get here?" Russell demanded.

"Long story. I brought some mules up, somebody that got stuck in a truck said he thought you two were still up here. How come you didn't come down?"

"We were working. We didn't know anything till it started coming down, and it was too late. We figured we'd be safer here."

Len joined them, carrying a stack of papers.

"Walt, I want you to go down right away. They've got a truck waiting for you at the road end here. I've got a copy of Russ's list of employees and their housing. The sheriff wants it as soon as you can get it there."

Len turned to Russell. "And now it's time for us to catch a ride and go get something to eat."

9

Avalanche repairs kept most of the town busy for several weeks. Everybody agreed that it was great good luck that nobody had died, even better luck that everybody had been accounted for quickly. There were two broken legs and one possible heart attack but that man was on his way to Bishop and the hospital there.

To the great disappointment of the children, the avalanche had missed Independence altogether, so school was in session as usual. Now that the highway was paved all the way up the Valley, mail and groceries were being delivered by truckers who had a hard time believing that buildings had been buried in snowdrifts.s

But with the avalanche danger over, most people felt that life in the Valley was just right. The mines, at Pine Creek and elsewhere in the area, were hiring as many laborers as possible, because the growing threat of war was driving the price of tungsten higher all the time. Industry and trade were recovering in many parts of the country, which meant that the new highway was filled with ore trucks, and, more and more, trailer-trucks carrying the finished products in every direction.

Better jobs meant more money, and the movie industry was alert to that. The hills were filled, it seemed, with cowboys and soldiers and warriors in exotic costumes. There were even a few camels to be seen.

Walt couldn't decide whether to leave the gas station and go to work full time for the movies, or to look for a job as a truck driver.

Alf's family had settled into their new home, although Sara often felt that she was the only one living in Independence. Alf was gone now for days at a time, visiting mines up and down the Sierra, sending ore samples to Bishop for testing.

Cliff, at twenty-one, was in his final year of college at Caltech in Pasadena. He had planned to follow his father's interest in geology, but once at Caltech he realized there were many more subjects to explore. Alf was proud of his son's ability to grasp new ideas, but worried that he would never settle down and graduate.

Dana was absorbed in her airplane and her flying lessons. Her instructor, Tuck Watkins, was happy to spend his spare time with her as she learned the basics. Taking off from the airfield in Inyokern, they would fly a short distance before touching down, then lifting off again, throughout the Autumn and Winter afternoons.

When she was not flying with Tuck, Dana worked on her engine. At times, she was sure she could never take it apart. The engine was at least six years old, with parts which had settled into apparently permanent places on the "central nervous system" as she called the engine body. Tuck gave her monosyllabic hints from time to time but she gradually learned to trust her own intuition, separating the engine into smaller and smaller segments.

The project led her to her cousin Walt, who was working at Magnusen's gas station. He was delighted to help his cousin and tried hard to keep from criticizing her, even though he was convinced that girls were not cut out to deal with mechanical things.

She kept a notebook in which she drew each part as she identified it. The notebook, creased and grimy and finger-marked and oily, was one of her most treasured possessions. She carried it with her wherever she went, to her mother's occasional embarrassment.

Now the money in her flying fund was spent on fuel and the supplies needed to restore the engine, including solvents. small hand tools and special purpose gear, like a used micrometer caliper. One afternoon in late January, she arrived at the airfield filled with determination.

"Uncle Tuck," she called. The stocky figure of her instructor appeared at his workshop door.

"I want to schedule the test for my pilot's license," Dana said.

"So you think you're ready?" he asked.

"I'm ready enough to look ahead to having a test."

"You're just tired of cleaning the engine."

"Well, at least I know what I still have to do on it. But I don't know whether I'll pass the private pilot test. I'm ready to try it."

"Lord knows you have enough flight hours! Next thing you have to do is solo and get enough solo hours. Suppose we aim at one month from today for the test. OK?"

She beamed. "OK. Now when can I solo?"

"Tomorrow. Come as early as you can."

Dana arrived at the airfield just as Tuck dismounted from his bike. She would never tell him, but she had been awake much of the night, wondering what this morning's experience would be. The morning was sunny and crisp but no snow was forecast and there seemed to be almost no breeze. The cold air would give plenty of lift.

Together they pushed his little plane onto the dirt path that served as runway. They did their pre-flight check together, Tuck standing back as Dana carefully examined every part of the plane that she could reach. When she turned toward the rear seat he tapped her shoulder and pointed to the front.

"Pilot's seat. I'll be waving at you from the ground."

She had been sure that she would remember every second of the flight, but later she could recall only parts of it: calling "Contact!" before Tuck swung the propeller and she turned the key; the heart-stopping moment when she took off and the plane lifted into the air; the feeling of the wind against her face; the steady noise of the engine; the man waving from the front of the post office as she passed overhead; a crow approaching, then turning and flying away from the plane.

She followed the highway north for a while, then turned east to fly over the dusty remains of Owens Lake. There was a small herd of cattle in the pasture near Olancha. Dana turned the plane south again and all too soon she was back on the ground.

"Good job." Words Tuck almost never uttered.

Dana lost her breath for a moment. Then Tuck returned to his normal tone: "remember that turn you made when you were about three-quarters through the flight? You turned East, then South. You need confidence in the way you turn. If there'd been more wind, you'd have felt that."

She nodded. She'd do better next time.

10

Ralph Merritt had formed the habit of taking part in morning discussions around the big table at the Miners Café. He and Father Crowley had been working for months on plans to increase tourist activity in Owens Valley. Talking with the local business leaders was a large part of their strategy. Somewhat to his surprise, Merritt began to enjoy the mornings drinking cup after cup of coffee. Of course, the thickly sliced toast with homemade jam didn't hurt,

On this morning, in Spring, 1938, one topic was on everybody's mind. The chairs at the big table were always filled, generally by the same people: The Baptist and Methodist ministers, the manager of the Owens Valley Lodge, the editor of the weekly newspaper, and a few men who simply enjoyed talking politics and world affairs.

"Does anybody really believe our country is ready for war?" someone asked.

"I think we're ready, all right. Ready to give those Nazi bastards what's coming to them." That started everybody speaking. Voices were raised on all sides of the issue. Some wanted the President to declare war immediately; others felt it was not the place of the United States to fight Europe's battles.

"Do we have the army and the equipment and the money and everything we're going to need if there's a war?" Another murmur. "So Ralph, you get all over, down to Los Angeles and all, what do you think? Any signs of preparation for war?"

Merritt looked up as the door opened to admit Father Crowley. "Ah, Father," he said. "You're just in time. They're asking what we know about whether the country is ready for war."

"Sadly, I think we're all too ready in some areas," Crowley said as he pulled out a chair next to Merritt. "People are starting to point fingers and make hateful remarks about their neighbors. Especially in the cities, like Pasadena. I wouldn't want to be a German living in Pasadena nowadays. Or anywhere else in the U.S., for that matter."

"Not to change the subject," somebody said, "but what about things like food rationing, or gas, or making gardens? All that stuff we remember hearing about during World War I. What about army recruitment?"

"You know," Merritt said slowly. "I think that this valley is in better shape than just about everybody else. We're away from the city, which means that far from factories, airports, train stations, government offices. Yes, we complain that we don't have much in the way of jobs or things to enjoy, but we're not a big target for enemy fighters or enemy bombers, or enemies of any kind."

The room grew quiet. The idea of thinking seriously about a situation where nobody knew what would happen, or what changes would be coming, was frightening.

Finally, Father Crowley stood. "Nothing's going to happen any time soon. At least, I don't think so. But there's an atmosphere that is becoming poisonous. People are beginning to suspect each other. People are talking about their neighbors and making baseless accusations, talking about disloyalty, secret spies, all kinds of craziness."

"I tell you what I think," a large man in overalls and leather jacket, sitting next to Joe Magnusen. "I was just too young for the first war, but my brother went, and he didn't come back. Shot and killed over in France. We never even knew he was in France. What kind of a country is that? He wrote home, once, said he couldn't understand a word anybody said over there. I miss him every day. But. When they're ready, I'll be first in line to sign up."

"But think of your parents," Joe responded. "They already gave one son to war. Don't you think your family has done enough?"

"Never enough. What if everybody felt like that? Then we wouldn't have enough soldiers and the Nazis would win. We can't have that."

Joe was not finished. "What does Maggie say?"

"We don't talk about it. She knows how I feel. We've got to finish what the Germans started. We all have to be part of this."

"But what if there's some kind of invasion or something?" somebody else said. "Maybe we should all be armed and trained. If they had done that in France and, I don't know, Belgium, maybe this would be all over by now."

Father Crowley held up his hand to quiet the others.

"We don't know enough to make any plans for war. We need to pay attention to the things closer to home, and not get all worked up about what might happen. For example, we need to plan our Fourth of July pageant. It's almost too late to get publicity out. We have just been bone lazy."

Enough chuckles greeted this to satisfy the priest, who pulled out his big notebook and began to read lists and assign

68

workers. Whenever Father Crowley was involved in a community activity, the big table at the café became the planning office. As in so many small towns, the men who gathered almost daily for coffee and chat were the same men who produced the community events, raised funds for decorations and improvements, and made sure that enough tickets were sold.

The idea of a summer pageant had been born almost a decade earlier, when the people of the Owens Valley, having survived drought and bank failure and theft of the Owens River water, decided (with Father Crowley's enthusiastic guidance) to create a Wedding of the Waters, bringing a gourd of spring water from the top of Mount Whitney to Death Valley.

The Wedding of the Waters was a grand success. The idea of a community celebration quickly grew into a necessary project for people from Bishop through Lone Pine and beyond. Isolated mountain cabin dwellers joined local businessmen to provide food, costumes and music each year. And each year, everyone expected the pageant would be bigger and better than ever.

"We've lined up some bands for the parade," Crowley reported. "And the fire truck from Bishop plus the Sheriff's horse patrol from there, and there's a whole group of children pulling even smaller children in little wagons. Let's see—who's in charge of that?"

Alf raised his hand. "It's not me—it's Sara who put all of the little wagons together. We'll be ready to go. She's already drilling them in back of the Methodist church."

The representative from the movie crews announced that they would sponsor a float AND a band. Well, it wouldn't be just any old band. It was going to be a drum and bugle corps that was preparing for a small role in a new movie. They wanted practice and some extra publicity, and they thought this would be just right.

The food committee chairman reported similar success, as did the games chairmen. It would be a splendid party, maybe the best so far. They were all happy. The men pushed their chairs back and began to leave, to return to work. Watching them, Ralph spoke into Father Crowley's ear.

"Do you always have luck like this?"

"Like...?"

"Well, you start a project and everybody jumps in. They're doing a lot of hard work for this Fourth of July, and I don't hear any grousing."

Father Crowley laughed. "I've given this a lot of thought over the years. But I think that the answer is, I'm not their pastor. Most of the folks here are Baptists or Methodists or maybe they don't go to church. My parishes are tiny, and spread far and wide. None of these people have to meet me in confession, or even attend church -- I wouldn't know whether they did or not, mostly. So, I don't think any of them feel I have any authority. I'm just a guy who occasionally gets a good idea."

Merritt nodded. "So when something gets started that looks interesting, they pile on because..."

"Because up here in the Owens Valley there's really not all that much to do. Somebody who'll be baking cookies for the pageant will be using a recipe she read in a magazine last year and has wanted to try. Somebody else has saved some materials that will come in handy for a costume. And the children will have a chance to put on a performance."

11

Walt decided that the best part of his job was meeting the people around him. Joe Magnusen had always prided himself on giving full service to anyone pulling up to the gas pumps. His customers expected to exchange a few words at each visit. Walt loved the opportunity to chat, and had quickly learned the names of most of the regulars. They in turn were happy to give him their opinions on many subjects.

One day, Walt came to Joe with a question.

"Did you know there are people asking about the Pine Creek mine?"

"Not again! There was an article in the Bakersfield paper, and maybe others too, about how Pine Creek is the largest tungsten mine in the country, maybe in the world. I think that has got people all excited again. So, are they talking here?"

"Yeah. There was a car this morning, two men and they asked directions."

"So did you talk to them?"

"Well, you know, the usual. While I was checking their oil and that. The thing was, they just didn't seem *right*. Like they aren't just sightseeing. They had a route they were following -- they got out their map and asked me to point out the mines. And not all the mines. They weren't interested in the Yellow Aster mine or Bodie or whatever. Just tungsten. But they didn't ask about tungsten. So, I didn't say much. I want to be polite and all, but I don't want to get me or us in any trouble."

Joe was quiet for a few minutes, then answered. "It's only going to get more like this. Your brother probably told you about the Germans who were here earlier. The thing is, our country needs the tungsten for armor, for the planes and ships and all that they need for defense. Right now, these strangers are just a nuisance. But when we *do* get into war, the enemy could want to damage the plants, or the mines, or who knows what? Safer to stay away, don't talk to them."

"Shouldn't we have some kind of rules about what we say?"

"Walt, I just don't like to have any more rules than what we absolutely need. Ask your uncle Alf what he thinks. He's pretty sensible about these things."

Walt had a chance to talk with his uncle before much time had passed. He confirmed Walt's observations.

"I think it's impossible to tell whether there are spies around, or maybe we're just imagining things. This valley is so isolated that any stranger stands out. Probably the best thing is just to be polite and not say anything meaningful."

"Well, *that's* boring."

"I know, and it may all work itself out, but not soon, I'm afraid. And not happily, either. Do you read the papers?"

"Sometimes. Mostly they just have football scores and road closures. There's not much that's interesting. Lots of bad news from Europe. I know that."

Alf sighed. "Walt, you are the complainingest fellow I ever met! Here you have a terrific job and all you tell me is you wonder about spies. Try to keep your mind on your work for a while and maybe you'll amount to something."

Walt shrugged and headed out for the string of mules he was to take up to the works. At least *they* wouldn't make trouble, he told himself mournfully.

During the summer of 1939, the people in the Valley became more aware of the war across the Atlantic. Radio broadcasts and the local newspaper kept them informed of the major stories. Young men started making plans involving joining the military or exploring the alternatives which might keep them closer to home. The idea of planting vegetable gardens, or raising a few chickens, became popular. Even people who paid no attention to newspapers found their neighbors exchanging recipes and talking about Meatless Mondays—for just-in-case.

Then in September the news came: Germany had invaded Poland. In Europe, the War had begun.

12

Dana's practice for her pilot's license had continued without stop. Now that she could fly solo, she stashed fuel money from each babysitting or fruit-picking or store-keeping job, and spent most of her free time in the air. Now she could tell the subtle changes that indicated storms or winds and she could read the cloud formations which warned her about unstable air currents to avoid. One of her favorite games was "buzzing cows" – flying over a herd in a pasture, just low enough to get their attention and send them scattering.

At the same time, she was studying and practicing for additional certifications. Knowing that her instructor had his heart set on making her the first female pilot from the Valley, she pushed him to push her along, and spent many hours memorizing the rules and requirements. At the end of each lesson their reward was air time, as Tuck taught her the first barnstorming routines and shared his vast knowledge of the fine points of piloting.

As a result, she found herself qualified as a commercial pilot. She was certified for just about anything her single-engine plane could do, and could see that eventually she would want to graduate to a larger plane. She eagerly awaited Charles' next visit home, when she could demonstrate all her new skills.

Dana was eager to talk with Walt, too, so one day she visited him at the gas station where he was happy to take some time for a chat. He heard her stories about her flying experiences and gave her some suggestions for routes she could fly next. Then he told her about the man he had just met.

"There was this man," he began, "pulled up to the gas pump with this great motorcycle. He filled his tank, and then kind of stretched and walked around some. I could tell he had driven a long way, and had a long way to go. So, I was curious."

"You're always curious, Walt," Dana smiled.

"Well. So, I asked him where he was headed and he said he was on leave before his next ship, and spending some time in the mountains. That didn't make any sense to me so I got him to tell me.

"He's in the merchant marine. He might be a ship captain someday. He goes on freighters. He goes all over the world, Dana! When he comes back from a trip, if he wants to change ships, he looks around to see where the other ships in his port are going, and then if they have a job for him, he can just go there."

She thought for a few minutes.

"It sounds like the absolutely perfect job for you, Walt. But what kind of a job is it, really? He doesn't just ride around on ships. Did he have to have college for this job? I don't see you in college, frankly."

Walt bristled momentarily.

"I don't know exactly what he does, but I know he didn't go to college, because he told me he started right after high school and got promoted by taking tests. I could do that, definitely."

"Yes, you could. So, are you going to see him again? Learn more?"

"He'll be back this Sunday sometime, on his way to port. Which I don't even know where it is. But it's either Los Angeles or another port down there. I think. Anyway, why don't you come to the gas station Sunday? I'd kind of like it if you would meet him because you can ask good questions."

Dana agreed. She had privately worried about her cousin Walt, who had shown an alarming tendency over the past year of threatening to enlist in the Army, simply out of boredom.

On Sunday, Dana was sorry she had promised. The weather was perfect; she had worked more than the usual number of hours at the Miners Café, which gave her some extra money in her flying fund, and she wanted to practice barrel rolls. But a promise was a promise.

Walt had brought sandwiches and some of Barbara's pears, so they made a picnic in the gas station office, finishing just as a motorcycle pulled up.

"That's him," Walt said.

He was tall and blond, in jeans and a light jacket. He placed his helmet on a rack behind his seat.

"Hi again," Walt called, bounding out to the gas pump. "Good to see you again. Back to your ship now, right? I hope you don't mind. I was thinking about what you were telling me, about your job and all, and it seemed like something I'd like to do. So, I asked my cousin to come over and meet you. She's very good at asking questions."

The young man smiled and shook hands with Dana, introducing himself as George Taylor.

"I'm happy to talk about my work, Walt," he said. "It's a terrific job and I know you'd like it. You seem like a person who enjoys variety and adventure."

"That sounds too good to be true," Dana laughed, thinking she had never met anybody with eyes that blue.

"The pay isn't great, and sometimes the working conditions are pretty awful. But the job is an important one. I've been working on freighters and we go all over the world. My last trip we took a cargo of farm equipment, like tractors and threshers, to Australia. And so, we had a chance to go ashore several times, and see kangaroos and stuff."

"Wow" from Walt and Dana simultaneously.

"So here's what I think. When you are ready, come down to Long Beach – that's my home port – and find me. If it's not too long, I should still be in port because we have some repairs to make on our ship before we leave again."

He handed them cards with his name, address and phone number.

"I'll be hoping you'll call. Then I can take you around, sign you up and you can make your first cruise. After that, you can either rack up experience on the ship or go to the maritime academy, although that's kind of expensive. I started by getting experience points."

"It's like learning to fly," Dana said. "Learning by experience, I mean."

"Yeah, sort of. I guess. I could never fly, but even though I'd never been on a boat, the minute we first pulled out of the harbor I knew this was where I needed to be. It's funny."

Walt spoke up. "That sounds like you, Dana. She flies," he explained to George. "Here, George, something for your ride."

He pulled out a bag of apples.

"Are these Manzanar apples? They smell so good. I'll enjoy them."

He finished checking his motorcycle, zipped his jacket, and retrieved his helmet.

"Hope I'll see you, Walt. Bye, Miss."

And he was off.

"You never even asked any questions," Walt said.

"I didn't have to. You know and I know that this is what you are going to do. Right?

"Right."

But one evening in August her father reported at dinner that Walt had left home, on his way to a new adventure, and did Dana know anything about what he might have had in mind? She told the family about the meeting with George Taylor.

"What is that boy going to do on a ship?" her mother sputtered. "Half-cocked. He is always going off half-cocked. I'd better go see Barbara soon. She must be just frantic."

"Sara, I think Barbara feels good about this," Alf said. "Walt has been struggling for some time to find work which is useful and independent. He is happiest when he is learning something new, and goodness knows he'll be surrounded with new things for a while."

"And it's not something he has to stay with forever," Dana added. "George says he can sign on for a cruise and then if he hates it, when they get back to port he can just collect his pay and leave, but if he wants to stay in he can continue to earn points toward advancement."

"Can you imagine Walt at sea?" Howard said. "I wonder if he has thought about being seasick. Or what he would be doing in bad weather? Will he wear a uniform? What kind of jobs do they have on ships?"

"Now, here is something," Dana said. "There's something I want to do, too. Not on ships, though. There's this pilot, Jacqueline Cochran. She has flown all kinds of different airplanes, and she has won air races, all across the country. She wants to set up a group of women pilots to help the war effort. If she gets it going, I want to be part of it."

Seeing the shocked faces around the table, Dana stopped speaking.

"Well, I do," she said, but her voice wobbled.

"Oh, honey," Sara said. "We are just surprised because you usually are so quiet. And now you are practically giving a speech."

"I think that's great," Howard said. "But it's not ready yet, right? So you'll still be at home for awhile, right?"

She nodded.

"Then you'll still be able to come to my ball game next week." Satisfied, he helped himself to another piece of pie.

13

One September afternoon, Dana took her airplane up for a run over Walker Pass, looking for sheep or burros. She noticed an odd shadow on the ground and dropped down for a closer look.

Tuck Watkins, minding the ground station at the airfield, caught her anxious message over the radio.

"Tuck, Tuck, there's an accident on the highway! Toward the Panamints! Send the sheriff and an ambulance!" The spotty radio reception cut off her call for several minutes, while Tuck paced frantically around the office.

"Tuck, can you hear me? It's right on the highway, east of us. I think it might be Father Crowley's car. It looks as though he hit a cow or something!"

Dana followed his orders to return immediately to the airfield. When she landed, she was less upset than he had feared. But once on the ground she began to weep.

"He's dead. I know he is dead," she said. "He would have been waving to me if he could. He always did when he saw me. It's a terrible sight over there."

She volunteered to guide the Sheriff back to the crash site but was easily persuaded that she had given enough specific details to get them to the right place.

By the next morning, everybody in the Valley knew the sad news. Father Crowley had died while driving his old car too fast over a road all too familiar to him, on his way to another small parish too far away. Somehow, just about everybody in the Valley felt diminished, as though a family member had died.

14

It took almost a month for Independence to be ready to hold a memorial service for Father Crowley. For a town with very few Catholic families, the interest in his passing was surprisingly deep.

"It's because he was such a nice man," people said. "It's because he was such a large part of our lives. Remember the Wedding of the Waters? He basically planned that. Remember when he was the first priest to hold communion up on Mount Whitney? If he hadn't died, we might be famous someday."

The decision to make a memorial was essentially unanimous. The decision of what to do and make was much more difficult. Everybody had an idea, from a parade and pageant to a multi-church service to a big community dinner or a fund-raising show to provide scholarship money.

"All up and down the Valley, there will be memorials," Spence reminded the men at the big table at the Miners Café. He had made a special trip, staying with Tony and Barbara, to participate in the planning. "This means we don't have to worry about making it the one official ceremony."

"You know, I think he would hate a big show, if he knew about it," Barbara said as the family discussed it one weekend. "I think we should have a simple memorial on the highway, with a sign telling about his good works and all the distances he covered."

"I agree, Cliff answered. "Somehow having a big party just isn't something I want to do to honor him."

The community finally settled on a solution which pleased most people: create a permanent memorial, with a plaque telling of his life and a cross to be provided by the Catholic diocese, and a gigantic picnic to celebrate the unveiling.

Ralph Merritt, who managed to be present at most of the meetings, thought it was a grand plan.

"The best part is that it sounds like something Father would think up himself. He always loved our big picnics and gatherings. And he wouldn't mind the memorial—he just would never admit that he might like it. And, best of all, planning a community picnic means we need to advertise it in advance and that means we'll have a deadline to meet."

It was an ambitious deadline, because it would be a Thanksgiving picnic which required lots of preparation. But it caught the imagination of many in the Valley. Some made costumes, some prepared foods, some made music. More than one song was composed, such as The Father Crowley March and Minuet, which, sadly, proved too complicated for local musicians to play.

The movie studios, of course, promised to provide short scenes from the movies they were making, plus make-up artists to decorate the faces of children. Barbara commandeered Howard to work after school to help her pick the last of the Manzanar apples to be offered as a prize in the auction (proceeds to be added to the Father Crowley Scholarship Fund).

As the time approached, everybody began to relax. The various parts of the program were going to mesh well, thanks in part to Russell's reports—he was learning how to make complicated schedules.

The picnic began at midmorning, with tables and chairs set out on the town square in front of the Post Office. The churchmen had decided that the most appropriate service would be simply music, with a short unveiling ceremony to follow. Ralph Merritt, representing the Inyo-Mono Association, read a brief biography of Father Crowley. A small girl, whose pigtails were braided so tightly they stood straight out from her head, pulled on a cord which opened a curtain so that everybody could see the memorial itself: A simple cross cemented into a low pile of desert rocks, with his name and dates.

Then they heard the motors. Three small airplanes came into view. Tuck Watkins was first, flying a plane no one had seen before. It was a sleek two-engine plane, looking long and slim, darting across the sky to disappear, then reappear again before coming down into the nearby field. Second was Dana, flying her bright yellow plane Jackie. As she reached the crowd, she dipped her wing, then turned into a barrel roll, her first before an audience. Finally, Charles, who had arrived just in time that morning, flew overhead, turning to drop confetti from a large sack onto the picnic grounds.

The rest of the program followed the Valley's idiosyncratic pattern. Guests were called to the waiting tables to pick up lunch: cold ham, cold fried chicken, potato salad, pickles, fruit—in short, all the necessary ingredients. For dessert, there were pies and cakes and the melons from Ray Gardner's patch, which seemed to grow all year around.

Finally, it was time to stand up and stretch, and find friends and catch up on news, while the movie crews set up a screen against the wall of the high school auditorium where they showed films for most of the afternoon.

Alf struggled through one group after another to find Dana and Charles at the edge of the field. Charles gave his brother a quick hug and gestured toward Dana, who smiled and trotted away.

"Do you know what she's doing now, Alf?" he asked. "She's over there with the movie crew, negotiating to get her plane painted. She's calling her Jackie; did you know that?"

"You're not jealous, Charles, are you?" Alf laughed. "Yes, it's Jacqueline Cochran she's named it after. And did she tell you what she's hoping to do? This Jacqueline Cochran is trying to get a women's pilot group to help the army air force. These pilots, like Dana, will ferry planes from the factories to military bases, and they'll also test them and do things like that. Dana has made this her goal in life."

"Is this the same Dana who would sit at the edge of the group no matter where, and never say a word? All of a sudden she is a businesswoman and an adventurer."

"I'd worry about her, but first of all she wouldn't let me, and secondly she is actually very careful. And Tuck has taught her well when it comes to handling aircraft. Have you seen her do a pre-flight check?"

Charles smiled. "I am proud to say I taught her first, but Tuck's carrying on. "

"How long will you be here this time, Charles?" It was a question asked by many at the picnic.

"I can't stay long. I heard about Father Crowley and felt I should come pay my respects. And I wanted to make sure Dana was off to a good start. Did you see that barrel roll? But I'm off again, maybe by the end of the week."

He moved off quickly before Alf could ask more.

As the picnic wound down and people began to pack away their dishes and chairs and head home, the family made plans to re-assemble at Barbara's house. They wanted to hear about Charles's adventures.

Dana was the last to arrive, explaining that she had taken one of the artists from the movie crews to the airfield to discuss her plan for the name he was to paint on her plane. The rest of the family were still getting used to hearing this shy girl speaking so often and so confidently.

Charles was proud of his niece, happy that he had set much of this change in motion. When he started talking, after everybody had found a place to sit and Barbara had passed cookies, he found himself next to Dana.

"It took me awhile to figure out where I wanted to go," he said. "I knew flying mail routes was not for me--too much repetition. But I've got some friends who went North, and it became something I thought I'd like to do. So, I headed up toward Canada, and then I started thinking more about Alaska and the next thing you know I was headed that way.

"It took longer than I liked, to get paperwork that would satisfy Canada and then the Alaska Territorial government, but I'm finally learning that I'd better not take any short cuts that might bite me later. When I got into Canada I found two things: one, that there are lots of jobs for pilots, and two, there are many, many pilots looking for jobs. "

His audience chuckled.

"But did you find some good work?"

"It's the same as here. Hang around the local air field and you'll find work eventually. But you won't get rich. Or famous. So far I've been working with a group helping European refugees who are trying to find family or friends but they don't have any connections. Or they don't even know where their family might be. Last week I flew a family who had just escaped from France. They're Jewish and they have had a terrible time. Now they are scared to death of everything. They have a relative in Alberta—that's one of the Canadian provinces. They wanted to go there but they thought it might just be a short train ride from Winnipeg to Alberta. Of course, it's none of that.

"And there are some wonderful people in Canada working with refugees, besides the group I'm working for. Like the Red Cross and a bunch of churches. It turned out that I flew them to a city not far from the Alberta border and somebody else picked them up and was going to drive them farther."

"But isn't it expensive? Who paid for your fuel?" Molly asked.

"Oh, mom, it would break your heart. They had a couple of suitcases where they were carrying things like their silverware, and some fancy picture frames, and things like that. That was all they had. But the Canadians have some special funds—they have been raising money like crazy—and they paid me. Canada seems to be more interested in refugees than our country is, which is crazy because we think we welcome everybody. Well, we don't."

Seeing their faces, Charles hurried to change the subject.

"I'll tell you what's more fun, and pays better, too. And it's why I'll be going back soon. They're making maps!"

"Don't they already have maps in Canada?"

"You'd be surprised. There are lots of places, the farther north you go, where nobody has ever traveled. So now the

Canadians are working hard on making their maps better. And the Americans are, too. So, there's lots of work for pilots."

"What's it like up in Canada, Charles?"

"I can only tell you about the parts I've seen so far, because it is such a gigantic country. Right now, it's snowing and there's already snow on the ground. The mountains that I've seen have more snow than our mountains have here, but that only makes sense, doesn't it, because they're so much farther north."

"Have you seen any bears?"

"Several times. And lots and lots of caribou and moose and elk. I've eaten moose stew. I didn't like it much."

"Did you see Eskimos?"

"Plenty, so far. Kind of like seeing Paiutes here. I have mostly been in the villages and they live in the wild for the most part. But they come in, with their dogsleds and sometimes on skis, and sell their game and their fish. But I don't speak their language yet. So, I don't know them."

Barbara finally asked, "are you going to stay there? In Canada?"

"Barbara, when do I ever stay anywhere?" Charles laughed. "I've got some plans I'm not ready to talk about yet, but I'll write you when I know more."

Dana had been sitting quietly, watching and listening. Now she spoke. "Uncle Charles, what are the people in Canada doing about the war? Are they being drafted?"

"No, not now. A lot of the men have already volunteered, including some who fought in the first war. Nobody knows what's going on, you know. Not here, not there."

Dana looked around the room. "I'm just wondering how many of the men in our family will be drafted. Have you all registered?"

The men nodded. Everyone sat silent for a moment. Then Barbara, as always, stood and offered cookies.

15

D uring the Winter of 1940—1941, the people of the Owens Valley seemed, on the surface, unaffected by the war in Europe. After surviving the worst years of the Depression, most people wanted to relax and enjoy life. Some people had invested in automobiles or trucks, and enjoyed driving the newly paved (since 1937) highway which made going to Mojave much easier than before. But most people concentrated on saving as much as possible and tried to find new ways of becoming self-sufficient.

In the mountains, Pine Creek Mine was busier than ever. Ore prices were more stable than they had been in the past decade, even with higher prices. Their parent company back East kept inventing improvements to separate the tungsten from other minerals, and found uses for those minerals, which meant that the conveyors rattled on their high platforms day and night, and trucks carrying ores of various kinds filled the highway.

Barbara and her friends made plans for vegetable gardens, frustrated by having to wait through the long winter till the snow melted.

Dana found pickup work with the movie studios and some local businesses. She developed a delivery service by flying small packages between the Eastern Sierra and an airfield in Van Nuys, north of Los Angeles. She patterned it after the air mail system, with a more or less regular schedule; thus, a merchant placing a package with her in the morning could expect it to arrive in Los Angeles that afternoon. A package given to Dana when she arrived at Los Angeles was ready for its customer by supper time that evening.

But Dana had the same temperament as her Uncle Charles. Once she had successfully flown the package service for a month, she was ready to hand it off to another pilot.

She roamed restlessly about the Valley, sometimes hiking the foothills, sometimes frightening cattle and goats as she flew above them, experimenting with landings in snow and ice (her parents were unaware of this). After she gained her commercial pilot license, her flights became longer. Sometimes she tried to persuade relatives to fly with her but only Howard was enthusiastic about the idea.

She began to use Howard as her sounding board for her plans. After all, he was the youngest in the family, and as eager for adventures as she was.

"There is this woman pilot," she told him one afternoon as she helped him with his homework. "Remember when I first got my plane, and I named her *Jackie*? Well, this woman, Jackie Cochran, has been a stunt pilot and she won a race from Los Angeles all the way across the country to Cleveland. She is starting a program for women pilots. She believes that woman pilots can take some non-combat jobs. I could do that."

"You wouldn't fight, though," Howard said worriedly.

"No, women don't fight. But we can be in the background."

"Like repairing planes? Or like what?"

"One of her plans is that women pilots can fly new warplanes from the factories to their airfields."

"Even if it's all the way across the country?"

Dana smiled. "Even if it's all the way across the ocean!"

She opened their big atlas and showed Howard how she would fly, North and East, across New England into Canada, stopping at Gander, Newfoundland, then over the water to England.

"That's a really long way! How could you do that?"

"Stops every few hours to refuel and rest. People have already flown that route. I know I can do it, too."

"I don't want to be around when you tell Mom and Dad."

She laughed. "I'll persuade them. I'm getting better and better at persuasion."

But the arguments between Dana and her parents continued over many days. There would be times when she would storm off, slamming the door and frightening Jack-the-dog, only to return in a couple of hours, calmer but still determined.

Sara's discussions with Alf took place at night, after Dana and Howard were in bed.

"I hate this! She's our only daughter and she will be far away and in trouble and what will we do?"

"We knew that once she started flying, she'd leave the nest—oh, what a terrible metaphor! But it's true," Alf said.

"Maybe we shouldn't have let Charles take her up. That very first flight with him changed her ideas, her goals. But I don't think we could have stopped her."

Alf thought for a moment. "If she weren't flying, she'd be on a horse, or climbing a mountain, or something. You can get killed by falling from a horse."

"I know. But now Howard is talking about getting her to teach him to fly when he's old enough."

"And she would be a good, careful, thorough teacher."

Sara sat still on the bed, remembering all the times she worried about her daughter. "Alf, that's what she wants to do, and it's not that different from what this woman pilot is planning. She's looking for all kinds of pilots, including instructors. Dana's right—she could add a lot to the program."

Alf said, "She wants to help the war effort. She wants to fight Hitler. How are we going to tell her that we won't let her?"

Sara sighed. "I wanted her to go to college."

"Let's face it, Sara. Dana and college are not meant for each other. It's like trying to make a champion football player learn the oboe."

"Barbara says it's very hard for her to have Walt gone to sea, even though he is not in a war zone. But she says she feels better since he seems to have found the right life for him."

"Hard to imagine," Alf said thoughtfully. "I think we should tell Dana to go ahead and apply for this women pilots' program, whatever they call it. First she'll have to be accepted, and then she'll have the hard decision whether to take it. By next Spring the whole war may be changed."

Cliff graduated from Caltech in Spring 1941 and returned home for a breather, giving the family an opportunity for a picnic. Alf and Sara, with Howard's help, had been gardening steadily ever since the snows had melted.

Barbara had her own secret. In his last letter, Walt had written that he hoped to be able to get to Independence at least for a quick visit. The letter, sent from a Central American post office, had taken almost a month to reach her, so she had no idea when to hope he would appear. So, she kept the letter folded in her dresser drawer. *What a wonderful surprise,* she thought, *if he does come while everybody is here.*

The family admired the new garden and, helping themselves to iced tea with fresh mint, they found chairs in the shade of the house.

"I've registered for the draft, and I know Russell has, too," Cliff said. "Walt probably has, too, or he'll plan to when he gets back on shore. What will we all be doing in a year or so? I thought I'd tell you my own plans, and I think we all want to hear what everybody else is thinking."

He had not come home often during his college years, spending vacations in Pasadena at the college labs, working on the jobs which paid part of his tuition.

"I've been offered a graduate fellowship," he announced proudly. "It means I'll be teaching some chemistry sections and helping in the labs and stuff like that. And all of my tuition will be paid."

Alf ceremoniously shook his son's hand. "You never told me anything of this. I'm pretty proud of you, son."

"It's a good school," Cliff responded. "I know that you think so, too. Even though I just can't get interested in geology."

They laughed.

"What I'll be doing is directly related to the war effort, so they tell me I'll be able to keep doing it whatever happens. I can't really tell you much about what I'll be studying, but I can tell you I think it's useful and very exciting."

Spence had been listening quietly. Now he spoke up.

"Well, I have to say I'm a pretty proud granddad. Looks as though you have made good choices. But my big question is this: is this the beginning of a time when everybody has secrets? Your dad would bring his fellow students to study the rocks around here, and he often brought me samples that we'd look at together. Far as I can tell, we've always shared whatever we learn with each other. I don't know I like this secrecy."

Russell defended his cousin. "We are taught at the mine that we don't tell anybody anything, but it's not personal. It's just that there are so many people we don't know any more. There isn't a week that somebody doesn't come up to the mine and want to know all about our processes. But we have a huge investment in them, and we don't want to just give our techniques away."

"Hasn't it always been like that?" Tony said. "There are always secrets in business, but to have secrets about what you're studying and learning—that's different. My question for you, Cliff, is: Do you feel good about what you'll be doing? Is it the right kind of science to be learning? Or is it just how to build a bigger bomb? Or is the bigger bomb the *right* thing to do, now that we know about Hitler?"

Their voices grew louder, their gestures more dramatic. Then a new voice broke in.

"Hi, everybody!" It was Walt, his sea bag over his shoulder, standing at the gate.

16

W alt burst into the room, where he was immediately surrounded. Only Dana noticed that he had brought someone with him. She pushed past cousins to greet George.

"Welcome!" she took his hand and pulled him toward a table loaded with food. "Wherever you two came from, you must be hungry!"

He took a handful of cookies and chewed happily.

"We want to know more about your trip. We want to know everything. Walt doesn't write very good letters."

"We none of us write good letters from shipboard," George answered. "It's hard to make time for it, and then it still takes a long time for mail to go back and forth—just an excuse, I know, for being lazy."

"Where did you go? I guess you go to different places each time, right?"

"Well, sometimes. Depends on which ship we sign up for. Walt and I both like the *Dora Henley*, and so we've signed up for her next trip."

"What makes her a good ship?"

"The food is really good, and they have lots of it. And a couple of the guys play guitar, so we have some music in the evenings. And she's a pretty new ship, so she's pretty clean and tight."

"So where...?"

"Central America. All along the West coast. We didn't have time to go ashore this trip, but they said we'll have some shore leave on the next trip down."

"But what is it like on board? For instance, what do you do?"

"We all do anything that's needed, but we have specialties. I work in the engine room, keeping the machinery in order, cleaning and lubricating parts. When they need me, I also help with the loading and unloading."

"How long have you been in the Merchant Marine, George?" Dana beckoned to her mother to come join them.

"I've been doing this for almost two years now, and I'm looking forward to getting a promotion. Walt's more involved with the deck operations and he's learning about navigation. Pretty neat for him, but it's not something I'd like."

At the other end of the room, Walt's hands were waving wildly as he told his adventures.

"Dolphins! Big ones! They came up to our ship and swam along right beside us for maybe half an hour! And we saw whales, and we had a bunch of flying fish! And the birds!"

Dana laughed, looking at George. "I think you convinced him a sailor's life is the life for him," she said.

She expected he would laugh, too. But he grew solemn, staring at his tea cup, crumbling a cookie.

"It's all very well now," he said. "But when war comes, we'll be in the thick of it. You know we'll be officially at war sooner or later, probably sooner, and then the merchant marine will be part of the Navy. And if it's like the last war, we'll have the most dangerous work."

"Does Walt know that?"

"Yes, they keep telling us."

"Why do you stay in then? Can't you resign or something and do something safer?"

George nodded. "Lots of reasons. And we do talk about it, every time we hear about a ship being sunk, or something. But I guess there are three major reasons we stay. First, the work we're doing is important and there aren't nearly enough men to do it. Second, it's just the best adventure there is. When we're your dad's age, and we tell our own kids about what we did, we'll have such stories!"

Walt had joined them. "Actually, the third reason is that we just can't believe anything could happen to us. We've got a good ship and we know pretty much what we're doing. What could go wrong?"

He made a face and shrugged. "I heard you telling Dana about the war news."

Dana frowned. "Walt, you just started in the Merchant Marine. Do you feel right about this? You could come home, try something else."

"Oh sure. Everybody knows I can't stay at one job more than a couple of months." When Walt was sarcastic, everybody knew it. "Anyway, I really like what I'm doing, and I heard George tell you what all the guys say. So, I'm going back. Our next cruise will be terrific! We're heading North this time, up to Alaska!"

Dana stopped him. "But what about the war, Walt? What if you have to move through an ocean with enemy ships and submarines."

"It's an adventure, Dana. It's the best adventure I can think of for myself. Why do you fly?"

She shook her head. "I have to admit it—you're right. It's the adventure. And the idea that I'm learning something useful."

The voices in the room had gained volume. Tony stood and tapped on his iced tea glass with his knife.

"They'll be here another couple of days, everybody, so let's let them get some food and relax for a spell. How did you get up here, anyway?"

Walt beamed. "On our motorcycles. Anybody want to see them?"

The group headed outdoors.

17

George was happy to stay in the Owens Valley, visiting the places Walt had told him about, meeting people who had never seen the ocean—he had to wonder about that, since it was a trip of only a day to get to a beach. But people, he decided, generally stayed where they felt comfortable, even if they never did anything exciting. And no two people were the same. For example, he told Walt frequently, he just couldn't understand why anybody would like a mule. They were stubborn, ugly and stinky, especially after they had had a lot of grass to eat. He'd stick to his motorcycle.

Dana offered to take him flying, but he turned her down as well. He wouldn't tell her, of course, but he was afraid of getting airsick in the open cockpit. He had heard too many stories about pilots trying tricks with their passengers, just because they could. Dana was disappointed, but she was more intent on becoming admitted to the WASP corps, and decided to worry about George later.

She thought she would never hear from the WASP project. She worried that there would never be a WASP project at all, because nobody answered her letters, and nobody at the airfield had any idea that anything was in the works. She realized that, after all, she didn't know any other female pilots; maybe there weren't enough to make the project work. She considered giving up her waitress job at the Miners Café and maybe going to college, as her mother wanted, but she hated to give up her dream.

Up at Pine Creek, Russell cornered Len one morning to pose a new question.

"I hear there are some Germans going to move to Independence," he said. "Is that going to be a problem and what should we do?"

Len stopped filing his papers and stared at Russell, with the look of someone who is thinking about something very far away. He liked Russell and enjoyed working with him, and goodness knows those reports he designed surely helped impress the bosses, but he kept asking questions! And thinking of different ways of doing things! And wouldn't let a man just go about his business!

He turned back to Russell.

"You'd better tell me what you know and what you want to know," he said.

"Well, I heard that the Crawfords—they're the family owns the bakery next block past the cafe—their grandmother is German and the father went to bring her to come live with them."

"Doesn't seem like much of a problem," said Len.

"But what if more Germans move here? Her friends, maybe? And what if some of them are spies? The guys were talking about it. What if they want to come work at the mine?"

"Russ, for crying out loud, this is a *Grandma!* Just one person. What would she do at the mine? If Mr. Merritt finds out that you're getting all steamed up about this, he'll blow a gasket. Now, go work on that report."

In town, at the Miners Café, Ralph Merritt was being asked the same question. The big table was filled and extra chairs had been drawn up. Nobody knew much about the Crawford family, except that their cakes were delicious and their bread was chewy and tasty.

"How can they be Germans with a name like Crawford?" somebody asked.

"It's Mrs. Crawford's mother." Joe Magnusen said. "Crawford is English—well, American, of course. And so is she. It's her mother who's German."

"Well, why is she coming here?"

Everyone at the table turned to look at Joe.

"She's old, and getting frail, according to Crawford. And there's been some trouble in the place where she's living. Some vandalism, some fights, that sort of thing. It's a German neighborhood and there's been some trouble. Kids getting out of hand, that kind of thing."

"So why is he going to get her? Why not his wife?"

"Who do you think does the actual baking?" Everybody chuckled.

"Seriously," one of the ministers said, "there will be people here who might not like this, somebody new in town, speaking a foreign language—Joe, does she speak English?"

"I have no idea, but I don't think so from what Crawford told me. Guess we'll find out."

"We keep being told to not give away secrets—not that I know any. Our bank always seems to be the last to know anything. But I do wonder, how would we know if somebody was a spy, just from seeing them on the street."

"Or buying bread from them."

"I think we don't have much to hide from anybody, anyway, except maybe the mines." Everybody at the table had something to say to that; for several minutes, there was general discussion with rising voices.

Ralph Merritt had been sitting quietly, watching each speaker in turn. Now he spoke up and from habit the others fell silent to hear him.

"I like the Crawfords. I think you all like them, too. Right? Then why not just wait and see what happens. They surely don't seem like people who would jump at the chance to bring an enemy into our midst. See what this grandma is like, and what she does."

Dana reacted to the Crawford news somewhat differently. As soon as she could, she went to the bakery to find Hilde Crawford, for whom she had been a babysitter when she had been in high school. She had heard Mr. Crawford was away, planning to bring her mother home; did the bakery need help while he was gone?

"Oh, Dana, I wish I could hire you! It's much harder than I had thought, managing everything with Henry gone. But I can't afford to hire anybody, especially since we don't know how we are going to manage with my mother here." She sighed. "At least, I think she will be able to help with the little ones. It's all happening so suddenly."

Dana didn't know what to say. It seemed impolite to ask questions, but she was curious. What had happened to drive an elderly woman from her home? And why has she been living so far away from her daughter's family anyway?

"My mother can be difficult. She and I came to America after the First World War, because I met Henry in Germany—he was a soldier there. We fell in love and after the war he returned to our village to visit me. We knew we had fallen in love, so he arranged for me to come to America. We—my mother and I—came

103

on a boat across the ocean and then took the train all the way across the country and there he was, in Los Angeles! We got married as soon as we could. But my mother was not happy—she missed her German friends and family. We found her a little cottage in Anaheim. That's south of Los Angeles. She found German-speaking friends and a church she likes.

"But now, with the new war starting, there are problems. Some young boys make mischief. They ride on their bicycles along the streets and throw eggs or tomatoes or even rocks, sometimes, at the houses and sometimes at people.

"My mother is frightened. She says that that is how it was in Bavaria when the first war started. She says she wants to go home but of course she doesn't, really. She's just unhappy.

"Henry and I hope that if she comes and stays with us and our children, she will understand that it is safe here. And she can help us, too."

Dana said, "Let me come help till they get here. And you can pay me with—let's see—a loaf of your good bread every day. That would be wonderful for me because I'm just waiting around to hear about a job I've applied for."

Hilde Crawford laughed, and reached across the counter to shake hands. "When can you start?"

18

A t Pine Creek, Russell and Len found that their work became busier almost every day. Demand for tungsten had risen sharply as American factories began turning to armament and military vehicles. The mine absorbed every miner who applied, and management considered adding to the available housing for miners and their families. Sarah's school was bursting at the seams, and some classes of smaller children had been moved to rooms in local churches. Barbara and her friends scoured the Manzanar orchards of parched trees for usable fruit and made applesauce and jams and stewed fruit to supplement the groceries shipped from the city.

"I'm pretty pleased that we built the tramway with wooden braces," Len commented as he and Russell prepared invoices. "I've been checking suppliers for replacement parts for our equipment, and nobody will sell any metal. Of course, we should probably worry that we'll start running out of wood next."

"Always looking on the bright side, right?" Russell laughed. "Well, we'll just have to warn all the workers not to break anything."

"I've been in this business long enough to know that it won't be long before there's a big slump. Suddenly there will be too much tungsten, or somebody will come up with a better or a different way of manufacturing, and we'll be back to the sleepy days again."

"If that means it's a short war, it would be worth it," said Ralph Merritt, suddenly appearing at the door. "But I'm afraid this will be a long war indeed. And we're not even officially at war, although I'd be surprised if we stay out for much longer."

"Nobody I know wants to go to war," Russell protested. "I surely don't. I wish Walt wasn't so far away. These are not our problems. We should stay out as long as we can. I think."

"And what do you suggest should happen to the people overseas who are being bombed and murdered? Just turn our backs?" Merritt, who almost never showed a temper, said angrily.

"Well..."

"Let's get on with the paperwork," Len advised. "We've got a big stack of stuff to work on today."

In Independence, the men at the big table were deep in discussion of the war. All the news reaching the Owens Valley from Europe concerned takeovers by German forces. The earlier lunchtime discussions, in which most of the group agreed that it was a European problem, had recently become more contentious. Those who had fought in the Great War reminisced about their experiences and vowed never to fight again, while those who had been too young to enlist were eager to have America put its power against the German forces.

"We should be seeing more soldiers, hearing more about how we're preparing to fight. We never hear anything about how America is going to help our neighbors overseas."

"I heard," one of the ministers said, "that they have so many men volunteering that they can't take care of them all. A friend of mine was in Los Angeles the other day and he told me that the line at the recruiting station was out the door and down the block."

"Why don't you have more news like that in the newspaper," somebody asked.

"We take what we can find, but we're not making things up," said Sam Norcross, from the newspaper. "You hear anything, tell us, we'll follow up."

19

Dana had begun working at the bakery in the afternoons. As far as she was concerned, it was the very best accommodation she could make while she waited to become a WASP pilot. In the early afternoon, when customers were scarce, she and Hilde tended the stock, re-packing and re-pricing whatever hadn't sold in the morning, deciding what to make the next day, and ordering any supplies they needed. By midafternoon, the store would fill with schoolchildren hungry for cookies and gingerbread men, to be followed by customers ready to pick up bread for dinner. Midafternoon also brought the Crawford children home from school, to be fed cookies and milk and set at the big dining room table to work on their schoolwork.

Dana was surprised to see that in addition to the reading and arithmetic work familiar to her, each of the Crawford children had a large workbook.

"It's their German language book," Hilde explained. "We try to speak both English and German with them, but Henry's German is not the best and it is hard for him. So, we supplement with these workbooks. My uncle sends them from Germany. I think they like them."

In fact, the children were eager to show Dana the stories and puzzles in the book. Sophie, aged eight, showed Dana the story of Hansel and Gretel and they both admired the pictures, which Sophie had decorated with colored pencils. Henk, two years older, was charmed by the chapter on maps. One of the exercises was to make a map of his home town, and he was well on his way to drawing streets and buildings, cars and people.

"What a good project!" Dana exclaimed. "I wish we had had that when I was going to school."

"He must write in German what the businesses do, and maybe make up some stories about the people. It's language and geography at the same time."

"Do they mind doing this extra work?"

"Of course they fuss because they want to go out and play with their friends. But they know it's my rule. And they like to do the assignments."

Just then the door opened to a flurry of children. Sophie and Henk quickly cleaned up their table and lined up for their cookies, then they all ran outside.

20

As Autumn began to give way to Winter, the family wondered whether Charles and Walt would be able to come home for the Christmas holidays. They had each written Barbara to tell her they would be coming if they could. Walt said that if he could get home he would probably bring George with him.

Quite by chance, both Charles and Walt arrived the same day just before Thanksgiving, when the morning sun quickly melted the overnight frost on cacti and sand and the clouds were soft streaks in a bright blue sky. They met each other in the Mojave bus station waiting for their bus to take them north to Independence, the weather and their limited time ashore forcing them to store their motorcycles for the indefinite future.

"I didn't recognize you at first," Charles told Walt, giving him a quick hug.

"It's the uniform, I'll bet. What do you think? I'm going to surprise Mom and Dad, because I never told them I'd actually signed into the Merchant Marine. The last thing I said was that I was signing on to one more cruise, but they really need men, so there it was. Have you met George?"

He waved to his friend who hurried over for introductions.

"George is basically the reason I'm here," Walt explained. "He told me about going to sea, and it was exactly right. Didn't you feel the same way when you were learning how to fly?"

Charles nodded. "Yes, exactly. They say that's true about pilots in general—they take one flight as a passenger and immediately sign up to learn to fly. Probably the same for you two, except you were on the ocean. But what are you up to, exactly?"

"George got a chance to sign up for Cooks and Bakers school, so he'll be starting as soon as we get back. I'm learning to be a deck officer—do you use Morse code? Dit-dit-dah-dit and all that? I'm getting pretty good with the sextant and I can make four different kinds of knots."

Charles laughed. "I think you are underselling yourself, Walt. I've met enough mariners to know they do a lot more than that. And George understands how vital a cook's job is to the success of a crew."

"You bet." George smiles. "The first ship I signed up for couldn't fill its crew without new guys, because the food was so terrible. And at the end of our cruise, just about everybody walked off and found another ship. I think the captain was in big trouble. But mostly I just like to cook and this is a good way for me to learn the business."

The bus was called and the three hurried to board. Charles looked at the two young men ahead of him, in their blue shirts and white caps, sea bags hoisted over their shoulders, and took a quick photo. *It's times like this I miss having my own son,* he thought. He considered asking them to pose for him, then decided against it. There would be plenty of pictures taken, he knew, during the next few days.

Dana met them at the bus stop in Independence, taking a photo of the three men at the moment they saw her. She felt like jumping up and down for sheer excitement but restrained herself. They slung their luggage into the back of the truck and climbed in. On the way to Independence they all seemed to speak at once, asking questions and telling tales.

George asked first about the menu for the Thanksgiving dinner, taking the opportunity to tell Dana about what he was learning at Cooks and Bakers school. This allowed Dana to tell him her experiences at the Crawford Bakery—it was the longest conversation they had ever had, and the most comfortable.

Walt and Charles were happy to let the front seat pair chat on, giving them time to exchange tales of their own experiences. Charles had been flying over the ice fields, the permanently frozen landscape near the Arctic Circle, and described the shadows on the ground which might—or might not—indicate human-made structures. There were many places, he told Walt, where he was sure he and his passengers were the first people ever to see those sights.

"Once, and only once, I saw a polar bear galumphing across the snow. The photographer was even more excited than I was. I thought for sure that he would fall right out of the plane because he was half outside anyway, shooting away with his big camera."

"So you are out in the open, basically, while you are flying?"

"In the plane we were using that trip, yes," Charles said. "And how about you. Do you have to climb up the rigging, like they do in the movies?"

"Yes, and it is even scarier than I thought it would be," Walt answered. "You have a harness to use, but that makes it harder to do the work. So, it's tempting not to use it but if an officer sees you, you get a demerit. And I'm kind of glad I'm in the habit of using it now. There are so many other things to keep track of."

"Speaking of scary, have you had any dealings with enemy ships?"

Walt shrugged. "Sometimes we see something in the distance. Nobody has shot us yet or anything. I'm learning how to spot German ships and subs and planes for when I'm on watch. So far I haven't been on watch all by myself, but as soon as I've learned enough, I'll be out there alone, and *that's* scary."

Just then they pulled into the driveway at Spence and Molly's house, and were enveloped in hugs once again.

Thanksgiving Day began with a trip into town to attend the Thanksgiving service at the Methodist church. Infrequent churchgoers, the Richardsons tried to make the effort to participate in the major holidays and special occasions. Mollie and Barbara, especially, enjoyed the hymn-singing, while Tony and his sons took pride in their work rebuilding the church steeple; the next project would be repairing the fittings on doors and windows, where the aging wood yielded to winter winds. They enjoyed the service and seeing friends, but on this day they were eager to return home; there was simply too much family news to discuss.

The Thanksgiving dinner was the best ever, they all agreed. First, everybody was there, including a few special guests—Len Reyes and Ralph Merritt from the mine, Hilde Crawford and her two children from the bakery. There was no way anybody could design one table to hold everybody, so they cleared away most of the furniture from Spence and Molly's parlor and kitchen and dining room and set up a dozen small tables, adding packing cases and stools to the available chairs. Additional seating could be found by the desperate by using the front porch and its steps. The food was spread over the larger table tops and the kitchen counters; as each platter was emptied, it was taken outside and counter space became available.

Such a feast! Celery stalks stuffed with peanut butter or cream cheese, radishes, cucumber slices, zucchini spears; ham studded with cloves, oven-baked chicken pieces, roasted vegetables; mashed potatoes and sweet potatoes; pickles of many shapes and colors; fry bread (Len's contribution); Hilde Crawford, aided by Dana, had produced loaves of crusty bread and two pies: sweet potato and chess. There was apple sauce and apple pie and stewed pears and apple crisp, rhubarb pie and cookies. Walt and George had brought two large boxes of chocolate candy which had melted only a little bit on the long bus trip.

When just about everybody had found a place to sit and had begun to eat their favorite dishes, Spence rose and tapped his knife against his glass.

"It's times like this that I really miss Father Crowley," he said. "This is a special time, one of the first in a long time when we have all of our loved ones together, so I want us to take a moment to think about those we love."

The room quieted.

"Now, we all have a lot of catching up to do," Spence continued. "I want everybody here to meet, if you haven't already, our special friends. George Taylor has come up with Walt from their merchant ship."

Shyly, George stood and quickly sat again.

Spence continued, "Now we have the wonderful bread baker Hilde Crawford and her children Sophie and Henke. Their father will be coming from Los Angeles soon, bringing their grandma.

"And last but not least, Len Reyes, a long-time friend, and his colleague at Pine Creek Mine, Ralph Merritt. We welcome them all to our feast.

"Mollie and I are so happy to be close to our family again. We have always felt at home in the Owens Valley, and it's like we had been on a long trip but finally returned. So, this is a special time for us, too.

"Now, we know what a difficult time it is for our country." Spence paused to take a deep breath, then a sip of apple juice. Then he continued. "We know that during the next who knows how long, we'll be separated and those of us at home will worry about those who are away.

"I just want to say that Mollie and I are darned proud of all of you, and we know you will all be brave and do your best, no matter what difficulties you might face. And we're here to help whenever and however we can."

He stood for a moment silently, then cleared his throat. "Now we want to stand, all of us, and thank God for the blessings of this past year, and affirm our faith that we will continue strong and loving through the year ahead."

The silence seemed to last for minutes, until Spence spoke again.

"It's time to get second helpings and dessert and talk, all of us to everybody. Happy Thanksgiving, all of us!"

21

Howard thought he was the first person to hear the news, but it later appeared that everyone in the Valley learned about the bombing of Pearl Harbor at just about the same time. Most people were just waking up, thinking about what they would do later that day, half-listening to the radio.

"It was like when we had that big earthquake," Mollie said to Spence as they sat by the radio. "We could walk down the street and hear the news from everybody's radio."

Howard had been earning spending money by working extra hours at the gas station. He heard the news from a traveler and raced to tell his grandparents. He regarded them as the calmest and most reasonable people in his family; his mother, he thought, was too ready to weep and his father slammed doors when angry. It was possible the rest of the family shared his opinion, because before long everybody in the family who was not at work was gathered in Mollie's kitchen.

As each one arrived, the first question was "Where is Walt?"

Barbara and Tony came, with Walt's latest letter. "They are both safe, in San Pedro," she said. "Actually, George is in Cooks and Bakers School. Walt is also in San Pedro but in a different school. He's studying navigation and says his instructor is very interesting. I know they are safe because I just got this letter yesterday and they say they have two more weeks to go."

It seemed then that everybody could relax a bit. But the next question was harder.

"Where is Charles?"

Alf handled that one. He and Charles had had some long discussions at Thanksgiving, Alf told them. Charles had contacted several organizations and individuals in Alaska and was in demand for a wide variety of flying jobs. But he could only talk about a few of them; the rest were more like spy stories. Alf said Charles would not even tell him about most of them, but did say that his clients were interested in mapping the unknown lands above Canada.

"He did have some funny stories," Alf remembered. "Some of the scientists doing the mapping had never been in an airplane before and couldn't handle it. They'd lean way out and get sick and Charles had to be careful they didn't fall all the way out. Once he looked around and found a scientist taking off his shoes. Then he pulled off his sock. Then he was sick into it—he didn't want to disturb Charles, or damage the plane.

"Or they would look down and be sure they saw a wolf or a penguin or something and he would have to tell them that there weren't any within hundreds of miles, but he would have to be very polite and careful so they wouldn't get mad. The best story was when they had some famous scientist go up in the airplane with Charles and take lots and lots of photos and when they were developed they weren't any good because it was just photos of snow and all the landscape, for hundreds of miles around, looked the same, so they had no idea where they had been taken."

Barbara had brought some apples, as she always did when visiting her parents, and Sara, with help from Dana, had prepared two large coffeecakes. Now the women began clearing space and setting out food.

Cliff arrived next. He had driven up from Caltech and immediately grabbed an apple and a mug of coffee. "I thought there would be traffic, for some reason, but the roads were just about empty. So, I made pretty good time, but it looks like more weather is coming by late afternoon. I can't stay long."

He had come mostly to tell his parents what the school had urgently told the graduate students that morning.

"I think they knew already that this would be happening. It's just that nobody knew when. Or exactly where. At school, they rang the big alarm bell and sent runners to find anybody who is living off-campus, and got all of us assembled in the main auditorium within an hour.

" I don't know what else is going on at the school because I was on my way up here as soon as the meeting ended.

"I was surprised. What they thought was the most important thing to tell us was that we should not rush out and enlist. You know we have all registered, and some of the guys in my classes are already in the military reserve, getting ready to be called up someday. But the chemistry department has been working on some special projects..."

Alf nodded.

"And they don't want to take any chances of losing time or talent, as they put it, because what we're working on is needed as soon as we can get it finished."

Sara smiled. "So this means you'll be in Pasadena for a while, then?"

Cliff remained serious. "Maybe near Pasadena. But not very reachable, I'm afraid. We have several labs where we have essential equipment. I may be traveling places and I still can't talk much about it. But I'll let you know whenever I can."

His hand hovered over the table. "Can I have some of that potato salad, do you think?"

Russell was the only family member missing. But just as they were finishing their meal, he arrived.

"I knew you all would be here. I just knew it. But we had some work we had to finish for Mr. Merritt. Where is Walt?"

So, they told Russell all they knew, with repetitions and reassurances and worries mixed in. Then they fed him and everybody returned to sit near the radio and listen for any more news.

The days and then the weeks passed. The people of the Owens Valley, like the rest of the country, stopped concentrating on the radio bulletins and returned to work, to school, and to their own private interests, making small changes as they began to understand that life was going to be quite different for an unknown period. Victory gardens which had begun as Depression relief gardens were renamed and enlarged. Women pulled their sewing machines from their closets and tried to remember how to make blouses and children's outfits. Rumors of shortages and rationing floated through conversations in grocery stores.

The country was at war with Germany and with Japan; both coasts were now enemy targets.

22

D ana was tired of waiting to be admitted to the WASP program. She wondered whether it was simply a fantasy, or somebody's unfulfilled project. She heard that the two famous women pilots, Nancy Love and Jacqueline Cochran, were feuding over the position of WASP commander. Would the whole thing collapse because of jealousy? Would the whole war be over before she had any chance of participating?

She had been corresponding with Jacqueline Cochran for almost a year. She had described her flying experience in detail, and had repeated her fervent desire to serve her country. She wrote about how she had been a waitress and a babysitter to earn gas money for her flying trips; perhaps her stubborn determination to make flying a permanent part of her life would begin to interest the famous pilot.

Finally, just a few weeks after Pearl Harbor, she received a letter offering her a position with the nascent WASP project. She was waiting at the door of the high school as her mother finished work.

"Mom, look!" Dana cried. "I'm going to get a job with Jackie Cochran! Right now!"

Sara was almost equally excited. She read and re-read the letter. Even though the project had yet to interview or hire its first pilots, Dana was offered a position on the staff to help with the initial organization.

"You'd better get ready and go," Sara said. Later she told Alf that she had never seen her daughter smile so broadly.

By the next morning Dana was airborne. When she arrived at the airfield, she found Tuck and his pals waiting to shake her hand, and when she completed her takeoff and flew over Independence and Manzanar she looked down and found her family waving to her from their front yards.

Alf was spending more time at Pine Creek Mine, because the need for tungsten ore forced the company to concentrate on improvements in processing and delivery. All the problems were complicated by the need to deal with rapidly changing conditions, from security issues like patrolling shipyards and ports to simply issuing enough gasoline rations to support the trains and trucks carrying the tungsten ore to the mills. He spent his days closeted with Len Reyes and Ralph Merritt. Russell was more directly concerned with day-to-day matters of schedules and payroll and personnel.

At the end of one day which had been entirely spent in a closed-door meeting while Russell paced and fumed and worried in the next office, Ralph Merritt came out and led him into his office.

"I've got to talk to you about some issues which must not leave this room," he said. "People will be hearing soon enough, but I have spent too much time thinking and worrying and I'm in danger of running out of time to plan for the work which I will be doing, and which I hope you'll be doing with me."

Russell studied Merritt's face. Normally expressionless, the older man now was frowning thoughtfully. *This must be really important,* Russell thought.

"You've been talking, Russ, about how everything seems changed since the Japanese attack. And you're quite right. We are being threatened from both the Germans and the Japanese, and we're going to be pushed to the utmost to fight back and win. It happens that I have been asked to take on a new job. For the duration of the war, however long it is, I'll not be part of the Pine Creek Mine at all.

"But strange as it may seem, I'm going to be part of the Owens Valley. Now this is the part you can't talk about to anybody, until I tell you that you can."

Russell stood up and then sat down again.

"The President is going to issue a special order. All Japanese people, including American citizens of Japanese descent, must be moved away from the Pacific coast. This is partly for their protection, but partly also because we cannot take any chances that any of them may be working for the Japanese government. We must protect our country from sabotage or any other kind of damage that the Japanese want to inflict. They will be identified and moved to special camps away from the coast. And one of those camps will be near here."

"But. Whole families? Or just the men? Or just the parents?"

"Whole families, Russ. They will live in the camp."

"But what about their jobs? Their houses? What about the old people?"

"All good questions, Russell. And there are good people working on answers to them right now—and they have been, for months and maybe years already, just in case of attack."

Merritt held up his hand to stop Russell. His voice took on the tone, already well familiar to Russell, of a man impatient to get on with what he had planned to say.

"I'm going to be the camp administrator. I'm going to be ultimately responsible for just about everything that goes on there, from how many beds to buy to how to make sure the children go to school, to how to keep the place secure.

"I'm telling you this because I have learned that I can trust you to do what I say. You won't tell anybody about this because we can't let people know yet what will happen. We don't want the Japanese in America to know because they will run and hide and maybe hurt themselves or us. We don't want the people in the Valley to know because they will try to make deals, or protest, and we can't afford to have anything slow down the establishment of our camp. I'm telling you all of this in confidence because I am now going to ask you to come and work for me on this project."

Russell could not move.

After a moment, he asked, "What would you want me to do?"

"It will be more of the same. Use your eyes and ears and brain and figure out what *I* need to know. Make reports. More and more reports. Tell me what we need to buy or make. Tell me where there are problems. Tell me how to make this work if we have to be behind barbed wire for years—five years, ten years."

Russell blinked. "But I don't see how we can imprison American citizens who haven't done anything wrong. That's not what Americans do. The enemy, I get that. But not just storekeepers or fishermen, or..."

123

Merritt rubbed his forehead, scowled. "That's the big issue. I don't have any answer for that at all, except that my President has decided this needs to be done, and I have been asked to help. And it's a job I know I can do well. And we are at war in a way we haven't been before. I don't understand it and nobody else does, either, even if they say they do."

"Well, sure, I'll be honored to work for you. And I'll do the best I can, but I don't know how I can explain this to anybody."

"That's partly why you can't tell anybody, at least not yet. There will be publicity and we will be told what to say and what not to say and the people who really know us will just have to trust us."

"Does Len know about this?"

"I talked to him and to your uncle Alf, because when we both leave—assuming you will come with me—they will have to make adjustments in how the company works here."

"What does Len think?"

"The same as you do. And, truthfully, the same as I do. There is no justification for imprisoning American citizens who have not been charged with any crime. We can say that it is for their protection, and I suppose there is some truth to that, because we know already that there is vandalism in the Japanese neighborhoods, and ugliness, with people being beaten on the street. This is not the answer. But it is the decision our President has come to, and we must obey."

"That's not right, either. The German people could have stopped Hitler, but they all just obeyed his orders when he began to take over other countries. Just obeying, when it's wrong, is not being a good citizen. I think."

Merritt smiled ruefully. "Exactly what Len said, and your uncle Alf too. They can't believe that you and I would take this on. You should know that, so you don't walk into this Buzz saw blind. When I think seriously about refusing the job, I start wondering who *would* take it, and then I picture the kind of person who would just love to lord it over the Japanese internees. And then I think, well, I've got to do it."

"Yeah. OK."

They shook hands and Russell went to look for Len and Alf.

23

Alf and Sara were beginning to think of
Independence as their home. Sara's teaching load
was heavy because new families were flocking to
the Owens Valley in search of work. Many had come with
unrealistic, romantic notions of life in California.

But when families reached California and started to settle
down, they began to understand that life would be just as difficult
to deal with here as it had been back East.

The jobs were mostly laboring work on farms or in the
mines. There weren't enough houses or roads or stores or banks or
sports fields. The people who already lived in the Valley had been
there forever and were not eager to learn from newcomers how life
back East was so much better. The children just coming into the
Valley missed their friends and their old homes and were
frightened about the war, which frightened their parents also, of
course, but the adults chose not to talk about it.

Everybody was confused and there was a lot of grumbling.

Sara, an experienced teacher, tried to use her class time to
encourage all the students to get to know one another and share

126

their experiences both in the Valley and elsewhere. After weeks of small group sessions, assigned papers, assigned readings, making plays and poems, she began to see the beginnings of new friendships emerge.

"I thought English class was supposed to be just for reading books," one of her students told her. "How come you're having us talk all the time?"

"Tell me, Peter," she replied. "Would you have asked me that question a month ago?"

"Well, no. Because we only got here two months ago and I didn't know anything. I didn't know what you might want."

"You didn't trust me yet."

Peter was silent. Then he burst out, "It's not that I didn't trust you, or didn't like you. For a teacher, you're not bad."

A small eruption of laughter.

"Good. Well, I didn't trust you either, nor anybody else in the class, because I didn't know most of you. So, I wanted to get to know you all and the way I do it best is to listen to what you have to tell me."

"OK."

"I suspect that you've learned a bit already about your classmates, just from our activities in class, right?"

She included the remainder of the class with an outstretched arm. "And the rest of you? Are you learning some names, some ideas about your classmates?"

One girl raised her hand. "Yes, but I didn't want to come here, and a lot of others didn't want to, either."

Sara nodded.

The girl continued, "We're here because my dad needs to find work. If he gets a job somewhere else, we'll be gone. So, I don't care about this class or this town. I miss my friends and I want to get back to them, but there weren't any jobs there."

Other voices spoke up.

"My dad keeps talking about the Army. He's pretty sure he'll be called up. He's worried the Japs will invade us."

"Hey, I've lived here all my life and I'd like to know where you all came from and why you ended up here."

"My brother was called up for the Army and he's in training camp. We send him cookies when we can."

"Is there any football here? What sports do you guys play here?"

"Do you ever go into the mountains? Can a guy go fishing here?"

A small voice from the middle of the room: "My mom just cries and cries."

Sara spoke quickly. "Good. We need a list. Who will write on the board?"

Soon their list of questions had more than a dozen items, from sports to other, more difficult subjects. Sara called on volunteers, and before the bell rang each student had been assigned an item to study.

That night she told Alf and Howard that it was one of her most satisfying days of teaching. "And we didn't even open the textbook!"

After she had summarized the discussion, Howard said, "I remember when we moved up here from Pasadena. I thought we had gone to the end of the earth, and I already had kin here."

"And I had a job," Alf said. "There are a lot of angry and frightened people around and it won't get better."

Howard said, "We talked for a bit about trying to get a Boy Scout troop going, remember? Because I really liked it back in Pasadena? But we got busy and I got busy and nothing happened. Maybe we can put something together now."

Sara smiled. "You have just landed on the list on my bulletin board. Great idea!"

24

At Pine Creek Mine, every worker knew that there were changes coming. The managers routinely sent messages telling the employees that their jobs were secure, that tungsten was more in demand than ever and that they would see additional visitors and activity related to the war effort. These notices made the employees feel even less secure. The fact remained, however, that the Depression's lasting results were still being felt. Jobs continued to be scarce. So, the men shrugged, pushed worry to the back of their minds and continued to work.

Russell could see that Len was upset, even though nothing was said. Len looked thinner and spoke even less than usual, and his normally jovial manner was gone. Russell wanted to talk to him, but since he had no information to give, he, too, remained silent.

One February day, Ralph Merritt appeared unexpectedly on the train. Russell took a mine truck and met him at the station. The older man had even more luggage than usual.

"Good thing you brought the truck," he told Russell. "I'm moving in, at Manzanar. And you'd better start making plans to move yourself."

They loaded the truck and set off, not for the mine works but to Manzanar. As they reached the old warehouse which had served as the final town office when the City of Los Angeles cut off all water to the orchards, Russell noted several cars and trucks parked along the street. It was a most unusual sight; Manzanar had been a ghost town for almost a decade.

"Do you want to stop here?" Russell asked.

"Yes, and I would like you to wait in the truck while I see who's here and what's what."

Russell rolled down the windows and took a deep breath. Even though it was still late winter, he thought he could smell traces of apples from the orchards. Many of the trees, now old and bent, still showed traces of green along the branches. *Maybe they would leaf out, he thought. Maybe we'll have apples here again. It would be nice.*

He wondered about Len. Would he feel that Russell and Mr. Merritt had abandoned him? And how did he, Russell, feel? Did he want to leave the mine for this new, ugly, job? No, that was an easy decision; Russell loved working at the mine, and was beginning to think he might make it his permanent lifetime job—if he didn't have to go below ground. Then why had he agreed so easily to leave with Ralph Merritt? Because it was a new adventure, because he was flattered that this important man wanted him, and because, like Merritt, he believed that when the President wanted something, the citizens should help.

Suddenly Ralph Merritt appeared and climbed into the truck. He handed Russell a sheet of paper with penciled directions written on it.

"This is the address of the house they've arranged for me," he said, "and you'll be able to stay with me till they finish the building they've assigned to you."

With the exception of the highway, none of the roads in the area were paved. The last traces of snow in protected corners or under trees made the soil slightly moist, but dust soon covered the bottom edges of the truck. They rattled along a road which, Russell was positive, had not existed the last time he had visited Manzanar. Other roads branched off on either side, and trucks rolled past in all directions.

They passed the dirt road which led to the home where Russell had grown up. Now it looked forlorn, with cheat grass and some coyote melon growing along the abandoned path.

"That's the road to the house I grew up in," Russell said.

"Want to stop by?"

"No. I don't go back there anymore. Mom comes by fairly often, does some gardening, makes sure the house is still standing. I don't know why, really. They'll never be moving back. It's such a waste, really. That's a big reason why Mom keeps picking the fruit and packing it. Not so much for the money, although that helps a lot, but to keep the fruit from just rotting on the ground."

"This will be near the camp but separate." Merritt was studying the map he had been given. "They're planning for ten thousand people. I find it hard to believe, myself. And they expect to have this all up and running in a month."

They turned off the main road onto a narrower dirt road and stopped at a barrier staffed by a uniformed military guard. Merritt leaned out and showed his wallet, open to his identification card, to the guard, who waved them through.

Inside the gate, the land had been scraped until it was almost bare of plants. Little trails of dust lifted from the sandy ground and spun around before settling. Men and machines were raking branches and uprooted plants and collecting rocks to be piled.

They could now see the beginnings of roads within the camp. Tractors pulling logs traveled up and down, causing the sand to be slightly more compact at each circuit.

At one square, several building structures had been completed; wooden, unpainted one-story affairs with two windows on each face. Workmen had just completed inserting glass into the windows, and had already installed the front door.

"They're all going to look alike, huh?" Russell said.

"Like a model home in the suburbs," Merritt growled.

"What?"

"Never mind."

It was in fact their block.

They unloaded the truck, stacking boxes and suitcases in one of the back rooms. Already the floor was dusty and more dust blew in from cracks and knotholes in the walls. Merritt shook his head. He tested the light switches, turned on the faucets, looked carefully at the heaters in the bedrooms and living rooms.

"We'll go introduce ourselves, see what we need to do to get going here."

They walked back to the gate and received directions to the military headquarters from the guard. By this time their shoes were white with sand and they could feel it in their hair and on their faces, kept sneezing it as they walked. The noise of the road-building machinery was a constant irritant, along with the hammering of the builders. A train of trucks deposited stacks of building materials here and there according to some plan not easily understood.

Ralph Merritt had already met the commanding officer so it was not long before they were head to head, over a stack of papers. Russell, uncomfortably aware that he was probably seen as a tag-along without much use, wandered back outdoors and strolled up the street. The few uniformed men he met were not interested in sending him away; he gradually relaxed and began to look with more interest at his surroundings.

There was a dreadful uniformity about the neighborhood; maybe that might change when it was all complete. On each block rows of buildings stretched from one side to the other. A few were finished sufficiently to show doors and steps regularly placed along one side. He figured that this indicated the number of families that would be living there. How would they manage to have so many people so close together?

A construction worker passed. He was a large man, with long arms and legs, carrying a ladder which he leaned against the building where Russ was standing.

"Pretty grim housing," Russell remarked.

"Well, they're not here for fun," the man responded. "They're Japs going to be living here. I'm not giving them Japs any more than I have to."

"They are Japanese Americans for the most part," Russ objected.

"They're Japs to me and they always will be. I'd drown them all if I could. They're killing our boys right and left out there and *we* have to build *them* houses?"

He spat on the ground and walked away.

Ralph Merritt emerged from his conference and waved Russ to the truck.

"They've assigned a house for my family and me, over in the administration area, so let's go check it out before we move anything we don't have to. This will be your quarters, and probably your office space as well."

Up one street and down the next they drove, slowly, in order to keep the sand as quiet as possible. Merritt had taken out his small notebook and was jotting in it; Russ knew he would be hearing about each note. The streets seemed endless and identical, but at one point the buildings were slightly different.

"This is the central area. This is the school and here is the dining area and the kitchen. Over here we find the medical area. Finally, the offices and the houses of the managerial personnel."

He counted out the order of the houses. They stopped at one towards the end of the row.

"That's mine, for the next who knows how long. Let's see."

The house was distinguished from the nearby barracks by being separate from its neighbors and somewhat larger. They checked electricity and plumbing and walked the wooden floors of each room, hearing the occasional squeak of boards.

"They say they can provide furniture, but I think we'll bring what we need from home." He began a list in his little book, muttering "curtains" "curtain rods?" "bedding" "dishes" before giving up. "We'll just have to make it up as we go along."

That proved to be the motto for many of the early days. The Army knew very well how to construct military buildings and design military camps, but this was very different. Each of the next days brought several adjustments to plans. Russell started keeping a little notebook just like Ralph Merritt did, but his contained lists for reports and memos needed for the running of the camp. They sandwiched the moving-in chores between the errands and meetings and phone calls and letter-writing that would fill every minute. They started work around sunrise and fell into bed, sleepless and twitching from exhaustion shortly before midnight.

135

Suddenly one day, after they had been working for almost six weeks without stop, Ralph Merritt entered Russell's office, a mug of tea in each hand.

"I realize we don't need the caffeine," he told Russell, "but that's what I found. Time for a break. I looked at our schedules and the lists we've made of preparations before the families arrive, and now we are right where we should be."

"It doesn't feel like we've accomplished anything," Russell objected.

"Well, we've got a lot organized, so when we want to find something, we'll at least know where to look. We know a bit more about what our responsibilities will be. We have a good feeling about what it is like to live in this windblown place. Be patient, you'll find you know more than you think you know."

25

Now that Alf and Sara and their family lived closer to Barbara and Tony, the two women frequently met at one or the other's house for tea and conversation. One day, both of them had just received a letter.

Barbara had prepared tea and ginger cookies, which they set on a table on the front porch. The Spring wildflowers were just appearing although there were still small, dirty, patches of snow in sheltered places. They watched a family of ducks march across the yard toward a small puddle.

Barbara pulled her letter from its envelope to share.

Dear Mom and Dad, sorry I don't write more often, but they really are keeping us busy now. I hope I already told you that I have been studying navigation, on my way to becoming a deck officer. It is so interesting. You can tell by the way the planets line up at night where you are, even if you are completely surrounded by water. Of course, you need to know exactly what the time is, and you need to have some special instruments, or else anybody could do it.

I'm getting pretty good at it, and I have learned Morse Code which is tapping long or short taps—dit, dit, dah-dit—that's what Uncle Charles was teaching me when I told him what I was doing.

The reason we are extra busy is because of the war now. They are trying to teach us what we need to know quicker, because they need so many of us on the ships. We're still getting the same lessons, but each day is longer, and we don't have the chance to do a lot of the exercises—we have to work homework drills whenever we can. We saw a cargo vessel limp into port here at Long Beach last week, and it was a wonder it stayed afloat till it reached its mooring. It had a big hole blown into its side, and even though the captain was so careful and slow about moving her, the water would slosh right inside her.

Our class went to the port to watch her come in, because it was a good lesson in how the deck officers made her move to increase her chances of reaching safety.

Mom, I know you worry about me. But I wouldn't be any other place, because for once I can really do something important. And I'll be helping our Navy, almost being part of it.

George finishes Cooks and Bakers next week, just about the same time I finish this class, so the chances are pretty good we'll be on the next ship together. I haven't seen him for more than a month, so we'll have some stories to share

Love, Walt

Barbara carefully folded the letter and replaced it in its envelope. The two women sat quietly for some time, then Sara unfolded the letter she had received from Dana just a few days before.

Dear Mom and Dad, I'm a Woofteddie! I'll bet you never knew that! It's very good news because I am officially signed up and enlisted and already working! Actually, it stands for

Women's Flying Training Detachment. (Mom, I know you'll have a fit about the grammar!)

We are busy assigning women to schools and jobs. We have to verify their ability as pilots by checking their logbooks, just like Tuck would do at the airfield for any new pilot. We have a lot of new women, who have somehow managed to get here by paying their own way to Texas. I had no idea how many of us there are—many are experienced pilots, and can be test pilots or instructors without much additional training. We all need some training just because we have never seen these particular airplanes before.

You'd laugh to see what we are worrying about now. What should we wear for uniforms? Or hats? Or shoes? Those of us who are here more or less permanently are staying in a local hotel; will the Army find us barracks on the military base? Fortunately, it's Jackie Cochran's problem, not ours, but it gives us lots to talk about!

I guess you can see that I am loving what I am doing. Even though we haven't even seen the new military planes, we know we will, and we'll learn to fly them soon. I am so proud that I am doing something for our country.

Love, Dana

The two women smiled at each other. Their children had left home; that was clear. And they were engaged in adult activities with adult responsibilities. They would be missed, and welcomed home with cookies and hugs. But Barbara and Sara were relieved as well; they had made it safely through their children's childhood—at least these two children—and felt they could look forward with pleasure to the next steps.

If, of course, the children continued to be safe.

26

Spring in the Owens valley is the most challenging time of the year. Temperature obeys no laws—hot, dry days may be followed by gray days leading to showers or actual rain storms, before the endless sunshine of the desert summer begins. The winds can be ferocious. Sometimes it blows so strongly that a grown man must stop walking and simply lean into it before proceeding. Sometimes it will pick up sand and scour cars and windows and skin.

On a windy Spring morning, Russell stood near the entrance gate to the Manzanar Relocation Center. He was wearing a light jacket, its collar turned up against the sand, and his favorite baseball cap, grateful for the long bill which shaded his eyes and kept some of the sand away.

Behind him, the noise of the construction machinery continued but he had become so used to it that he heard it as background noise, like the trucks rumbling past at Pine Creek Mine. He was suddenly homesick for the mine, apprehensive about the arrival of the first internee residents who were due any moment.

Squinting down the highway, he kept thinking he could see vehicles approaching, but for more than an hour there was only the usual traffic.

Then he became aware that a chain of cars and trucks were moving together and slowing as they neared the Manzanar sign. The first car in line carried four men, a driver and a civilian passenger in the front seat and two uniformed soldiers in the rear. The car stopped at the gate and the two soldiers got out, opened the gate, and waved the rest of the procession through.

Russell followed the cars to their designated parking area. The civilians gathered in silent, confused groups, looking around them. They were tired, frightened, dusty from the long drive. They were probably thirsty and hungry. Russell suddenly realized that more problems required immediate attention than he or Merritt had realized.

Beyond the shiny chain-link fences they could see the mountains, running like a wall, unbroken, impassable. The fence was capped at its corners with guard towers, not yet occupied. Rows of single-story, unpainted buildings stretched down street after unpaved dusty street. The ground had been scraped smooth for the construction, leaving loose sand to blow in directions which changed from moment to moment.

Most of the barracks were only partially complete; that was part of the reason for this first wave of settlers. They were to complete the construction for the thousands of people who were to follow.

Well, his job was to direct them to the appropriate areas. He climbed onto the back of a truck and called for quiet.

"Good morning," he said loudly. (He had earlier decided he was NOT going to say, "Welcome to Manzanar.")

"Good morning," he repeated now that the groups were quiet and paying attention to him. "I am now going to tell you where each neighborhood is located. We are making every effort to keep neighbors together. Since you all are from the Los Angeles area, you have been assigned to Block 1, here." He gestured.

"Please come with me."

He realized he was speaking slowly and clearly. He was unaccustomed to speaking to groups and knew his voice was shaky. Did they hear him?

"Come," he repeated loudly. "With. Me."

A voice from the group called, "We are Americans, you know. We do speak English."

"Sorry." Russell's entire day was in ruins.

At the block assigned to Los Angeles, the group reassembled. Russell could speak in a more normal voice, and quickly summarized the situation. The internees were to work on the facilities which would be used for shared activities: the mess hall, the medical quarters, the auditoriums and school rooms, and the gardens.

"I know you have brought tools and supplies that you already use, and that you already know how to build areas like these. So, I leave you to organize yourselves. Please tell me what I can get for you to help you with your work. I'll be over here, in the last room of this building."

He turned and left, leaving a quiet murmur of voices behind him. He very much wanted to know what they were saying—about Manzanar, about him, about the war, about the soldiers, about their families—but the hours of discussion he and Ralph Merritt had been having convinced him that they must allow the internees the most privacy and respect they were capable of giving.

He busied himself with paperwork, occasionally taking a break to stand by the window to see if he could see any signs of activity, but, apart from the continual construction activity, the place was quiet and seemed deserted.

Then it was lunchtime. The construction workers put down their tools and opened their lunchboxes. Russell found that he was quite hungry. He went to Ralph Merritt's office but found it empty. He wondered whether he should see to lunch for the new internees; it had not been covered in their lengthy discussions.

He walked down the dirt path to their buildings. As he got closer he could hear the sounds of conversation. Opening the door, he found Ralph Merritt, teacup in hand, surrounded by the internees.

"Hi, Russell, come on in."

One of the men offered him a cup of tea.

"We have sent a couple of the guards to the Army mess to bring us some lunch," Merritt explained. "By tomorrow, I'm assured that our own mess will be up and running, although you might want to double check about dinner tonight and breakfast tomorrow."

Merritt's voice was calm and steady but Russell noted that he gripped his tea cup so tightly that his knuckles were white. They were well aware that this situation was new to everybody, including the American government, and its success or failure would affect many people, up to the President himself.

He introduced Russell to the Japanese crew, carefully pronouncing each unfamiliar name and identifying Russell as his associate and a trusted member of the staff, ready to accept

143

information, complaints and questions. As each introduction was made, Russell found himself echoing the Japanese custom of a short, quick bow.

Their lunch appeared, in large tubs and covered pots. A search of the building turned up plates, bowls and silverware, and, even better, a box filled with wrapped chopsticks. They were soon a quiet group eating noodles and vegetables.

Ralph turned to Russell and said softly, "So far, so good, I think. Right?"

Russell, his mouth full of noodles, nodded. It was going to work.

27

The Owens Valley seemed to calm down for the next few weeks. People in Lone Pine and Independence became accustomed to seeing uniformed soldiers in town. In Lone Pine, they watched the almost-daily processions of buses and trucks bringing people and goods from the railroad station to Manzanar, to the camp. Those driving by could see the miles of fencing and the guard towers which were intended to reassure the local inhabitants of their safety; generally, it made them sad and nervous.

Some of the residents of the Owens Valley were offered jobs at the camp. Some of them accepted. Sara Richardson, happy to be rid of her fractious students at Lone Pine High School, became an English teacher at the Manzanar School.

At Manzanar, each day brought surprises. The construction effort, building the buildings which would house the internees, was coming along quickly but absorbed most of the labor and funds. The internee council, established by Ralph Merritt, realized that they needed to establish a vegetable garden as soon as possible, to make sure there would be a harvest that summer. They assigned work crews led by men who had been farmers until they arrived at the camp. The Army had furnished materials including fertilizer and some hand tools for preparing the gardens which would supplement the rations for the residents.

Some of the families had brought seeds and gardening tools, understanding that they would, as the government had told them, be like pioneers settling into the wilderness. But this garden effort was larger than anybody could imagine.

They needed more. The camp administration found them a tractor, somewhat old and wobbly but still working. But nothing else seemed to be available.

One morning, a representative of the Internee Council found Russell and explained their need. It took him no time at all to understand that this was a place where he could help.

"I've been talking with the gardeners," he explained to Ralph Merritt. "They need some support equipment we don't have. They have to pull heavy carts, pull plows, that sort of thing. Now, what does that remind you of?" He grinned. "I'll tell you what—my grandad!"

Ralph Merritt scratched his head, puzzled. "Your grandfather can pull a plow?"

"No, but my granddad knows every mule wrangler around. If you give me the go-ahead, I'll see what he can do."

Spence listened to Russell's long tale of life at the internee camp at Manzanar. Normally a patient man, he seemed even more patient now, fixing his eyes on his grandson and nodding slightly every now and then as Russell described the Japanese families and their responses to their new environment. Finally, Russell came to the part of the story where they were setting up the gardens.

"So you think it would be a good idea to find them some mules?" he asked.

"Well, yeah. They can't really use a lot of machines because we don't have the gas for anything extra. One of the men— he used to be a gardener before—he said he used to have a friend who used mules, but the friend died and he didn't know what had happened to them. But I thought you might have an idea."

Barbara and Molly, who had been listening as intently as Spence, began to smile.

"You're thinking about Jack Flanders' mules, right?" Molly said.

"Exactly." Spence turned to Russell. "You won't believe this, son, but I used to know some mules that understood the Japanese language."

He continued, "Jack was an old buddy of mine, had some mules he'd bought from a Japanese fellow oh I don't know how many years ago. Up around Bishop somewhere. Jack picked up enough Japanese to make those mules do just about anything. We used to take them to fairs sometimes, show them off. The people watching couldn't understand at all what Jack said to them, but the mules would start, stop, turn—folks loved it."

"Are they still around? Can you find Jack? Could we buy a couple? Or rent them?"

"Hey! Slow down! Can you get a truck? You and I can go up to Bishop tomorrow—how does that sound? We'll see what we can do. Will this camp get along all right without you for a day?"

"They don't know what to do with me now," Russell admitted. "Everything is so confused, people don't know what to do, or how to do it. And they are trying to get everything going all at the same time. And new internee families are coming in every day and they are so sad and confused and the children are crying and..."

Barbara said, "You definitely need a day away, just to get your balance back. Now go quick and get permission—can the Army buy these mules? Can you take the right paperwork? Can you get a truck?"

The family, always ready for a new project, prepared to make sandwiches for the next day's trip. Spence went to check out some old mule harness just in case.

28

Howard had continued Dana's babysitting job at the Crawfords, as a part-time substitute when Grandma Schmidt was not available. Since this almost never happened, Crawford news had slipped out of the family conversations in recent months.

But today both Howard and Alf had information.

"I was up at Molly's Place today," Alf began. "Howard, I'm sorry to say you're probably right. The men around the big table were just about jumping up and down. It was shameful, they were so excited. See this?"

He pulled from his pocket a folded piece of paper and passed it to the others. Howard took one quick look, then returned it to his father.

"Well, this is silly. Where'd you get it?"

"This was the big excitement at lunch. Can you believe it? Somebody said it must be a spy map, to prepare for invasion."

Sara said, "Invade the Owens Valley? Whatever for? This is madness!"

"I'll say it's madness!" Howard said. "That's Henke's homework paper! His mom gives him extra homework assignments so that he'll remember his German language. It's a neat idea—see, he's made a map of his neighborhood and has labeled houses and stores and stuff. That's all it is."

He thought for a minute.

"And I know how they got it. He was running to catch up with me, the other day, and he dropped his book bag and everything spilled out. We thought we'd picked it all up, but we must have missed this."

"And somebody found it, and couldn't read the simple German words, and decided to make a lot of noise about it. Alf, you'll have to make sure they understand what that piece of paper really is." Sara was indignant. "But what does this have to do with the bakery closing?"

Howard sighed.

"It's the same thing, really. People are saying that they don't want to support Germany by buying from the bakery. They hear Grandma Schmidt talking, and sometimes she can be pretty mean anyway, and so they are saying they'll just get their baked goods somewhere else. Even though it's the only bakery in town. They say it's patriotic to buy American, and not German."

"Don't they know the Crawfords *are* American?" Sara asked.

"I don't think they care, Ma," Howard said. "They're all wound up about the Jap camp—sorry, the Japanese camp, and now they have something else to get worked up about. I sure wish Father Crowley was still around. He'd set them straight."

Alf stood. "Well, we'll have to do something. Can't just sit back and let a good family suffer. I think I'll pass by Molly's Place again tomorrow."

The following morning, Alf walked along the main street toward the offices of the Chalfont Tribune, the local newspaper. He was still undecided about what he could or should do, but the sight of the bakery, open but empty of customers, pointed him in that direction.

"Good morning, Hilde," he said, selecting a pastry. "How're the children?"

"They're fine, Alf," she answered. "In fact, they're pretty happy just now. I've stopped making them do their after-school work so they think they are on vacation."

Her smile was confident, but her eyes looked tired. Her husband, Henry Crawford, waved from the back room but did not pop out to greet him as he ordinarily would have done.

"I heard about those silly rumors," Alf told her. "Some people don't have any sense."

"My mother says it's like it was in Germany in the last war. Nobody would talk to anybody. Nobody trusted anybody. Even close friends. Even relatives. I was just a small girl then, but I remember people looking out their windows, watching, watching. But not speaking. I think we did wrong to bring mama here, but Henry says it will get better. I don't know."

"Just keep making these beautiful pastries," Alf said. "Nobody will be able to resist them for long."

He felt sad, knowing he had not thought of anything better to say. *What a trivial and insensitive comment I just made*, he thought. *I haven't helped one bit.*

Just outside the bakery door, he encountered a man carrying a homemade placard which read GERMANS GO HOME DO NOT SPY HERE.

Alf stood in front of the man, staring at him. "What are you talking about?"

"Well, you know—didn't you hear about the spy map?" the man said loudly.

"Do you mean this paper?"

Alf unfolded Henke's map.

"Right! German words all over—see?"

Alf moved closer, so that he could stare at the man, whose face grew even redder. He plucked the placard from the man's hands and set it down against the store wall, so that the writing was not visible.

"It is a child's homework assignment," he said quietly. "This is a drawing by a ten-year-old, a boy interested in maps and map making and learning about the town he lives in. Do you want to tell everybody you were afraid of a child's drawing?

"And, by the way, this is the drawing of an American child. My son has been his babysitter and we are friends of his family. They belong here as much as you do, maybe more. Do you live here? Do I know you? Do you have work here in Independence, or are you just coming to make trouble?"

The man picked up his placard and stormed away down the street. Alf continued his walk to work, shaking his head sadly. The only thing he could think of was to try to remember to get Russell to put the bakery on a list of places for Manzanar to purchase bread and pastries. Not a lot of help, he thought.

29

C liff arrived home from Caltech to announce that he had a project that would occupy him for the indefinite future. Although he enjoyed his teaching responsibilities, he had discovered that his real interest lay in the chemistry lab, where he was working with a team trying to build reliable rocket fuels.

He cornered his father at breakfast his first morning home and told him how much he was enjoying chemistry.

"I thought I really liked geology, and I do, and physics, too," he said earnestly. "but there is more to chemistry—much more. For example, you find a rock and want to analyze it so you assay it. You do some chemical tests and maybe you make some scrapings, see how hard or soft it might be. Make a note of where it's found and what it might resemble. Stuff like that.

"But chemistry! You start off with a substance you think you know, and then there are so many ways to study it! You can heat it and cool it and combine it with other things. You can change its color and change what it can do, what will make it more useful, what will destroy it."

"Sounds like you think it's just right for you," his father commented, pouring coffee. "and you think there will be some way for you to turn it into a business or a career of some sort when you finish school?"

"There is so much to do, and the university is happy to pay me to do whatever looks interesting to me—at least for now. I'll still get my graduate degree but along the way I'll be working on projects that are important to our soldiers. Can't beat that!"

Alf said, "You've never said you wanted to be a soldier. You don't want to be a soldier now. Are you sure you want to discover better ways of hurting or killing people, or killing even more people?"

"What they tell us is that by improving our rocket science we can actually shorten the war. If we shorten the war, then fewer men will be killed. That's what they say, anyway."

"Who is 'They'?"

Cliff stopped, thought, then grinned sheepishly. "They are the people who want me to build better rocket fuel. Guess there's some self-interest there, right? I hadn't really thought about that part."

"It's glamorous work, Cliff. And technically interesting—fascinating, in fact. You've got a good brain for this, and you have developed some excellent lab skills. Just be sure you don't mislead yourself. The result of your work will be that men will die."

"But I can't turn my back on something I've started learning really well. I can't unlearn it. And I want our country to have the best weapons we can give them. I surely don't want the Germans—or the Japanese—to get any advantage over us. If we don't make them, the enemy will."

Alf sighed. "I can't argue with that.   I just wish circumstances were different, so you could spend your talents in another direction. But you're an adult now, Cliff, and you'll make your own decisions and whatever you decide, your mother and I trust you and support you."

It was a short hug, then both men went to their cars to go off to work.

30

Dana's next letter home contained a photo of herself in her new uniform—or clothing as close as possible to a uniform worn by a woman who was as close as possible to being in the military but without a rank or official position.

Dear Family, Here I am in my new outfit! Let me explain some of the parts to you. Up on top you will see my headgear—a white scarf which we fold into a turban to capture our hair from flying out. We call them Urban's Turbans in honor of one of the officers here.

Next, we have the dashing coverall for when we climb into and out of the airplane. Does it look like farmer's pants? Just your imagination, I'm sure!

And, since we are each providing our own uniform, there is only one rule about what shoes are allowed: everything except cowboy boots!

Seriously, we are quickly becoming more military, and very quickly learning what we can do—and that is a lot! Some of us are already flight instructors and are very much welcomed by the pilot trainers themselves, because they want to move on to more complex jobs.

Some of us, including me, are learning about the engines and the instruments on the dashboard, like altimeters and thermometers and just all kinds of stuff, all of it absolutely essential if we want to stay up in the air. This is the part I'm just loving. The large planes are altogether different from my Jackie plane. Just figuring out what those differences are, and why they are there, and how they were designed is exciting.

I may not have much time for writing because we're kept busy from morning to night, and I wouldn't honestly change that. There is so much to learn, and it is all so important. So please know I am safe and happy and will write again when I can.

I think that George wants to come up to Independence for a visit to you all, maybe in a couple of weeks. His class is almost finished but he missed getting the ship he wanted to be on, with Walt, and he's kind of lonesome and his family is far away. So, don't be surprised and I hope you will be extra welcoming, because he is a very nice man.

Love,

Dana

31

When the mules arrived at Manzanar Camp, they were an immediate success. There were three of them: Tango, Pete, and Flossie. Spence explained to Ralph Merritt that although the original plan was to purchase a pair, this particular trio had been together for almost fifteen years, so the owner refused to separate them. And they were, indeed, special, because they understood both English and Japanese. They would be uniquely suitable for this setting.

Spence led them down from the truck. Flossie was first and moved cautiously down the ramp, shaking her head to wave away flies. The other two mules followed her. Spence fed each a carrot from his pocket.

A growing cluster of people gathered around the mules. Russell returned the truck to the Army and trotted back, seeing that the half-dozen watchers he had left had now been joined by just about everybody who could press in: administration staff, including Director Merritt (holding a carrot); Mrs. Merritt, looking rather apprehensive; Army guards who were off duty; the Japanese men assigned to the garden project; children (who knew how they escaped from school?); several construction workers.

The mules were accustomed to gardening work, so it took almost no time, with Spence's help, to harness Pete and Flossie and set off digging rows for planting in the garden beds.

One of the gardeners took charge of Tango and soon he was pulling a log to smooth the paths between the barracks buildings. As the residents began to understand what was going on, families emerged with small sacks of seeds, and soon Tango was called from one space to the next, to help prepare the ground for small flower and vegetable plots.

Russell watched, fascinated. It seemed that people were settling into their new lives, coming to grips with the fact that they would be here, in these drafty, ugly buildings next door to strangers, for a long time to come. And they would make the best of it. *Maybe it would all work*, he thought. *Maybe.*

He turned back toward the administration building, but stopped. A young Japanese woman was walking quickly toward him, her hand outstretched.

"Are you part of the staff?" she asked. He nodded.

"I'm a teaching aide with the fourth-grade class," she said. "There are several things we really need for our classroom and I don't know how to go about trying to get them."

She handed him a list: crayons, unlined paper, lined paper, pencils and erasers.

"There's more, much more, that should be on this list. Books, for instance. Cups for drinking water. Paints and easels."

Russell frowned at the list. "I'll do what I can, but I'm not sure how much has been allowed for these supplies."

She scowled. "You have enough power, you in the government, to move ten thousand people out of their homes, destroy their workplaces, deprive them of their freedom, and you can't buy crayons for their children? I find that hard to believe."

She marched away.

Russell took the list to Merritt's office, where his boss added the items to the agenda for the next day's meeting.

"She has a point, sir," Russell said. "How can they require schools and not provide paper and pencils? How can they think we will have a library without any books?"

"I agree, but the problem is how we'll fix it," Merritt said wearily. "Some anonymous clerk in some office in some city, maybe in Washington or maybe in California—or even maybe in Nebraska, who knows?—forgets to add these items to a list, or maybe just doesn't feel like making the effort. And they never will see that anybody is hurting as a result. Sometimes I wonder how we ever get anything done."

He rubbed his eyes tiredly, stood and stretched.

"Did you find out the name of that aide? The one who gave you this list? I'd like to meet her. She seems to have a lot of spunk."

32

Nobody had heard from Charles for weeks and weeks. It seemed odd, with so many events swirling around the Owens Valley, to think about Charles, who would ordinarily be right in the middle of any excitement, now so far away and doing whatever mysterious work he might have found. But there was no big war news from Alaska, or even from Western Canada, so what was he doing, anyway?

Barbara made a special visit to Spence and Molly, bringing a short message from their younger child. It was a picture postcard of fishermen in a small boat on a wild sea.

"Just looking at the picture makes me seasick," Molly said. "Do you think he is trying to scare us?"

"He doesn't think like that," Barbara laughed. "He probably thinks we should all be jealous because we can't be out there in the waves like that."

"Looks cold, too. I wonder what they are fishing for," Spence said.

They absorbed the words on the reverse: "Having wonderful time. Now I have two planes to fly, and I'm eating lots of salmon."

They decoded the message, following the routine that had become familiar by now:

1. He is alive and healthy, or at least healthy enough.
2. He is still flying, so he is happy.
3. Apparently, he has not fallen in love.
4. He has not made his fortune, because he is still sending the cheapest possible postcards.
5. But he has enough money to eat salmon and buy postage stamps.
6. He does not want us to worry.

"I wonder what his second plane is," Alf said when they showed him the postcard. "I wouldn't be surprised to learn that he is involved with something chancy, maybe smuggling."

This led to some entertaining discussions about possible items Charles might want to smuggle. Howard was the most intent, studying newspaper reports and suggesting some quite unlikely items—hot dogs (as a fashionable new food); sleds and sled runners; apples (this was said with bitterness because Howard greatly missed the apples from Barbara's trees. The family had decided to stay away from the Pershing's old house, now that the camp had been built.)

The family was happy to see Howard's interest, because he had been unhappy and distracted lately. The anti-German attitudes in town were difficult for him to cope with. He continued to baby-sit Henk and his sister on occasion, mostly as a favor and just to give the parents a little treat. The Crawford bakery continued to lose customers. Hilde and Henry Crawford were trying to decide whether to give up and return to Southern California, where her mother would be back in familiar surroundings.

"We have to deal with anti-German prejudice wherever we are," Hilde sighed, over coffee with Barbara and Susan. "It's different from the feelings people have about the Japanese. Here, they are behind fences and people believe they will be safe from the enemy. But there's all kinds of anti-German propaganda out there—posters and songs and cartoons in the newspapers. You can't escape the idea that the Germans are traitors who want to kill us all."

"I think it is harder here, in some ways, than it would be in a larger city, or in Southern California where there are already large German populations," Sara said. "At least, there are ways to find friends and have a social life. Not to mention that Grandma Schmidt would have people she can talk with."

"But oh! How I hate to think of giving up the bakery! Before all this happened, we were so happy here, and we had friends—we thought we had many friends but many have dropped away."

"It's probably only temporary," Barbara soothed. "People are so upset about Pearl Harbor, and about how we are actually at war—we weren't officially at war until just about Christmas so it was easier to try and ignore all of the hate. Can you stick it out here for a while? See what happens in the next, say, six months? The war won't last forever."

Hilde finished her coffee and prepared to return to the bakery.

"We're going to try. We were just feeling that this is our home, and we want to make it really be our home, so if that requires extra effort, so be it. Henry has found a job at the mine up in the mountains, but he'll be able to spend weekends with us, and bring home enough pay to cover losses at the bakery. I'll need help from all of you, especially Howard if he is willing—with Henry at the mine, I can afford to pay for more hours."

"I'll check with Howard. I'm sure if he can, he'd be happy to spend time with Sophie and Henk."

But Howard was not happy. When Sara opened the subject he tried to ignore her, turning her comments aside with jokes or simply not responding. Finally, she stared at him over the dinner table till he spoke.

"Ma, I can't do this. I can't be spending time at the Crawfords' house, or taking care of their children, or anything. You should understand this, Ma. It was bad enough that Dad told off that guy about the map that Henk made. But people know he did that because I told him, so now I'm a marked man."

His voice was so intense and loud that he startled both parents; Howard was ordinarily the least talkative in the family.

Alf understood immediately. "Howard, I'm sorry I didn't consider you before I acted. It never occurred to me that you'd become labelled."

Howard began to calm down.

"It's because we're new here. Most of the guys in my class have known each other since they were babies. Now I come in and they don't know anything about me and all at once they hear I'm some kind of Nazi-lover. And now they know that you're teaching at the Jap camp, Ma, and that makes it even worse."

Sara and Alf looked across the table at each other. Neither could speak. Finally, Alf cleared his throat and said,

"Howard, you know how your mother and I feel about both of these situations. And you know they are not exactly identical, but similar. Right?"

Howard thought for a few moments. "Yeah, I guess. The Japanese-Americans are interned behind fences and treated like criminals, but they haven't been convicted of a crime, so it is unjust. And Mrs. Schmidt is German, but she's living in our country and is not a spy for Hitler."

"So far, so good," Alf responded. "Both alike and different. The important thing is to figure out what is the right way to behave."

"The people in the camp don't need me to do anything, really. And I don't have to go around talking about how my mother is working there, and my cousin, or anything."

"That's right," Sara chimed in. "Nobody outside the camp should be paying any attention to what goes on inside the camp."

"But Mrs. Crawford, she does need me. That's a lot of work she does at the bakery, and Mr. Crawford will be gone. That's something I should probably do. And she'll pay me, you told me."

Sara nodded, smiling. "And maybe she'll teach you how to make bread, someday."

"But Mrs. Schmidt only speaks German. And she is fierce. And she also doesn't like me anyway. And she yells. And she smells bad. I think Henk and Sophie are a little afraid of her too."

"So maybe," Alf said, "you can find a way to do your afterschool babysitting away from the Crawford house. Maybe at our house? Or the park? And have you thought about whether you actually can do this babysitting? It's summer now, but what about sports or whatever else you want to do? You're not required to do this, you know."

Everybody thought about this for a few minutes. Then Howard laughed.

"We all got so carried away about how we can save the world here that we forgot that this is real life. And most of this is on me. And I want to have the rest of the summer as free as I can. Swimming, say. I've made plans for a bike ride up the canyon tomorrow. And maybe baseball."

Howard continued more seriously. "I do want to do some babysitting, partly because I like Sophie and Henk a lot but mostly I can use the money. And I don't want somebody else to get that job away from me. So tomorrow I'll go over to the bakery and talk to Mrs. Crawford about making a schedule, maybe an hour, two hours a day, maybe in the afternoons when she's tired and I'm finished with what I want to do.

"And I just thought about this: I know a couple of kids who could also use some money. If it's ok with Mrs. Crawford, maybe I'll line them up, too."

Sara and Alf smiled. "Howard," his father said, "you have the makings of a real businessman. I have no idea how you learned that."

33

Walt and George came home to the Owens valley together, Walt because he had a week's leave before shipping out, George because he had one more week of Cooks and Bakers class and was bored and homesick. His parents lived too far away to visit, he explained to Walt, and so he would like to go visit the next best thing—Walt's family.

It was a great excuse to take their motorcycles on the road for the day-long ride up to Independence. Barbara, happy to be a substitute mom, was ready with a big dinner when they arrived.

"Mom, I packed my uniform so you can see me all dressed up," Walt told her. "You can take my picture in my new outfit, my cap and all."

It was a most impressive uniform, everybody agreed. "You look kind of like a sailor," Howard said, "but a little bit different. Do you wear it every day?"

Walt laughed. "Oh no, hardly at all. It's only for parades and impressing people. On board, we're in jeans and work shirts—kind of like George here."

Barbara, remembering the request she had received from Dana, took a photo of the two young men together, then one other of George. She would send them both on as soon as they were developed.

Of course, it was time for family to gather over coffee and dessert, to hear stories of their adventures. George was modest about his class, but made special plans to visit the Crawford bakery and discuss bread dough. Walt told about his latest cruise.

"They talk about a 'cruise' but it's really hard, very hard, work. Not like rich people on a yacht, not at all," he began. "I'm a deck officer now, and that means much of the time I'm looking for trouble. We can be moving along in calm seas—yes, Ma, I'm finally over being seasick all the time—and then there'll be some alert, like the watch thinks they see an enemy ship on the horizon, or there'll be sudden storm clouds, or, let's see, something in the engine will seize up, or seem to, and we have to get an engineer to check it out. So, it's either boring or scary, nothing in between. I love it.

"In Summer, we sailed from San Francisco to Honolulu, taking materials to rebuild the harbor where the Japs attacked us. It was an easy crossing, partly because we were in a convoy guarded by some Navy ships, but then when we got to Honolulu we saw all the damage, even after months. Pretty awful."

"Is that pretty much the route you follow?"

"No, we go just about anywhere where they have cargo to ship. They say we may carry troops at some time in the future but I hope not. For one thing, we'd have to completely rebuild a lot of the cargo area of the ship. I think that may be why they aren't trying it now. Who knows?"

"Can you still quit if you want to, Walt?" It was Sara, saying what Barbara was afraid to ask.

"No, we're under the command of the Navy now, until the war is over. We're in it, even if we don't wear their uniform."

George spoke up. "Actually, it's a good thing. You don't want everybody and his brother giving directions and orders. And the Navy knows what needs to be done to win back control of the oceans. For myself, I'm pretty proud that they've taken us in, and I just wish I could be back on a ship."

He stood. "If you all don't mind, I'd like to excuse myself and go see Mrs. Crawford. If I bring back some of her tips for making bread in quantity, I'll get some points for my grade in class."

He wanted to leave the family for a while, to give them a chance to send Walt away again, backed by their love and concern. He and Walt had talked for many hours about the differences in family life, how his own family did not seem to care about his safety but was more interested in the small amounts of money he could send home, how Walt's family chewed away at philosophical and moral issues, while his family, he said, probably didn't know or care who was president as long as they had food in their own bellies. He knew Walt would not tell his parents how frightening it was to be on a ship in the middle of the ocean, knowing that underneath your berth lay tons of explosives.

George walked downtown to the Crawford bakery, wondering what he would find. Walt had told him about some of the problems, but he found it hard to believe that people would boycott a business which had been such an asset to the town.

The front door of the bakery had a sign in large bright letters, printed on a sheet of white butcher paper:

"Welcome friends! The Bakery is Open!"

But no customers were in the shop, and the display racks held only small amounts of the cookies and pastries which George remembered.

As he tried to decide whether to call out, the curtains to the back kitchen parted and Hilde Crawford entered, holding out her hands to him.

"Ah, George Taylor! How good to see you! Would you join me in a cup of coffee?"

He was relieved. This visit would be easy and enjoyable. He took a seat at one of the small oilcloth-covered tables as Hilde joined him with two mugs of coffee and a plate of almond cookies.

"I'm taking a cooking class, Mrs. Crawford," he began. "Because I'm in the Merchant Marine, and I'm learning how to be a cook for the crew on the ships I sail on."

"Oh, that's fine," she exclaimed. "I remember your last visit, with young Walt. You were interested in many of the details of my bakery."

"Yes, and I have come to ask you some questions. I have learned that you can't just take a recipe that serves four and multiply everything and it will serve twenty-four. Or sixty. Sometimes we have several dozen men on board, and when we carry passenger traffic that's even more. That multiplication works for things like stews and vegetables, but not for bread, or quiche dough, or cakes. Or maybe it does? What kind of rules do you have?"

She leaned forward, smiling. "What good questions! You're right, you can't just expand everything, and you need to also think about how, when you bake one batch, the oven will be hot, and so the next batches take less time and burn more easily. Oh, there is so much to think about!

"I think we should divide the question into parts. Bread first, then cookies, then, maybe, puddings? Do you ever make puddings?"

Soon they were into a serious, detailed discussion, with George's pencil flying across the pages of his notebook. They didn't notice the curtains parting until a voice broke into their dialogue.

"Hilde!" Her mother stood at the table, wrinkling her apron.

"Mama, Ihr ist meine freund. George, this is my mother, Mrs. Schmidt. Mama, er heist George Taylor."

Mrs. Schmidt scowled, and sent a burst of angry, rapid German toward her daughter. George listened carefully, then spoke up.

"Mrs. Crawford, do you mind if I talk to her?" At Hilde's nod, he spoke quickly in German; the older woman's expression began to soften, then she smiled and patted him on the shoulder.

"How did you do that?" Hilde asked.

"My family lives in Cleveland, Ohio, in a part of the city where there are lots and lots of German people. I grew up knowing more German than English. I would be happy to talk to your mother, any time I can. I get homesick for my family sometimes."

Hilde gave him a big hug. "She is so happy," she said. Her mother beamed.

34

To Russell's relief, a thorough search of the warehouse revealed that a shipment newly arrived at Manzanar included paper and notebooks, children's scissors, glue and library paste. Even better, dozens of boxes of crayons were found at the bottom of the big crate. He lost no time in carrying the supplies to the schoolroom.

"I'm looking for the teacher aide who requested some supplies," he told the teacher on duty, who pointed him toward the room next door. Inside, he found the young woman who had presented him with her list.

"Hi. Here are lots of the things on your list, and we're working on the rest," he said with a big smile.

She pulled the box from his arms and set it on a nearby table.

"Where are the books?"

"Well, that's harder. Apparently, the government is not crazy about reading. But wait and see."

"That's another thing about you people in power. It's not possible to wait and see when you are spending your life in prison.

Try it sometime. Do you really think we will ever get books for our schoolrooms, or books for our own use? Do you?"

Her voice was thick with sarcasm. She folded her arms across her chest and stood in front of him, tapping her foot. Russell had never met a woman like her. He was enchanted.

"And another thing." She began to shake her finger at him. "Rice."

"I beg your pardon?"

"Rice. Rice, rice, rice. The meals we must eat, here in our prison, they have potatoes all the time. No rice. We do not eat potatoes. We eat rice. Shall we all starve?"

"OK. I'll be back."

Ralph Merritt heard Russell's report and put his head in his hands.

"Of course. She's absolutely right, and it is a terrible mistake. We'll have to fix that at once."

As with the school supplies, the solution was at hand: sacks of rice were sitting in a warehouse at Manzanar, ready to be prepared, offering the opportunity for internees to take jobs as cooks.

But the question of the books was much more difficult. Local schools and the county library were interested in helping but needed time to organize a book drive.

"Go tell the young woman we're working on the book question," Merritt told Russell. "And tell her we found the rice. What did you say her name was?"

Russell had no trouble finding her. Everyone in the school building knew her.

"My name is Joyce Takahashi," she told him.

"And mine is Russell Pershing." They shook hands.

"You should have rice in your meals soon, but probably not today. Lots to organize." He smiled.

Joyce did not smile. "If it was your dinner, it would be done today."

"It is my dinner. We eat here, too."

"But you don't have to stand in long lines."

"We stand in the same lines. We just pay attention to when is a good time to go, when the lines are shorter."

Their voices were rising, their hands gesturing. People passing by turned to see who was making such a fuss. This time it was Russell who stormed away.

35

Cliff made a special trip home from Caltech to talk to his father about the guayule experiment. Alf was a geologist by interest and profession, but he had a great curiosity about other kinds of scientific subjects and botany was high on his list. These little blossoms would be intriguing to him, and the connection with Manzanar would be a subject to catch the imagination of other family members. And Cliff missed his mother's cooking.

"So, Dad, there's this man who teaches in the botany department and he has been working on one project for a really long time without much result. But he was able to talk the government into letting him have some money and it's pretty exciting and I wanted to make sure you knew about it."

There was something in the intensity of Cliff's usually calm voice which caused Alf to wave him into a seat on the porch and continue talking.

"It's guayule. Ever heard of it? I didn't think so. Nobody has. But with the war on it could be really important. See, we used to get all our rubber from, I think, Singapore—anyway, Southeast Asia. Now, of course, that's out of reach but we still need lots of rubber.

"So this professor knew that there is one plant that only grows in desert areas, but if anybody could figure out how to get the sap from it, it makes really good rubber. Like for car tires and airplane parts and such.

"But getting the sap out is tricky. There are different experiments going on but nobody has come up with anything. And it's really a race, because rubber supplies are needed all the time."

Alf was listening intently but somewhat skeptically. "So how did you get involved, and why are you telling me this?"

Cliff laughed. "I'm not involved in it, not really, except that sometimes I play tennis with him, and he was telling me. And he knows that I live close to Manzanar."

"Now I'm starting to be interested."

"This professor believes very strongly that Manzanar was a terrible idea. In addition to the losses they've suffered, and the fact that they are American citizens who should never be treated like this, the people now living at Manzanar include scientists of various professions, including botany and biology and chemistry. And there's a big government-funded push to find new sources of rubber, it's called ERP, the Emergency Rubber Project, and it's based at Salinas, in the Central Valley. He thinks the Manzanar scientists can make some real scientific progress, prove that they are loyal and want to help us win the war, and earn themselves some money at the same time."

"Now I'm interested," his father said.

"Good. I hoped you would be. They need all kinds of help getting equipment and supplies, and apparently in setting up their work space. I was thinking maybe your company could help, and maybe, if you know this guy, you might offer him some Caltech contacts?"

Alf, as always, needed to find and feel the objects he was thinking about before he came to any conclusions. He wasted no time in reaching Ralph Merritt, who gave him and Cliff permission to visit the camp, assigning Russell as their escort. The next morning the two arrived for their first experience inside Manzanar War Relocation Center.

"Dad, he's wearing a really large rifle," Cliff murmured as they stopped at the gate. The unsmiling guard motioned them to park their truck in a specific spot near the gate, then waved them to approach.

"Purpose of visit?" Alf explained that they were guests of Mr. Merritt. They waited in the guard shack while phone calls were made. The two Richardson men stared around them, shocked by the sight of guard towers topped with giant lights and the barbed wire coiled across the top of the fences.

Soon Russell appeared, carrying a note from Ralph Merritt, and the guard unlocked the second gate, allowing the three to enter the camp grounds. It was the middle of the morning, and there was activity all about. They could hear sounds of recitations from the open school room window as they passed; cooks were preparing lunch in a vast shed; gardeners were busy in several sets of community gardens, some planting, some weeding, some establishing drip irrigation lines. Alf was especially pleased to see the three mules hard at work in the vegetable beds. They passed a large building with blocked window openings, hearing women's voices singing softly.

"What's that?" Cliff asked his cousin.

"The women are making camouflage nets for the Army," Russell answered. "Keeps them busy and they earn a little bit of spending money. They like to feel they are helping the war effort."

No answer to that.

Before long, they arrived at the guayule shed. It too was a large building separated into several sections. In one part, stands had been built about four feet off the ground and were being filled with glass containers, each holding a tiny seedling. Elsewhere sacks of plant cuttings were waiting, and at benches in a third room several Japanese men were quietly talking together, using a blackboard and several notebooks.

"Not exactly laboratory glass," Alf commented, pointing to the seedlings. Their containers were of different shapes and sizes, from tumblers to jam jars.

"They gave us several sacks of cuttings for starters, because we need so many for the experiments. But glass is really, really hard to come by, so everybody gives us whatever they can find. See those jars?"

Russell took them to a corner where several women were washing glass jars.

"Can you tell what they were used for? Jelly. Peanut butter and jelly. We're all eating as much as we can of anything that comes in glass, so that we can add them to the supplies. We need about ten thousand plants to provide good experimental material."

He led them outdoors to the next building, which looked only partly finished, its walls composed of planks separated from each other by several inches.

"This is our lath house," he said. "The seedlings will be put in here, on shelves and broad platforms, when they have been well established. They'll stay in here maybe a year. In the lath house, we can protect them from the worst of the winds and temperatures, and make the sun at least a little bit less bright in summer. We can keep them moist more easily than if they're in the ground, and the scientists can watch and study them."

"And then what?" Alf asked.

"Then, it's kind of like at the mine. When the plants are big enough, we can produce some sap from them, and then figure out how to process it so it is efficient and won't be too expensive to make. Since there isn't a good substitute for rubber now, anything would be better. But we are looking for a permanent solution, just like at Pine Creek, where Len and them figured out how to get the tungsten out."

They moved on back to the gate, where the soldiers checked them carefully for contraband ("What on earth would we want to bring OUT?" "Shut up, Cliff"). When the outer gate had been closed and they had returned to their truck, they both sighed.

"How does Russell do that, day after day?" Cliff wondered.

"I think Tony and Barbara have taught him patience," his father answered. "Let's get out of here!"

36

It was time for George and Walt to head their motorcycles back to San Pedro to return to duty. George carefully packed a dozen rolls he had baked with Hilde's help; Walt added a jar of applesauce from his mother's supply to his own sea bag.

"Are they able to save the apple trees at Manzanar?" George asked.

"From what I understand, the Japanese gardeners are doing amazing work. Already they've planted fruit and vegetable gardens and have pruned some of the apple trees. We saw some of them at work this morning," Alf reported.

"Do you think I could go into the camp sometime?" Barbara asked. "I'd like to see whether there's anything I could do to help out. Manzanar is my real home, I think."

Alf frowned. "It was hard for us to get in, and we needed authorization from Mr. Merritt himself. I'm afraid that for the near future you'll just have to wait."

Cliff looked at Walt fitting his heavy sea bag on his motorcycle. "Watch out for that jar of applesauce. Better bring it back when it's empty!"

Barbara quickly produced cookies and lemonade for the last goodbyes as Sara read them the letter she had received from Dana.

Dear Mom and family,

You'll be glad, or horrified, to see what I have been doing lately. I have soloed in three military airplanes, and I have repaired engines in each of them (no, not because I was flying—repairs have to be done routinely). It all helps me learn more about what we're doing.

Two of my roommates have already flown new planes from the assembly plant to air bases on the East Coast. From there, the Army pilots have flown them to—well—somewhere where they are needed. I'm on the list for the next batch of planes and it will be pretty special, because they are a new kind of plane, so we'll be test flying them before we make the official delivery.

On the not-so-good news side, we have lost two of our sister pilots. One just couldn't pass the tests, and had to wash out. The other was good, but it turned out she was more interested in finding a man, and got herself thrown out!

We have our new uniforms now, and so we look more official. I have enclosed several copies of a picture of me, all dressed up, in case anybody would like one.

I'm learning so much, and getting stronger all the time, because we have to do exercises and go hiking, just like the soldiers (only somewhat shorter distances and lighter packs!)

Please give my love to everybody. And keep writing me! And please tell Aunt Barbara thanks for sending the photo of George. We are now corresponding several times a week.

Love, Dana

They finished off the cookies and lemonade and began to say good bye. George quietly followed Sara into the kitchen.

"I wonder, if you have an extra copy of Dana's picture, could I have one?"

"I was saving one for you, George. I know she'd like you to have it."

He gave her a quick hug and trotted out to join Walt.

Suddenly everybody was gone. The house was silent. Barbara and Tony sat on the front porch where a slight breeze had begun to cool the air.

"Sara gave George one of Dana's pictures. He asked her for it just before he left."

Tony smiled. "I like watching that begin. I don't think Dana has had any romance yet, and he is a pleasant young man."

"He's good for Walt, I think. Even though he did start him on that motorcycle."

"Yes, Walt looks more serious, more mature. I think he's had some scary times at sea, even though he doesn't tell us," Tony said. "I dream about him, sometimes—I hadn't done that since he was little."

"I know, I'll be doing something, or maybe just reading a magazine, and suddenly I'll wonder how he is. Oh, I wish he were home."

"He wouldn't be at home, Barbara. You know that. Walt would be out on some adventure that might be just as scary. This way he's part of the war."

"What do you remember about the first War, Tony?"

"Not a lot, actually. How about you?"

"I never felt it was part of my life. I was so involved in growing up and of course we got married before our country entered the war, and then we had Russell, and you didn't have to serve and then it ended."

"And nobody in our family went to that war," Tony added. "And now look at us. All our young people are affected, one way or another. And for the life of me, I can't figure out how it all happened. Or what will come of it all."

They sat silent. Far away, a car honked, and a coyote howled as if in answer. A small airplane crossed to the East and was lost to sight in the trees.

"We never had airplanes before, or cars honking. Our world has changed, Tony, and I am not ready for it."

37

Russell thought he would always be exhausted. These days, he rose before sunup, grabbed a quick breakfast, and was in his office shortly after seven a.m. It didn't matter. There was always a stack of papers on his desk and each paper was a job, or a problem to solve, or an angry internee or soldier or civilian, or something he had forgotten to do earlier. The only good part was that this job was never, ever, boring.

He was learning, learning all the time. He had picked up some Japanese, both language and customs. He no longer felt silly making a bow in greeting or when apologizing (he felt he was spending all his time apologizing). He loved a lot of the Japanese food which was becoming more regularly available at mealtimes. Even though he spent much of his time carrying papers from one place to another, he was in motion more than he had been at the mine He missed the satisfaction of preparing reports and lists of items; here at Manzanar there was no time for reports.

As always, Joyce Takahashi was his first visitor of the morning. As always, she appeared with a fistful of notes. As they became better acquainted, she began to trust him to take her worries and demands seriously. The items she requested seemed to him to be reasonable supplies for people suddenly dislocated from their environment.

This morning, she seemed less confident and walked slowly toward his desk.

"Well, good morning, Miss Takahashi," Russell said, practicing his greeting bow. "I see you're carrying no papers today. Can I believe that all of your concerns have been addressed?"

He had just begun to mildly tease her. He hoped she would understand. He found he was holding his breath.

She smiled. Russell grinned and pulled out a chair for her.

"It's quite the reverse, Mr. Pershing," she said. "I have a dilemma and I hope you can help me. I may have to break a rule or two."

"Oh, not that!" They had quickly agreed, weeks ago, that there were far too many rules and regulations for any of them to be taken seriously.

"There is a man, here, a cousin of my aunt. I hadn't met him until we all ended up here. He is a famous photographer. He has—he had a studio in Little Tokyo, in Los Angeles. He has taken photographs of parades and weddings and other ceremonies, all the important events. All Japanese in Little Tokyo wish to have this man take their photographs."

Russell had almost become accustomed to hearing about well-known internees. But he had not heard of any photographers.

"My problem is this. He has brought a camera lens into the camp. He knew it was not allowed, so he hid it very carefully. He and a friend have made a box for it, and he intends to take photos of life inside the camp. He says it is a historic event for us—for the

Japanese and for the Americans both, and it is important to have a record of the daily life here."

Joyce was unaccustomed to speaking more than a few quiet words at any one time. She found herself a bit out of breath.

Russell thought for a moment. Then he said, "But we have photographers here anyway. Already two famous photographers, Ansel Adams and Dorothy Lange, have visited, and they will probably come again."

"But those are government photographers, taking photographs for the government! And they are Caucasians! Mr. Miyatake, he takes pictures of real life, weddings and parties and people in shops, ordinary things. He wants to take pictures of ordinary things in the camp so that they will not be forgotten. That is what he means as a historic event."

"Well, I wasn't thinking it would be like a bomb going off," Russell grumbled, then stopped himself. "Gosh, I'm sorry, I didn't mean that. I was just trying to think of something really big and outlandish. I wasn't trying to insult you!"

Joyce smiled. "I know you well enough now to be sure you didn't mean to make me angry. And I know I am usually angry anyway. But what are we going to do?"

"I'm sure Mr. Merritt will say Why does this man think he deserves special treatment? We are trying to treat everyone fairly, and he wants to have special privileges. Is it just because he is famous?" Russell folded his arms and waited for Joyce to respond.

"He would say that he is bringing his skills to the camp, and making a record that will be available to everybody. The war won't last forever, and someday we will simply want to remember what happened in our lives. Having the pictures of the mealtimes and the gardens and all the other things, that will remind us of the good and the bad times, and it will be more honest than just thinking about the bad times only."

"Oh." Suddenly Russell found himself thinking how much he would like to have a set of photos of the camp. He could see himself showing his mother and father what he had been doing. He held out his hand.

"Come along with me, Joyce, and we'll see if he's at his desk. Can't hurt to ask him, anyway."

Ralph Merritt looked tired most of the time these days. He needed a haircut, and (Russell thought but would never say) clothing more appropriate to life in the desert. He wondered how his boss would look in jeans. They knocked on his open doorway and were called in. Merritt looked with interest at Joyce.

"I'm happy to meet you," he said after Russell's introduction. "I think it has been three times now that you have made valuable suggestions and have found us falling short in ways we have been able to correct. I wonder what you are bringing me today?"

"Sir, there is this man..." and Joyce told the same story she had told Russell. Ralph Merritt was silent for several minutes. Then he began to ask questions: What kind of photos had he already taken at Manzanar? What did he plan to do with them? Would Joyce bring samples to him? What kind of photos had he taken before the war? Are there samples for him to see as well? Did this man know Ansel Adams? Dorothea Lange? Would they vouch for him? If permission were given, the administration would have to review the photos before they were released. Would the man accept that? If the man were released to move away to a different part of the country, say, Minnesota, would he be willing to go?

By this time, Russell's fingers were twitching from his scribbling. He had become used to transcribing as well as he could all the meetings his boss attended. Today was harder than usual, because he wanted so badly to participate in the conversation.

"Why doesn't this man come himself to see me?" Merritt finally asked. "He doesn't sound like the kind of fellow who might feel too shy to speak for himself."

"Oh no, on the contrary," Joyce burst out. "He doesn't know I'm even here. He is so sure he will be turned down that he won't even try."

"Oh, wait, wait!" Russell threw his notebook on the table and dashed away, returning in a few minutes with a manila folder.

"I live surrounded by these folders and I had forgotten all about this!" He pulled out a letter.

Ralph Merritt read it, and then read it again. He shook his head and smiled, passing it on to Joyce Takahashi.

"It really makes me believe in the power of coincidence," he said. "Edward Weston is one of the most famous photographers in the West, he is found in museums across the country, and he has written in support of Mr. Miyatake. He hopes that we can include Mr. Miyatake in any photographic projects we undertake here. Russell, send off a letter to Mr. Weston at once, invite him to visit here, and when you have arranged a date with him, set up a meeting with Mr. Miyatake."

"No sooner said than done, boss," Russell answered.

The meeting between Merritt, Miyatake and Weston was a great success. Russell had arranged the conference room so that it appeared much less formal. He found some scraps of carpet to place on the floor in one corner, and coaxed Tony into lending him four comfortable arm chairs from the collection of furniture at the movie studio warehouse. A table against the wall held a hotplate with a kettle of water, a tray with tea cups and spoons, and some cookies on a platter. Joyce had volunteered for hostess duty and was ready to make pot after pot of tea, just the way Toyo Miyatake liked. Russell had found a small table and stool, where he perched with his trusty notebook and pencils.

Edward Weston arrived first, greeting Merritt warmly, reminding him of meetings the two had held while arranging a photography exhibit in Los Angeles some years before. He was met almost at the door by Toyo Miyatake, who was clearly happy to see his old friend. After Joyce served tea, the first part of the conversation began, led by Ralph Merritt, who reviewed the relationship between Weston and Miyatake.

"He was your student, I understand?" he asked Weston.

"Hardly a student. He is such a talented photographer. We met to discuss ideas we were both struggling with at the time, ideas about making photography do more than simply record events. Back then photographers could make terrific photos of individuals and groups, but they were more like records— marriages, company celebrations and the like. If you knew the people, they were wonderful souvenirs, but if you didn't, they were just pieces of heavy paper. I was then just starting to look at photos as art. If a painter paints a nude, or a landscape, then a photographer should be able to do the same transformation with his camera. Toyo agreed."

"Yes," Miyatake answered. "I have always taken photographs of celebrations and other big events, but it is because I can show the people reacting to the events around them. For me, it is the people who are important."

Merritt smiled. "And I suspect that you feel the same way about the project you want to do here. Tell me, Mr. Miyatake, what do you expect to accomplish by taking photos here?"

The Japanese man did not move for perhaps a minute. Then he sighed and reached into the folder he had brought with him, pulling out a small stack of photos. Weston and Merritt leaned forward. Russell, in his corner, wished for a telescope.

They took the photos to a nearby table and spread them out. Russell and Joyce tiptoed closer. The pictures were of a variety of scenes. In many of them the Miyatake family engaging in daily activities—the children dressing for school, the adults gardening, walking outdoors—while others were more varied. An old man sat on a wooden chair in the middle of an empty room. Two toddlers in overalls fought over a ball on the dirt street.

Edward Weston picked up one picture, then another, staring intently at them before replacing them. He looked at Miyatake, then nodded.

Merritt also studied the photos carefully. Toyo Miyatake stood silently, impassively waiting for the other two men to finish.

"I understand, Mr. Miyatake," Merritt said. "You are showing us not just *what* is happening here, but *how* it affects us. That old man, for example. He looks lonely but not frightened. It's a very strong picture."

He looked at Weston who said, "I'm hoping that you can find a way to make Toyo an official camp photographer. That way he can use his camera out in the open, and maybe we can even find a way to bring his own real camera, one of the good ones, from Los Angeles to Manzanar."

"Well, hold on! We have a lot of bridges to cross before we do anything! You've done a pretty good job of convincing me that we need our own visual record of life here at the camp. But why should that photographer be Mr. Miyatake? Why not have a contest to see who should be camp photographer?"

"Because he is the best! And we want to have a chance to have our pictures taken by the best Japanese photographer! We know about him already!" Joyce was almost weeping, her usually quiet voice rising.

"May I speak?" Toyo Miyatake stood. "Of course I want to have a chance to use my cameras again, to keep my skills fresh. But I don't want to be a disturber of the camp life. I have an idea. I can take photos and give as many to our camp newspaper as they want. They can publish them in the paper at any time. I can also teach young people how to be photographers. We can make a dark room and develop photos."

"Okay. I can see some good ideas here. But you all have to understand that we cannot afford to give the slightest impression of favoring one person over another, or offering special exceptions to the camp rules. We have to remember that Manzanar Camp was set up to protect the Japanese American population from attack by others, but also to protect our country from attacks by the enemy. We still don't know how all of this is going to work. We don't know each other yet. I need some time to think about all of this. Thank you all for coming, and I will have some decisions for you by—let's see—two days."

He stood, clearly indicating he was finished with this meeting. Everybody melted away, the two photographers in close conversation as Weston walked to the main gate.

191

38

Barbara was lonely. She felt at loose ends, with not enough to occupy herself. Tony was busier than ever at work, as was Russell, who came home only occasionally, to stay only briefly, for a meal or a short visit or simply to sleep. Walt was probably at sea by now, and she knew not to expect a letter from him till he reached port and George nagged him to write. Charles and Dana, her most faithful correspondents, had not written in weeks. *Blast this war,* she thought. *If only we could return to normal, even if it's just for a little while.* She had gardened, canned, stitched. She had pulled out her old stack of piano music and practiced, pleasantly proud of the way her fingers still responded after years of non-playing.

She was taking the morning's laundry from the clothesline in her back yard when she heard noises from out front. She walked around the house to find a large unfamiliar-looking man closing her front gate and walking toward the house. He was limping, relying heavily on a cane. His black beard was full, masking his face. He wore jeans and a battered leather jacket which looked hot in the California summer. He moved slowly.

Barbara continued walking toward him. She looked into his face and saw his bright eyes. She folded her brother into her arms and he seemed to sag a little.

She brought him into her house and sat him down in the kitchen bringing him a plate of cookies and a cup of tea.

"Well, Charles, what kind of sandwich for you?" she asked briskly. "I have some chicken and some cold roast beef."

"Do you have some soup on hand?" he asked. "I always love your soup more than anything."

"I just happen to have a pot on the back of the stove. Some now and some at supper? If you can stay?" She tried to be calm but he looked so tired. She hoped Tony would come home early.

He sat back in the wooden chair, stretching his legs out before him, and spooned up her soup, then wolfed down a cheese and tomato sandwich.

"Yes, I can stay for a while," Charles said. "I'm actually home for medical reasons. I need to rest up so my leg will heal before I go back to Alaska."

"You're going back?"

"Oh yes. I have to. There are people counting on me. And anyway I think the hardest part is over."

"Can you tell me? Want to wait till you're less tired? I love your beard! Want to take a nap? Can I call some people—Alf, Dad and Mom? Have them come over? What happened to your leg?"

He waved at her to slow her down.

"I really can't talk about any of this now. Not that it's secret or anything, but it's just hard. What I would want most, Barbara, is to talk to Dad. Just him, just the two of us. I think I want to see him listen to me. Can you fix that?"

"But are you really OK, Charles? Will you get better? Is there something wrong with you that you don't want me to know?"

"OK, big sister. I'm hurting right now, but I'll be better." He grinned, and the smile she remembered from his childhood was still there.

"Then I'm off to get Dad. You gather up some food because I'm sending the two of you off on a picnic."

When she returned with Spence, Charles had assembled a basket with apples, cookies and several sandwiches, along with two large jars of lemonade and some cups.

"Dad is taking my car. The two of you can go out to our old house—Tony's and mine—in the old orchard. It's been vacant ever since they chased us out of the orchards and cut off the water, but every now and then I just go out in the afternoons. It's really nice there, quiet and deserted. Come back when you're ready. I'll have your bedroom ready for you, Charles."

"You're a pretty good sister, Barbara."

She gave him another hug, figuring that he needed as many as he could get right now, and waved them off.

The little house in the orchard looked just like it had when Tony and Barbara lived there, except that cheat grass and rabbit bush had overtaken the front yard, and the gardens were dry and dusty. Barbara had given her old house key to Spence, so they lugged the picnic basket inside. Most of the furniture was in their new house in town, but they found two chairs in the kitchen. Spence poured lemonade.

"Charles, I'm glad to see you, safe and relatively sound," he began. "I'm ready to hear what you have to tell me. I'm assuming we will keep most of this between us?"

"Dad, I have killed some Japanese soldiers, or as good as killed them. I have seen things that nobody should see. I saw our men who had been bayoneted as they slept. I have been more scared than I thought ever would be possible. Just telling you this will make you sad, I know. But I keep thinking that my family needs to know how I spent my war, in case I don't see you again. And I can't bear to tell them myself."

Spence nodded. "And now you are back home, where you are close to a prison for Japanese Americans. Oh, it's not supposed to be called a prison, and Russell will tell you a more balanced story about Manzanar Camp. And these are Americans even if they look like the enemy. But it must be difficult for you to think about that."

"To tell you the truth, I haven't even been thinking about that. Before I went to Alaska, I don't think I had ever seen any Japs—Japanese. Anyway.

"You know, I was doing some flying for various agencies, people who are making maps of the far north. It started as a scientific mission, and then after Pearl Harbor it got to be more of a military mission. Instead of photographs of snow and mountains and such, we were taking photos of harbors and the waters around them.

"But I heard about this Army officer who was putting together a band of scouts. He is amazing. He's found prospectors, Indians, outlaws of various kinds, just anybody who is strong and tough and knows how to survive in the wilderness. I figured I could be useful with my plane, so I found him and talked to him and he signed me up.

"And I have been useful. See, the Jap army has been trying to invade all the way up there. They figure that we won't be expecting them. And we weren't, at first. But now our band of scouts goes overland and watches for activity that looks like possible landing parties and then we go and attack them before they can get established. My job has been to fly out ahead, or in the area, where I can see farther and give them some good directions. Sometimes I have a partner with me, sometimes I'm by myself."

"Sounds exciting," Spence said quietly.

"It is exciting. And for me, it started out almost like a game—can I spot them before they see me, that kind of thing. But soon it became real. I spotted a raiding party and called out our guys. They hid behind some rocks on the shore and shot the Japs while they were still in their boats. I saw them fall, and one fell into the water and we shot him while he was trying to swim back to his boat and then he drowned. So, I think I basically killed him."

He couldn't continue. They sat silently for a while. Then Spence said, "Tell me about your buddies."

"They've been brought together from all over this part of Alaska. They know how to live in the wild and they would rather be there than any other place. Let's see—the ones I know best are probably Iron Mac—he used to be a logger and he can throw an axe at a target and never miss. And there's Silent Slim—never says much but when he does, you have to listen. He's prospected for gold and silver, actually found enough gold to stake a claim but he lost it in a poker game. He can track just about anybody just about anywhere. And Whiskey Red—he's the best at leading us across snow when the drifts are higher than we are tall. They call me Mad Wings Chuck. Because of the airplane."

Spence chuckled. "Never thought I'd have a son named Mad anything. Now go on. How'd you hurt your leg and how bad is it?"

"I got shot. We were scouting. I flew up to a place on the coast where I could set my plane down on the water—I'm mostly flying seaplanes now, up there. I was just about to touch down when I thought I saw movement nearby. So, I lifted up and flew over this rocky place, and there were some Jap snipers there and one shot right up at my plane, bullet went right through my leg and out the side of the cabin. Man, that hurt! I put her down ok, and my buddies heard the noises and probably saw me go down and up and down, so they knew something had happened, so they snuck up and took care of that whole nest. I think they said there were four. They got to me pretty quickly, and rigged something up to pull me along till we got back to camp. I should recover pretty well. They say it just takes time and I have to do exercises."

"Have you had any more battles?"

"Not exactly battles. Mostly we try to stay away from them, because what we're supposed to do is indicate their location and strength to the regular Army patrols. And I think that it's slowing down some because they are realizing that the American army is here and strong. So, I think when I get back, there'll be more flying just to check on things, not to go out hunting. I hope so, anyway."

"Are you officially in the Army?"

"Well, yes and no. We all got sworn in, and we have numbers and all, we get paid, and we follow the orders of our commanding officer. But he's pretty loose with us. We don't have to wear uniforms, and we get to carry whatever weapons we want to carry. Actually, I don't carry any weapons. I figure I have my plane and that's enough."

Spence smiled. "I imagine you would be more of a menace than a help if you had a gun. I'm not sure you would know what to do with it."

"We had to learn how to clean it and load it and shoot it and all, and I was actually not bad. But I know I couldn't point it at anybody. My pals know that, too, so they don't give me a hard time. Now, if I didn't have my plane—that would be different!"

"Are there other things you want to tell me?"

"There are things that wake me at night, and things I hope I will forget someday, but no. Not to tell war stories. I know that I don't feel about the Japs the way the rest of you do, and that's a problem. I'm not going to change about that—no, I won't say why. But I don't want my experiences to influence how you all feel, and I don't want to give up my family. It has been so good to come home and see you and Barbara. And Tony too I hope. But I won't stick around. I'll be on my way tomorrow."

"Why don't you stay here for, say, a week? Barbara won't mind and she won't tell. It would be a good place for you to rest your leg. Maybe you could do some carpentry work for her here, to repay her."

"I'd like that. I've got a week's leave, so I can stay a couple of days. Would you come up and visit me again then, before I leave?"

"I tell you what. You know I must talk to your mother about this. You know I will tell her much of what you have told me. I haven't agreed to talk to anybody else, although either you or I should talk to Barbara, who has been so faithful. After I talk with your mother I'll see you again. How's that?"

"If Barbara will agree, I would really like that. She'll come this evening. I'll ask her then, and—you're right—I need to tell her some of what is making me act so crazy."

"Good. I'll be back in a day or so." Spence gave his youngest child a long hug, then walked quickly down the path away from the house.

198

39

When Ralph Merritt told Russell his decision in the matter of Toyo Miyatake, Russell had to bury his face in his handkerchief so that nobody could see his expression.

"Are you laughing at me?" Merritt asked.

"Oh no, sir—at least not out loud." He tried to keep a straight face but failed miserably. "I'm thinking about how it will all work, and mostly I'm saying to myself, please don't make it be me, please don't make it be me."

"And just who else do you think it could be?" Merritt tried to scowl, but seeing Russell's expression he sat up and tried to offer his reasoning.

"I want to make this work. But we must make sure that nobody thinks we are making life too easy for the internees. We don't want to give anybody a chance to complain that we are favoring them, or anybody in particular. We must be seen as the big, tough, strict, military Americans in charge. We must show we are in charge here. Not to the Japanese-Americans. They already know that. But the newspapers and the politicians and all. So, that's why I have decided on a plan that will actually be a compromise but will look like we are in charge."

Russell giggled.

"Stop that. It's up to you to make it work. I leave it all up to you and I won't be anywhere close. Now go off and get started."

The Miyatake building was familiar to Russell, who had become familiar with most families' quarters. There was a small vegetable garden by the front steps. Inside, the family had done their best to make the drafty, crudely-built building attractive by filling the walls with pictures from their collection and from magazines. They had arranged flowering plants in all the rooms.

The photographer opened the door, smiling at Russell.

"Are you bringing me good news?" he asked.

"Well, I think that in general, you'll agree that it is good news, and it's definitely a good start. But I must admit I'm embarrassed to tell you what he has decided.

"He's appointing you a camp photographer. Nothing on paper that says you are the official photographer. That must be worked out. You'll be expected to take photos of official visitors, camp events, and other photos you think should be part of the archives. He expects you to work with the young photographers we may have here, and teach photography. But that is in the future because you and I have to figure out a way to get them to have cameras and use them, but without any possibility of taking illegal photos. We'll have to get started on that.

"Here's the thing. For now, anyway, you'll use the camera you have rigged up already. But at least it will be out in the open. You'll line up the picture you want to make, and then, well, then, at least the way it's set up now, then..."

His voice faded away.

Miyatake stepped closer. "Then what?"

Russell sighed. "Then I will press the shutter button."

"What?"

"I told you. It's crazy. But I can't let Mr. Merritt get into trouble because he is trying his best to make this work. Maybe I can sort of just wander past your camera when you have it set up, or something. Or you can pretend to teach me how to use it. I think it's worth a try, and it's a start toward everything we would like to see in the future—getting your cameras up here and all."

The photographer sat quietly for a few minutes, then stood and left the room, returning with his bulky box camera.

"Let's go take a walk," he said. "Show me some things you'd like pictures of."

The two strolled out together. The first stop was the garden area, where the mules were working steadily on several different chores: delivering buckets of water to gardeners in the fields, plowing new areas for expansion, and pulling a sledge filled with stones to a place near the back fence.

"That's Yokio's project," the photographer said, waving to a man wearing a broad-brimmed straw hat. "He's making a water garden that will run through much of this part of the camp. He is a master of design."

Together they set up the camera near the water buckets. The mules worked on, ignoring them. The workers, who recognized Miyatake, seemed to work harder and more gracefully. Russell quickly pressed the shutter. They reassembled the camera and moved on.

Turning a corner, they found that the lath house so carefully constructed for the guayule plants was in ruins. The workers were on their hands and knees, carefully salvaging the broken shelves and re-stacking the boards which had been ripped from the walls. It was the wind, someone explained. The Spring and summer winds were so strong, stronger than anybody had imagined, and the wind seemed like acid, the way it blew through and dashed the walls against the floor. The only good news was that most of the seedlings had not yet been transplanted, and so were saved, inside the lab buildings.

"We learned another lesson," their guide continued. "We have now placed the lath house in the shelter of the lab buildings. We will rebuild it from the beginning. That should help."

So much work, Russell thought. *They are building things that won't be used for another ten years, when maybe this will be all over. And they are building things to be permanent. Why?*

They had made a half dozen pictures. They separated so that the photographer could develop them, and so that Russell could take care of some of the other chores he had undertaken.

40

Howard was not happy. He missed his friends in Bishop, where he had been promised a spot on the city's summer baseball league. He intended to become a major-league baseball player when he finished school, so he regarded this move as a thoughtless act on the part of the family, depriving him of his goal. Since he had never mentioned to them that he wanted to be a professional baseball player, they were innocent, but he felt that somehow they should have known.

The summer baseball being played in Independence was small-town baseball. The teams were composed of a mixture of all ages and even included two women who played fielders when needed to make up the required number. Howard was reluctant to approach them, but finally inquired about a spot and was selected to join the Independence Coyotes. He figured it would use up some free time and give him some exercise.

At his first practice, he sat in the dugout next to a couple of men he vaguely recognized. They were about the same age as his father. When they introduced themselves, he found himself between John Trent, manager of the hotel, and the Presbyterian minister.

"Having trouble filling up your time this summer?" Trent asked. "Not a lot of things to do here in the summer."

"Oh, it's not bad," Howard replied. "I've picked up a couple of part-time jobs. And I like baseball. I didn't know I could get on the team till just lately."

"What kind of jobs have you found?"

"Well, the regular one is more of a favor. I'm watching the Crawford kids when Mrs. Crawford needs me. They are pretty nice kids, and they can be darn funny, too."

"They're the ones running the bakery, right?" the minister said. "Maybe they'll teach you to cook!"

"Mrs. Crawford is helping to teach my friend to bake. He's in the Merchant Marine and has to cook for his whole ship."

"Who is the woman who is living with them? She doesn't seem to understand English."

"That's Mrs. Crawford's mother. She's German."

Just then, it was time to take the field. Howard was to play third base.

41

D ana had progressed in her training, and now was one of the pilot instructors herself. Her strength, she thought, was her insistence on studying the manual and thoroughly understanding the engine before ever taking off. This meant a careful pre-flight check including walking around the plane, paying attention to everything.

Sweetwater Field was not that different from the Owens Valley, she felt: hot, dry, windy, nothing special to see when you look around your area. She was about to test a new fighter plane, flying it for the first time. Notebook and pencil in hand, she walked around her plane slowly, carefully noting everything she could think of: any scratches in its paint, the treads on the tires, the joints where the landing gear folded into the plane's belly, the way the surfaces of the wings reflected the sun.

When she was convinced that the exterior of the plane was free of problems, she climbed into the cockpit to check the controls. Earlier, the mechanics at the airfield complained that she was taking too much time on her pre-flight checks: "none of the REAL pilots worried as much as you do" but last week, a pilot had died in the crash of a new fighter plane, brought down by an oil leak which had not been spotted and repaired. Now, as Dana went through her checklist, they busied themselves with little chores, just close enough so that they could see when she was finishing.

She climbed back out again and waved to the mechanics to come.

"There's a noise," she reported. "A kind of mewing noise."

They clustered around. At first no one could hear anything odd, because the wind itself was making fierce noises, but during a calm moment they all heard a small sound, like a squeak or a scratch.

"Maybe it's that new baffle," one of them said.

"No, I guess it's something in the fan back there."

"No," said a third man, "there *is* no fan back there in this model."

They stood and thought for a while. They had just spent more than an hour that very morning, running the pre-flight checklist prepared by the airplane factory. They had heard no squeak. There was a small, muttered argument in favor of deciding it was nothing wrong; the pilot should go ahead and test it, maybe with a short flight.

"Maybe it's like brakes when they wear down—they squeal for a while before they show any real damage."

"But," Dana countered, "this plane is essentially new. It shouldn't show any brake wear at all."

They stood for a few more minutes, thinking. Then Dana said, "If I'm going to get a flight in today, I've got to be in the air soon. Otherwise the winds will be even stronger."

"One thing. Start her up, rev the engine and see whether that affects anything."

She did. With the motor going, nobody could hear the squeak, but the instant it died, the noise was back.

The oldest of the mechanics spoke up. "The only thing I can think of, since it is a brand-new plane and unfamiliar to us, is to send for a factory rep to check it out."

They all nodded. Dana scowled. "That will set this whole program back a week, maybe more. Our men need this plane in the air, not on the ground."

"So, you want to go up in her? Or are you scared of a little noise?" It was one of the mechanics who did not like women in airplanes and found opportunities to test her whenever he could.

"I'm going to take one more look." She decided that this time, nothing would escape her. She took a small flashlight and a screwdriver with a long handle and re-entered the cockpit, examining every corner, every connection, every place where one object touched another object. She twisted handles, set and unset switches.

Suddenly she stopped and stared at the cover of a safety light attached to the base of the pilot's seat, listening. Slowly she reached down and pulled on the wire cover until it came free. She reached down with her gloved hand and pulled out a small kitten.

"This belong to anybody here?" she called.

Again, they clustered around.

"I wonder if she traveled all the way from the factory," Dana mused when nobody claimed the kitten. "Anyway, her name is now Sweetwater and she will live in my office."

42

Alf had made sure to tell Russell his idea about the Crawfords: that if the Manzanar Camp would buy bread and pastries from their bakery, it would surely help out. However, it turned out to be a really bad plan.

"First of all," Russell patiently explained to Alf, "The foods the Crawfords make are not foods the Japanese people like to eat. We love bread, but they don't seem to eat that much of it, and they *really* don't like the chewy bread the Crawfords make.

"They also don't eat many pastries like ours. They don't like donuts or pies or other things with stuffing, even fruit stuffing. They were polite, of course, when we presented the plan, but the committee in charge of ordering food just never orders any of the same dishes the Crawfords make.

"Thanks for the idea, anyway."

Alf felt embarrassed. He knew much of what Russell had said, or could have figured it out for himself. He felt that his meddling had only made things worse. Feeling sorry for himself, he decided to make a trip up to Pine Creek and see what was happening at the tungsten mine.

The first thing Alf noticed as he approached the mine was that everything was busier than he had remembered. A procession of trucks filled the road, which had been widened and smoothed. The employee parking lot was full. He found Len's office, where his friend was sitting behind a desk, looking harried and talking on the phone. He waved at Alf to come in and grab a chair, then continued bringing the phone conversation to an end.

"Haven't seen you in a long time," Len said as they shook hands. "What brings you up here?

"I don't actually have a reason. I'm just fed up with everything and mad at everybody in town, it seems, and so I thought I needed to get away and come up here and see an old friend. But here you are up to your elbows in work! I don't mean to interrupt—but do you have time for a cup of coffee?"

"Always, and with pleasure," Len said. They found the company canteen empty and sat with steaming cups. Len summarized his past few months for Alf. "Pretty much all the same stuff. But we've been busier all the time. Seems odd that we used to worry about whether we could keep the miners busy, but once we found this pretty rich vein, we're going great guns. It's still middling quality ore, but good enough to get good prices. I miss Russell, though. He has the ability to keep going at some really tedious work, without whining. How is he?"

"He's about as overworked as you are, these days. Ralph Merritt keeps him hopping from morning till night, sends him on the most hopeless errands. They're all trying to make this camp work, even though just about everybody thinks it is a terrible situation. You know they have so many different kinds of people inside the fence—scientists and landscapers and cooks and artists—so much talent and so many projects just cut off and going to waste. For example, just a tiny example, the government authorized a library building but never provided money for books, so they have developed a project to gather books from schools and libraries all over the country, and of course most of them are old and battered and useless."

"Your government makes a lot of assumptions without much evidence," Len remarked.

"Len, you're still talking about 'your' government. Just like when we were kids. You haven't changed much."

"I'm more careful unless I'm talking to somebody like you, or Charles. I'm Paiute through and through, always will be, and our situation hasn't improved any, either. So, tell me about Charles."

"I don't even know where he is. Last I heard, he was in Alaska, but now with the war going on, he won't say anything except that he is alive and well. We get the occasional post card but it doesn't say anything specific. Barbara worries the most. She has been his minder ever since he was little."

"And Russell's brother? I heard he joined the Navy."

"Walt? No, well, not quite. He has joined the Merchant Marine. No kidding. Has a uniform and all. He loves it, as far as I can see. He is becoming a Deck Officer, learning navigation. Walt is working harder than I've ever seen him. Now, I'm the one worrying about him, because the ships Walt will be on are the ones in the most dangerous waters. Keep him in your thoughts, Len."

"I will. You know the last time I saw him, I chewed him out for, well, he and Russ were having a fight on company property and I was embarrassed. Not very adult of me."

"Adult. We're none of us acting very adult these days. Did I mention Dana? She's gone off too, she's going to be a pilot. In fact, she already is a pilot. She's attached some way to the Army and ferrying planes back and forth and even doing some test piloting. I never would have believed it but there she is."

"OK. Go on. Your boys. Cliff and Howard." Len rose, brought back fresh cups full of coffee.

"Cliff and Howard are probably the least dramatic of anybody in the family. Cliff is in graduate school at Caltech, in chemistry, sort of, and Howard will be finishing high school this next year. Right now, he's playing baseball."

"I know," Len said. "I've watched him play a few games and he's pretty good. He's fast and he's got a good eye and that long arm of his just reaches out and plucks a ball from the sky. He's got some good times ahead of him I think."

"You know, Len," Alf said, "Just going through the names, just telling you my family news, makes me feel better. If you've got five more minutes, I'll tell you what was the final straw today, and see if you have any ideas."

He told Len about Hilde and Henry Crawford and Hilde's mother, her arrival in Independence and the dust-up about the map with German names. Len smiled, and even chuckled at some points, making Alf realize that part of the situation was, in fact, ridiculous.

"But I see what troubles you, Alf. The Crawford family has been an asset to Independence, good neighbors, friendly folks, and if they can't make a success of their bakery, it's a problem for all of us. Or it should be. I tell you what. I've got some friends who I know buy from the bakery fairly regularly. It shouldn't be hard for them to buy just a little bit more and a little more often. Maybe if you and Sara work out a way to introduce this Grandma to some people, that would help?"

"I can try. Sara has been trying. But you know people we don't know. Maybe something will turn up."

43

I t was time for Charles to leave. After only a couple of days, his leg was less painful. His wounds were healing well. He felt that the days of rest did a world of good, and the conversation with his father didn't hurt, either. He sat on Barbara's front porch waiting for the promised visit from Spence.

Spence soon pulled up in his battered pickup truck with Molly at his side. She was carrying a basket filled, Charles could tell, with food: cookies, sandwiches, sandwiches and a large jar of cold tea. Charles stood, balancing without his cane, and carefully walked down the porch stairs, where Molly thrust her basket at Spence and enveloped her son in a long hug.

"Ah, Mom, it's so good to see you!"

Molly held up her hand to stop his words. "Honey, I don't need to know anything more than that you are alive and will be getting better. And you're doing something that you feel strongly about. So, hush now and let's talk about what your plans are, and let your father take your picture."

Spence set the basket on the porch floor and pulled out his Kodak camera. "Now a big smile, if I can even see it through your beard," he said gruffly.

They spent a roll of film making different arrangements of themselves. Charles was in most of the pictures, sometimes with his warm wool cap, sometimes posing in funny attitudes. They all tried to pretend they were not a little tearful.

"Are you all packed, son?" Spence asked. "I'll drive you to the airfield, and I'll drop your mother on the way. And Barbara sends her love, too."

When Spence and Charles reached the Inyokern Airfield, they took some time for Charles to show his father his newest airplane. It was larger and shinier than the last one his father had seen.

"But the one that's waiting for me in Alaska is so much bigger than this one," Charles said enthusiastically. "While I've been here, I've been thinking a lot about what I want to do when I get back. I think my usefulness to Castner's Cutthroats—that's their nickname—is limited. But there's an outfit up there that has this great plane. It's fitted out for taking aerial photographs. The photographer stands in a kind of box in the front, with the pilot behind him. The plane can have skis for water or snow. It can go just anywhere. We'll be able to take photos of places nobody has ever reached on land."

Spence frowned. "Are you regretting your work with these Commandos, these Cutthroats?"

"Not at all. I know I saved some American lives, and I made the Japs understand that this is our country and we have forces beyond anything they expected. But the war is moving on. And now I want to be there with it, using the tools I know how to use."

"I will never understand you, Charles," his father said. "But I love you anyway."

Howard was finally enjoying his summer break. The baseball team had several players not much older than he was, including a couple he knew from school. His position at outfield gave him a chance to observe the personalities of his teammates while also providing an opportunity for him to show off his fielding and running abilities.

After the game, it was a habit of many of the players to stop for a snack. Usually they gathered at the little ice cream shop. Howard was ready to celebrate his catching two fly balls and joined the rest, feeling as though he was finally part of the team.

He took his time with his strawberry ice cream cone, enjoying the snippets of conversation around him. Somebody had been to the movies in Bishop, a Western, which started a lively conversation comparing movie cowboys.

"Have you all been out to the Alabama Hills?" he asked. "I guess you know that's where they film a lot of these shows."

In answer to their questions, he gave them directions to the site, and some tips: look for places where trucks and equipment are parked, because those might be movie crews; try to keep out of the way, because the movie companies have rented locations and don't want lots of people wandering around; sometimes, if you bring treats like donuts and lemonade, you can get them to talk to you.

"My uncle Tony works there," he concluded. "He likes them, says they are generally friendly as long as they're not having schedule or weather problems."

The conversation moved on. He relaxed against the wall, enjoying the feeling of being accepted by this new group of adults.

When he became a big-league ballplayer, he decided, he would remember to encourage young players to join in team activities.

44

They had been trying to put the war news out of their minds. There was no point in complaining about things, or worrying all the time, because what could be done? Nothing. Just about everybody in the Owens Valley felt that way. Now that the country had been officially at war for more than half a year, more families found that at least one relative had been drafted or had volunteered. They were becoming aware, too, of shortages. Each family had its ration books and each car owner had a special book for gas purchases.

One Saturday as summer turned into Fall, Sara and Barbara sat in Sara's kitchen sharing tea and cookies.

"These may be the last cookies you have for a long time," Barbara commented. "Now that we all have ration cards, there'll be a lot of ingredients we won't be able to buy whenever we want."

"I think the hardest part, actually, is having to figure out in advance what I'm going to need to buy. I'm so used to dashing in after school for just one or two things—a loaf of bread, say, or a couple of cans of tuna. I'm going to have to start making lists, and I'll have to get Howard to do the shopping, once this rationing gets up and running."

"How will you get to work?" Barbara asked.

"This is the one part that's actually good news. They're putting together a staff bus that will pick us up in the morning and drop us off at the end of the day. I just hate driving up to the camp, and it will be so much easier to ride the bus. They're still working out whether we all must contribute ration points, or whether we can pay our fare and how. But in the end, it will be simpler—for us, even if not for them."

Barbara said, "You know, the thing that makes me so mad all the time is that we really have things pretty easy here, and yet so many people in town are just complaining and grousing all the time. Today at the market they were saying that the Japanese in the camp were getting all the food they want including steak every day and they don't have to use ration stamps and how it isn't fair for the enemy to have all the best food."

"And that is so stupid!" Sara exclaimed. "If I had been there, I would have told them that the Japanese don't even like steak and wouldn't eat it if it were offered. They eat vegetables like us, and they make this tofu they eat, from soy beans I think. It's actually pretty tasty once you get used to it."

Inside the camp, the Miyatake family prepared for a visit from another photographer. Ansel Adams had permission to visit frequently because of his contract as a government photographer of this War Relocation Authority program, and always took time to have tea with the Miyatake family.

Joyce Takahashi was the organizer of the present meeting. Her idea had been to show the smallest children, orphans from the Children's Village, at play on the equipment built for them by internee carpenters. Russell helped her drag the miniature teeter-totters and rocking horses out into the yard next to the Children's Village rooms.

"Where'd they even find all these babies, anyway?" Russell asked as they wrestled a large wagon through the door.

"I wondered the same thing. So, I asked around and first nobody would tell me. Even though I'm one of them. But it turns out that the Army took most of them from three or four orphanages along the coast that specialized in Japanese orphans. There are others, though. Nobody wants to tell their stories."

"They surely don't look like anybody to be afraid of."

"Huh. I'm trying to teach myself to be less angry. You're not helping."

"Well, help me get these little fellows into the wagon."

Ansel Adams, like most adults meeting the group of tiny solemn children in identical overalls, was charmed. He and Miyatake took photo after photo of the toddlers playing in the dusty lot separating the barracks. One little boy had found a straight stick and was making tracks in the sand, when another boy came up with a wooden truck to drive along this new road. Together, wordlessly, they created a highway, then planted several clumps of grass at the road edge. The first child then went away returning with three wooden blocks which became houses at roadside. The camera's clicking made the only sounds.

"I wish they would talk," Joyce said. "I wish they would laugh or cry or yell. These are the quietest children I've ever seen. I think it is because they were in an orphanage. I'm thinking I will spend some time trying to get them to talk. Maybe I'll start reading to them. If I had some picture books."

"I know I can help with that," Russell said. "Mom has saved all our picture books and I know she'll be happy to have them used. The only thing is, you'll have to be willing to give them back, because lots of them were my brother's. Right now, with him

218

off at sea, it's the only part of him she has and she is pretty protective of them. She'll let us borrow them, though, I know."

"Is your brother in the Navy?"

"No, in the Merchant Marine. He's at sea right now, and I have no idea where in all the world he might be. I tell you, Joyce, sometimes I dream about him at night and that is tough."

Joyce put her hand gently on his arm. "I know," she said. "My brother is in the Army. Right now, he is in Europe but I don't know where. I dream about him, too."

45

Cliff made one of his unexpected visits home just before his Fall at Caltech started. He planned to see his younger brother play baseball but he pretended that was not the entire reason for his visit. After all, he had seen Howard play many times before.

He pulled up in front of the house just in time to meet Sara, Alf and Howard as they left for the ball field. Sara made sure Cliff had a hat to cover his head from the sun, and gave him a basket filled with bottles of water to carry to Alf's larger car. Howard was twitching with anxiety, hopping from foot to foot while trying to look calm.

"You're going to see," he told his older brother, "I'm getting to be a pretty good outfielder. The June Lake team can't get past me. I hope!"

"Will you get into the playoffs this year?" Cliff asked.

"Maybe. We are really good, or else everybody on the other teams has gone off to war. Bishop lost its star pitcher. He's in the Army now. Have you met George?"

He gestured toward a tall young man leaving the house. Howard introduced them, explaining, to George's great embarrassment, that he was "kind of sweet on Dana."

"Walt and I are in the Merchant Marine," George explained. "I'm going to be starting my next cruise in about a week, and I hope Walt and I will be on the same ship. But in the meantime, I came up to take Grandma Schmidt to the ball game."

He left to trot down the street toward the Crawford house, leaving Howard to explain to Cliff about Germans and bakeries. It helped take Howard's thoughts away from worrying about the game.

George and Hilde Crawford had created a plan to introduce Grandma Schmidt to the town by bringing her to every event they could think of. She had helped Hilde buy vegetables at the summer market stalls, she had visited church services, and had helped dish out ice cream for the Presbyterian Church social. The Richardson family helped as they could, providing escorts and persuasion when she felt shy. Now George was expanding Grandma's experiences by showing her about baseball, a sport which was completely unfamiliar to her.

The baseball field was near one edge of town, in a large lot bordered by tall trees which gave some relief from the hot sun. The bleachers were already partially occupied by fans. The Richardsons settled themselves on one row, making sure to leave room for the Crawford group. They soon appeared: Grandma Schmidt, Henke and Sophie, Hilde, with George Taylor. Henry had been left behind to mind the bakery.

Sophie excitedly waved to her friends on other rows, while Henke described the surroundings to George and Grandma.

"There's Howard," Henke called, checking the players. "See, he is in the dugout, only it's not dug out, really, it's just a row of benches. A real dugout might even be a canoe. That's what my book says."

"Language," George responded, "is always surprising and repays a lot of study."

"OK," said Henke. "And the man on the end there is going to be the pitcher. He has a special glove."

Grandma Schmidt sat very still, clutching her handbag. From time to time she stared at the other people on the bleachers, or out at the infield, where the players were warming up. She wore one of Sara's straw hats, which she patted from time to time, making sure it would not blow off.

Alf wandered off, returning with Len, whom he introduced to the Crawford group. After a short chat, Alf offered Len a pastry from their basket.

"Wow! That is tasty!" Len said, loudly enough for those sitting nearby to hear. "Grandma Schmidt, did you make those?"

George quietly translated. She smiled proudly, and waved her hand rather grandly over the basket, indicating her skills.

Targeting one of the men who had turned around, Alf offered him a pastry, then included his friends. Two of them accepted the little rolls and munched happily. The third muttered, "I don't eat German food."

"It's not German food," Sophie said. "It's Independence food. We made it, right here in our bakery."

"And it's delicious," Len added. "I think you should call those Independence Rolls, and make them a specialty."

Some nearby people who had been listening curiously, came over to meet Grandma Schmidt and sample her

Independence rolls. Alf said quietly to Henke, "go to my car and bring the big basket in the back seat."

It proved to contain several dozen more rolls, all of which were distributed just in time, before the game began.

Afterwards, driving home, Alf said to Sara, "In the Crawford car, I'm sure George is telling Grandma more about baseball than she wants to know."

"We accomplished step one of our plan," Sara responded. "We should just wait and see what happens."

"Did anybody notice I caught three fly balls? Again?" Howard asked. "And we won the game?"

46

To everyone's surprise, Grandma Schmidt turned out to be a baseball fan. George's quick explanations to her had taught her the basic rules, and the fast-moving athletic moves caught her imagination. She was eager to attend the next game, and even occasionally walked to the field with Henke and Sophie to watch practices. She became a familiar figure in town. Hilde noted that she was nodding to neighbors and saying, in heavily accented English, "Good day!"

"It almost sounds like guten tag," Hilde told her husband. "But mama never says that, it's always been Grüss Gott. So now she is speaking a different German and a very different English!"

They were able to laugh at that, because the bakery was doing more business. As people learned that Grandma Schmidt was not dangerous, but in fact had a merry sense of humor, customers began returning to the store. The Independence Rolls were a great success. They had even begun a daily baking of Grandma Schmidt's cookies, two sugar cookies pressed together with a spoonful of mincemeat in the middle.

Howard was particularly happy, because returning business meant more hours of baby-sitting time when the bakery was especially busy. He was beginning to expect that he would have coins in his pockets for sodas after practice.

"Step one of our plan is working," Sara told Alf. "Now we have to figure out what will be Step Two."

"I'm not as pleased as you are," he replied. "It's one thing to have folks relax about the German Invasion. After all, the war in Europe is far, far away from us. It's the Japanese that will be the big issue, for now and for a long time to come."

"Oh, I hope not. I can't imagine people would think there are any threats from Manzanar, not with the fences and those towers. Have you seen them lit up at night? How anybody can sleep there is beyond me."

"Merritt is trying to hold everything together, to get control of the loose ends and establish a community that can survive for, say, ten years if necessary. Will the internees have the patience and the trust to cooperate with his plans?"

"Oh, Alf, this is so hard. My kids in the camp school are worrying about whether they will be allowed to go to college, and I don't know what to tell them. Surely the war can't last that long!"

"Nobody thinks so, but still, we worry. I worry that it won't be over before Howard has to register for the draft. But I'm just feeling down tonight. Let's go get some ice cream."

47

Russell's days were so busy that frequently almost a week would pass in which he didn't even catch sight of his boss. While he was usually occupied in running errands, solving immediate problems and talking to people, Ralph Merritt was often shut in his office, dealing with larger issues, sometimes on the telephone for hours talking to people in Washington. Russell thought that other people, watching, might think this was exciting work, but at his level it was just a continual chase with no obvious goal in sight.

He tried to solve most problems himself, and was gradually becoming more successful at it, but this morning he felt his problem was out of his control. He knocked on Merritt's door, thankful to hear "Come" in that strong voice.

"It's not that I have a problem, but there's definitely something you should know," Russell began.

"Oh, not you too," Merritt said wearily, then grinned. "Actually, I've missed seeing you, now that you can manage just about everything that I hit you with."

"This time I'm really telling tales," Russell said. "I don't like to talk about it, and you probably already know about it, but the Japanese men are just boiling over and I think there's going to be trouble."

"I know there are problems, but I haven't been able to make much sense out of what I'm hearing. What do you know?"

"Well, you know that most of the people here are from the Los Angeles area. Of course, they are very different—fishermen, gardeners, and then the professionals. But Los Angeles is their home town. They go to the same church or temple. Their families may be related. They share a lot of the same history. And they belong to the same family organizations which are very, very strong. So, that's part of it. The other part is, do you know that many of the older Japanese don't speak any English at all?"

"I guess I hadn't thought about that, the Japanese language, I mean. I don't have a chance to meet most of the people, you know. I'm so involved with memos and meetings and orders from just about everybody, it seems. So, what's the point?"

"A couple, to start. I heard that one of your managers, I don't know who, has made a rule that all meetings of the internee councils must be in English. They can have a translator but the actual meeting must be in English. You see what this means. They are having meetings all the time, selecting block captains and deciding who does what jobs and how any money is spent. And they were beginning to get organized well, I thought.

"But all at once, with this rule, this means that the elders, the very men who they count on to make wise decisions, can't speak. Because they don't know the language. And when the translator translates, they don't trust that it is accurate. So, things have started collapsing. And there are other more minor problems, like petty little rules, that come up just because people are already upset.

"And finally, there are a couple of people here, who apparently were already bigshots in Los Angeles, and people tell me that these guys, who may be gangsters, are getting special treatment from us, from the administration."

"Oh boy. Just what we need. Can you show me a copy of the rule about the meetings? And get the names of the bigshots? I need those. As soon as possible. And no, I had no idea."

48

Ralph Merritt felt that the first year of the Camp had more problems than he had expected. He was experiencing the awful realization that although the camp appeared to be running smoothly, there were undercurrents of rebellion and criminal elements at work. Additionally, the ordinary stresses to be expected when a large group of people is forcefully detained were adding tension to otherwise unremarkable events. As Joyce put it to Russell one afternoon,

"We Japanese have systems of living that you Caucasians do not understand at all. Take my grandfather, for example. He is here, he is old, he has been a fisherman all his life. My brother and I know, like all his grandchildren, that he is the leader of our family. If my grandfather tells us something, it is true and we obey. If he says we should do something, or go somewhere, we do that."

"We are all taught as children to respect our elders," Russell said, believing that he was agreeing with her.

"This has absolutely nothing to do with respect, like in politeness and manners. He is our leader because he is our eldest relative. We know his council is wise, and we obey him because it is the right thing to do, not because we have been taught to do it."

Russell changed the subject. He felt he almost understood what Joyce was saying but did not fully understand; this was a familiar feeling by now. He sympathized with Ralph Merritt, who was being bombarded by complaints and accusations on all sides as the camp was settling into a permanent structure.

The same issues troubled both men. On the one hand, the camp had been open less than a year, up and working for only about seven months; how could anybody assume all the problems would have been solved so quickly? On the other hand, nobody knew how long the war would last. Would the Japanese-American families spend the rest of their lives here? Already, the first very old Japanese man was about to die and would be the first to be buried in this new, raw, ugly desert cemetery.

To Merritt, Russell felt he had to share his concerns:

"You look at these men who keep coming to you with demands to re-organize our block committees and our jobs councils," he said. "Mr. Merritt, some of these people seem to be real super-patriots. They tell you that so-and-so is a traitor, that somebody else is pro-Japan, that you need to lock them up. Well, half the time the stories you hear are from before the camp. There are businessmen here who have been ruthless. They have ruined their smaller competition, and now the big and little, the winners and losers, are together in the camp, living next door to each other. No wonder there is a scramble."

Merritt was a quick learner. He began to hold meetings of the managers who reported to him. They told him some of the same stories, and brought their own worries and demands. Now that food rationing was in effect, the camp's purchases had become even more complicated to manage. Gas rationing restricted travel between the camp and the outside. Internees, realizing that they would be imprisoned in the camp for years, became more vocal and anguished in their tales of lost homes, wages, property: What would the government do for them or for their families?

It was overwhelming. The guards assigned to Manzanar were angry because they had signed up to fight, not to do guard duty. The internees who had been selected first, before the camp was even built, turned out to have their own agendas; they captured the positions of influence simply because they were the first to move to Manzanar. But once in place, they antagonized their camp-mates by issuing orders and imposing petty rules. The elder Japanese, the Issei, often could not understand English and had a hard time accepting the new practices and rules imposed on them. And all the internees were angry at the distrust shown to them by their guards and administrators. They had had no chance to prove their loyalty and now their protestations were not believed, they felt.

Perhaps the largest problem was the managers of the camp. During the chaotic weeks between the President's Executive Order 9066 and the beginning of construction at Manzanar, the administrative staff was quickly—sometimes too quickly—selected. As Merritt reviewed the resumes of the men and women reporting directly to him, he began to find disturbing indications that some were not appropriate choices for these sensitive positions.

He was sitting at his desk, deep in thought, when Russell and Joyce knocked on his door.

"I hope you are bringing me some good news," he told them.

"Sir, we are bringing you good news, bad news, and a new idea," Joyce said. "Good news is, a big shipment of books for the library has arrived, from libraries in Los Angeles. They are books they no longer want, so they are somewhat battered, but they look interesting and useful."

"Bad news is that the seedlings in the guayule lath house are not responding well, and the planters want to put up additional protections against wind and cold," Russell contributed. "And the new project is that Joyce thinks, and I agree, that the wood shop could make wooden toys for Christmas presents for the children in Children's Village."

"And maybe the tailor shop can make children's clothing for Christmas too," Joyce added. "All you have to do is requisition the materials."

"Christmas! It's only Autumn! But it's not a bad idea. Russell, please make a requisition."

"Fine. But first, I think you have to requisition more six-part forms from the printer in town because we are just about out."

"And one thing leads to another! Joyce, I've been thinking about some of the things you and Russell have been telling me. I would like you to see if you know any of the men on this list. They are managing different parts of the camp, but you may have known them before."

Joyce took the paper reluctantly, skimmed the contents and handed it back. "I wish you wouldn't ask me, sir. I can't help you. I'm not going to give you rumors and stories. Sir, you are not my friend, you are the camp administrator. You are the Caucasian in charge of my people. I am working for you, and I like you a lot, even though I am still angry all the time."

Russell nodded at that.

"But I am not a, a stoolchicken. Stoolpigeon. I do not betray my people to the Caucasians, like some people here in camp might do. Here is your paper back. Ask somebody else."

She marched toward the door. "But. There is this one man. They call him The Merchant King. He thinks he is such a bigshot. He makes other people do his work, and I think he is one of the people who is stealing sugar. If your employees do not know who he is, they should. And they should stop his bad actions."

The investigations into the possible thefts of sugar and meat had became a confused, frightening puzzle. The Japanese leadership of the camp accused administration employees of bribery and theft, while the managers of the kitchen and transportation units reported suspicious behavior by their Japanese workers, many of whom were the political leaders of the internees. The internees, who had been generally calm and steady, began to take sides in the rivalries between the Japanese leaders. Debate started on the question of whether participation in work projects like weaving camouflage nets and growing guayule seedlings was giving in to the conqueror.

The easy social gatherings and cooperative projects became less frequent and attracted fewer people. It was clear that morale was hurting.

And the sugar and meat still vanished from the inventories.

Merritt decided that if he couldn't solve the food thefts, he could at least attack some of the other issues. He called a meeting of the supervisors who reported directly to him.

"My first point is about language," he began. "You know, or you should know, that although most of the internees speak at least some English, there are many older Japanese-Americans who speak only Japanese. These elders are well respected in the camp, and we must try to make sure that they are included in decisions concerning them. Now, for example, I understand that some of you have been calling block meetings and requiring everything to be in English."

"There was a memo. From the WRA itself. Said we were to insist on English for everything official."

"We don't speak Japanese, sir. And neither do you. Sir."

"We give them translations at the end of the meetings."

Merritt said, "Well, at least that can change. I understand that you are all getting too many memos. So am I. But these people's lives have been turned upside down in so many ways. We need to accommodate them whenever we can. If we use young internees as translators, we can have them sit in the meetings and tell their elders what is happening while the discussions are still going on. I think that would be a big improvement, don't you?"

There was a general muttering of disagreement, in which the words "Jap-Lover" could be heard. With difficulty, Merritt ignored the objections.

"I'll get translators assigned right away," he said. "And I expect you will begin to use them as soon as you get their names. Now, about the camp newspaper. I have authorized a Japanese-language edition, to begin publication immediately. You will make sure that both England and Japanese editions are distributed in all of the areas you supervise."

"Now how do you know that Jap paper will not be writing propaganda?"

"Do we really care? Are there secrets that the newspaper will be talking about? And how can we live without at least a small amount of trust between us and them? Use your translators to check the papers, have them read them to you. Maybe you will even pick up some Japanese yourselves."

His head was hurting. It hurt a lot these days. "Meeting adjourned." He said and left the conference room.

49

As the Christmas 1942 holidays approached, life at Manzanar appeared to be peaceful, even boring. Block captains had been selected, and in most cases elected by the residents, to manage the day-to-day decisions which had to be made. There was now enough rice to satisfy the requirements of the Japanese diet; excess potatoes were sent to military bases. The workshops were busy preparing items to be sold as Christmas presents, and making toys and clothing to be supplied to the children by the camp administrators.

There were still rumblings of discontent. The mix of soldiers, civil servants and Japanese-Americans was still uneasy. Occasional fights, especially involving young male adults, would break out. But in general, residents agreed, it was probably safer to be in camp than back in their home neighborhoods, where everybody was nervous because the war was not going well for the Allies.

One night, a fight broke out in the recreation area of the camp. By the time military guards arrived, several men had been badly injured and two were sent to the camp hospital. An on-the-spot investigation identified four attackers, who were sent to jail in Independence.

After Merritt and the commander of the Army forces reviewed the evidence, three of the four were brought back to Manzanar and put in the camp jail quarters, but one was held in Independence for trial.

During the following morning, rumors spread throughout the camp. The internee leaders wanted the man in the Independence jail returned to camp. By afternoon small groups of men were beginning to collect, and by mid-afternoon marches had started. The marchers were singing Japanese marching songs and folk songs and were waving hastily-made protest signs, mostly in Japanese. As they moved from one barracks area to another, they collected more followers.

Merritt, watching from his office, tried to think of a strategy to calm the situation, but could not find any useful plan. He met the largest group as they turned into the street by his office, and tried to talk to the leaders, but got nowhere. The noise grew louder, and now included horns, whistles, and alarm bells.

He now realized he had no choice. He called for support from the military, which sent a dozen of the guards, fully armed, to make a wall between the marchers and the administration offices.

There they stood, both sides facing each other, for perhaps an hour. The air was full of noise. Occasionally, someone would throw a rock in the direction of the soldiers, who stood stiffly, angrily, on alert, guns directed at the crowd.

Suddenly from a side street, a rumbling could be heard. A driverless truck was being pushed along the street, gathering speed as it went, heading for the corner barracks building in which families were clustered at their windows, watching.

Later, no one could say what happened next. Shots were heard, men fell to the ground. Two men had been killed by gunfire. Several men—both soldiers and internees—had been injured.

Those who had not participated in the uprising were confused and upset. A lock-down order was swiftly put in place. Everyone was required to stay in his home. At mealtime, military escorts accompanied each barracks wing to the dining hall, then back to the houses. People working on jobs had to apply for passes to continue working.

This situation lasted only two days. Those deemed responsible for the riot were transferred to a separate relocation camp, while those accused of breaking the law in other ways were moved to a different camp, this one run by the federal justice department. For all practical purposes, they disappeared from Manzanar forever.

Ralph Merritt felt as though he had come to the end of the earth. Everything he had worked so hard to achieve was in shambles. People he thought he could trust had turned against him. Men had been killed while he was in charge, unable to find a way to stop it.

He sat in his office, in the now-quiet, almost silent village, staring at his desktop, where his files were all-too-neatly arranged. There was nothing he could jump up and fix, nobody to see. He looked out his window, where night had fallen during the hours which had passed without his notice. The only light was from the giant lamps on the watchtowers *(he wanted to tear those down,* he thought. *He would, if he were still in charge here to do that.)* It had started to snow.

The knock on the door startled him. It was Joyce, as always accompanied by Russell.

"Sir, it's almost Christmas. We have boxes and boxes of decorations for the outsides of the barracks. The presents for the little ones are finished and ready for you to distribute. We think that now would be a good time to put up some Christmas lights."

It was something to do. He shrugged into his coat and picked up one of the boxes. The three went to the corner of the street and twined garlands around the pole of the street sign, adding a string of Christmas lights. A teacher, shepherding her class back to school from a late choir practice, watched them.

"Let's sing," she said to her class. And soon the carols began. "Oh come, all ye faithful", they sang, louder and louder as they saw the faces of the adults.

In the nearest barracks, faces appeared at the windows, and, one by one, then in groups, people appeared. They sang the first song twice, then someone started O Little Town of Bethlehem, then they were settled in. The music reached farther and farther, as extra hands grabbed garlands and light strings and sent them out into the camp.

Ralph Merritt stood in a corner, tears rolling down his cheeks. It was not, after all, the end of the world.

50

For the people of Manzanar, the December riot was, like the lancing of a boil, the release of poison. For many, it cleared out old antagonisms. The gang lords who had tried to exert their rule in the new situation had been, for the most part, vanquished, most of them transferred to camps better designed to accept lawbreakers. Most residents of the camp had stayed inside their homes and were soon able to resume their normal activities. Those outside the camp were largely unaware that anything unusual had happened.

Within the next weeks, several camp administrators were quietly replaced. Several were sent under guard to Federal facilities to await trial for misuse of government resources. Since these officials had not spent much time on their assigned duties, nobody missed them.

Sara had many long discussions with her students at the camp high school. As often happened in her classrooms, the assigned lesson took second place to debates about the proper roles of leaders in any organization. This led to some discussion about how to select leaders, and concluded at the end of the week with a petition to the camp administration to change the name of the camp's baseball team from Manzanar to Manzanar Coyotes. Sara sometimes suspected that they delighted in these discussions because they had not prepared for the day's assignment. But she delighted in them, too.

Sara had hoped that Dana would send more letters home. She knew her daughter's days were busy from wake-up to lights-out, but she couldn't help imagining dire events in the weeks between letters.

She was relieved to find Dana's latest letter one day when she returned from Manzanar.

Dear Mom and all,

I used to think the hardest part of this job was learning all the new airplanes, but I have to add to that all the military learning we have to do, even though we are not exactly in the Army. We march every day, carrying our packs, and we learn all the little rules, like who to salute and when, and what all the badges mean.

Now we are getting more and more different planes. We are getting fighter planes and spotter aircraft and some bombers and all of them can arrive the same week. So, we specialize in what we do. Some of us test the new planes—that's me! Along with a couple of friends. Some of us take the tested planes, make sure the manuals are accurate, and then ferry them out to the forward bases for shipment overseas. So far, I think we all have the jobs we want the most.

I had one plane last week. The Army pilots were complaining that it was too hard to fly it, that it did not respond to the controls. So, I took the manual and really, really studied it. I started from the beginning, just like Tuck would have made me do when I started learning to fly. And what do you think? I found that right at the beginning, right there in the manual, there was a big change from the way the old controls work. This change makes the new plane faster and stronger and just slicker than the old one, but you have to know a couple of things, involving the order you throw switches.

Well, I read that, and I got into the plane and tried it on the ground and found that I could make the switches work the way the manual said to do. So, I made a test flight and Boy Howdy! It worked!

The men didn't believe me, but then somebody else tried it and now they are saying they made this big discovery! But at least my officers know what really happened!

What do you hear from Walt? From George? Is Howard behaving himself? I'm healthy and happy and proud to help our Army—even if the men still take all the credit!

Love,

Dana

51

"Nobody cares!" Cliff was trying to explain to his father the frustrations of trying to work with the new rocket science. "First nobody had any idea of what to use them for. People who should have known better talked about rockets like they are party favors. Or like balloons. The people who spend money in the military want big guns and big ships. Not streamlined tubes.

"I tell you, it's like pulling teeth. And we grad students, all we can do is watch and wait for supplies and wonder if we should change to botany or something!"

Alf tried not to smile. His son was pacing up and down, fists clenched. Cliff had come home for a few days because work at the Caltech lab had been halted by a lack of supplies. It had taken almost a year to convince the military and university funding sources that rockets were worth developing. Now they had permission to go ahead, but the next step—developing appropriate rocket fuel—was at full stop.

"I'm glad to see you, anyway," Alf said mildly. "Want to go rock hounding with me?"

"No, I don't want to go rock hounding with you!" Cliff heard his voice squeaking with anger and frustration. He took a couple of deep breaths and began to calm down. "Here's the thing. Caltech has signed contracts with the Navy to develop rockets. And some other things. The Navy is building a lab right at China Lake where they tell us we can do some experiments. They call it NOTS—Naval Ordnance Test Station. If they actually get it going, it will be great."

He went on, "This isn't just a terrific weapon that the Navy should be learning how to use, it's also at the same time good science. It's everything that a Caltech project should be. And we're making it work! We've created the proper fuels, we know the difference between a rocket and a bomb, we've even built our own labs to test all of this, and now we can't run the tests because the money we need to build a test set safely is stuck in some budget office somewhere.

"I hadn't meant to tell you this," he continued, "but it's also seriously dangerous work. We had one man die at the lab last month. He was working on the components of our fuel, using some explosive elements, and another man, who thought that particular lab was empty, came in with just a small amount of just the wrong explosive. The next thing anybody knew, the first man went running down the corridor pulling his clothes off as he went, until he fell down, still all in flames. Then he died."

His father was silent.

"That particular event should never happen again," Cliff said, "and shouldn't have happened at all. It was a case where people were too complacent about safety rules. We have these stupid aprons we have to wear..."

After a moment, he continued, "But we have had some real triumphs. We've tested rockets that can be shot from under the wings of an airplane into the ocean. If we ever get permission to actually *use* an airplane for a couple of days, we all think we can demonstrate that they work."

He shook his head. "Now let's go up the canyon and look for rocks."

A thousand miles away, in Texas, Dana was having her own experiences with rockets. Later that week her father, who was hearing entirely too much about rockets and explosions, received her letter.

Dear Family,

"*It seems that we have begun to prove that we can be counted on, just like military pilots are. The airplane ferrying work is going well, and we are adding pilots as the numbers of planes being built increases. It's not my line of work, though.*

"*You know I'm too much of a wild woman to be content with doing the same job all the time. So, when the Navy requested some pilots to run target towing missions, guess who had her hand up first! They need to teach the gunners in the ships how to shoot enemy aircraft down. So we have been flying large targets on their gunnery range. The scariest part is when you're flying and you begin to hear pop! Pop! Pop! That's real guns, with real bullets, and big ones! We're supposed to call in as soon as we hear the noises, because that means they are close to their targets and therefore close to us, but we don't like to call stop until they get really close. How about that for military experience?*

Love,

Dana

52

Tony, running errands for the movie crew, stopped in Lone Pine for a short visit with Spence and Molly. Ever since his early childhood he had thought of them as his second parents. Now, it never seemed that they spent enough time just keeping in touch. As he parked the studio truck in front of their small cottage, he could see them sitting on their front porch.

"Just watching the passing parade, I see," he said. "I was in town getting some stuff they're having shipped up as props, and thought I'll stop by for a sec. Want to see?"

They followed him to the back of the truck, where he removed some tarpaulins, revealing several large objects.

"Looks like pure gold," Molly said. "But it can't be, right? Even for the movies?"

"The movies require only the best," Tony joked. "Or at least, stuff that looks like the best. Looking like, that's the real requirement."

"But what is it?"

"It's a golden throne. We left its packing box back at the rail depot because they had packed it so carefully down in Los Angeles that the package was too big for the truck. They never think!"

Over iced tea and cookies, the three discussed the throne, creating possible movie scripts that might include it. Finally, Tony set down his glass and stood to say good bye.

"Molly," he said quietly, "I'm worried about Barbara. Maybe you can come talk to her, keep her company or something."

"What's wrong, Tony?"

"She's so anxious about Walt. She won't even mention his name. It's like she's superstitious. She's knitting hats and socks for him and for George, and has a whole big pile already. But she won't send them off. Says she is waiting to see him, or them, to give them to. It's like she doesn't want to deal with wherever they might be."

"Oh, dear." Molly sighed. "Barbara has always been our good steady girl. She doesn't ever seem to get upset, even about the things that make the rest of us mad."

"Right. And now she's just, well, beginning to fall apart. We know Walt and George are on the same ship right now, but not which one and not where they are going. So, nobody has any reassuring answers to give her. Molly, she cries in her sleep."

"I'll go see her. Oh, the poor thing."

"Just, Molly, just don't tell her I told you anything. I can't bear it if she gets angry with me. And I can't tell any more what will set her off."

"Thanks, Tony, for telling us. We'll go up today."

Molly had a good reason to visit Barbara. She had only yesterday received a letter from Charles. He had been writing his mother much more frequently now that she had weathered his experiences in Alaska. Now she folded the letter into her purse and prepared for the visit.

Barbara was gardening when they drove up. She managed to find garden jobs to do throughout the year. The result was that something was always growing in the spaces around her house. Now she was planting the amaryllis bulbs she had been given for Christmas. Next Winter they would bloom, surprising everybody. Molly greeted her daughter waving Charles' letter.

Dear Family,

I'm getting lots of experience with the new airplane they want me to fly up here. I must be doing something right, because I've got more work than I can handle. It's funny to think about. For hundreds of years there have been people – Inuits and whites—exploring and hunting and living together and trading. And nobody worried about the fact that there were no maps. Probably because there were no roads!

Now because of the war, everybody suddenly needs maps of every place. We started at the coast, and of course there have been charts of the waters already. But once we got even a little way inland, there was just this endless sea of white.

Fortunately for everybody involved, I don't have to make the actual maps, because I wouldn't have the foggiest idea how to do that. All I have to do is fly around and let the Coast and Geodetic photographers do their stuff.

The latest job, though, was to rescue a trapper. He had been careless just one minute, just long enough to not see the bear in time to get away. He was pretty badly torn up before his partner managed to shoot the bear. But we got the radio call and I was able to get to him—and land, and then take off—which is

247

not always possible up here, on the snow. We even marked the place and came back after the bear, so now the trapper has the bear, even though he left part of his leg behind. The last I heard, he and his partner were having a big fight about which of them got to keep the bearskin!

So it's still definitely something new every day, although— Dad and Mom—I'm much happier with what I'm doing these days.

Love, Charles

Barbara read the letter quickly and laughed. "That Charles! He'll never grow up!"

Molly laughed with her, then turned to admire her daughter's gardening project.

"Are those the bulbs that Walt gave you last year?" she asked.

Barbara's smile disappeared. "Yes."

"Look, Barbara," her mother said, pulling her close. "I know you are worried about him. We all worry about him and pray for him, and for George, too. We hope they'll be able to come home soon and safely. But you have to make yourself let go of this anxiety. There are plenty of people who need you to be their happy, hard-working Barbara. Don't you think Walt would just hate it if he knew how sad you are?"

"Oh, I know, Mom. I just can't help it."

"Yes, you can help it! Do something different. Can you go volunteer with Sara at Manzanar? Can you volunteer at the hospital? Read to kindergartners? Something. Get out of the house and get into the real world, dear!"

Barbara turned her back and marched into the house. After a few minutes, Molly returned to the car, where Spence had been waiting and watching.

"She's upset all right. Poor Tony! He can't even share his own feelings with her, because she's all worked up. She needs something to do. I don't think she'll listen to me for a while, but I can try again in a few days."

53

Tuck Watkins phoned Alf in great excitement.

"The military is taking over my airfield! They are kicking me out of my airfield! Can you believe this?"

"Didn't you already sell your airstrip to the Navy? I thought you told me in December that you had done that? Now it's almost a year later and you're surprised?"

"Well, I did. But they said they didn't need to use it right away and they'd tell me when they were ready to start, but they never did seem to do anything. So, I more or less forgot about it, except they said we could continue to keep using the field so we did.

"And now they're moving in, with trucks and building materials and all, and it's not even the Army. It's the Navy! In the desert!"

"I don't know that you're going to be able to do anything to stop any of this," Alf said. "We knew something was going to happen, sooner or later. I'll see if I can get over there sometime.

Cliff is up there somewhere, working with the Caltech folks. I'll see if I can find him."

Inyokern, usually a quiet village surrounded by desert dotted by the occasional prospector's shack, had become a bustling village. Tuck's airstrip, where Dana had enjoyed learning the rudiments of flying, had been the original attraction for the scientists and Naval officers seeking space for rocket experiments. They were amazed, flying over the dry desert plain, to find the paved runway; even the county officials, who had caused the runway to be built as an emergency landing strip, had forgotten all about it, and Tuck had never been one to remind anybody of his business interests.

This Spring of 1943 saw some of the darkest days of the war, with an apparently unending string of defeats for the Allied forces. The military planners were caught up in debates—should all work concentrate on getting the best weapons out to the combat troops? Or should some major effort be placed on making a permanent laboratory presence for future research and development of weapons?

During the weeks and months spent in negotiating the boundaries and ownership of hundreds of square miles in the valley, the landing strip had been used perhaps a dozen times, mostly for impressing visiting Admirals. The real business was transacted by teams of military officers and Caltech scientists driving in from other Navy bases and stations, uniformly coughing from dust and alert to snakes and other unfamiliar dangers. Navy in the desert, indeed!

Alf had a feeling he would find Cliff near the administrative center, a group of Quonset huts being built about ten miles east of the air strip. He was not surprised to see his son trotting over to his truck. He was surprised to see his son's companion, a pretty blonde young woman in stylish slacks and a flowered shirt with a large straw hat perched on her head.

"Dad, I'd like you to meet my friend, Monica McDowell," Cliff said. "We went to school together in Pasadena, and now we're working together again."

"How do you do, Mr. Richardson," her words were quick, her voice pleasant. "It's so nice to meet you. Cliff talks about you a lot."

"All good, I hope," the words were automatic. Alf had never heard Monica's name before, he was sure.

"How you all survive this, this desert climate, I'm sure I don't know!" she waved her hat in front of her face, making a breeze.

"It's not even a hundred degrees out, yet," Cliff protested, laughing. Clearly he thought this woman was special, Alf realized. He told them about Tuck's worry over the Inyokern landing field.

"I can help you with the information about what we're building here," Monica said. "That's actually part of my job. I'm an administrative aide to the Yards and Docks office here. Actually, that's why I came up—to see Cliff at work, of course, because I just love to see him work. But my boss wants information about what is being built, and where. We keep getting conflicting information. So, he gave me this camera and told me to go out and take pictures."

"And what's happening at the air strip?" Alf asked.

"What airstrip?" Monica said.

Alf sighed. "There's an old air field, right next to the highway. Apparently originally it was going to be part of the range, but then the Navy wanted it. So, is it going to be restricted to the Army? Or the Navy? Or can it still be used by private pilots?"

"Oh, lordy, I don't know. I'll bet nobody even knows. I wonder how you can find out. Why do you even care?"

Cliff pulled on her arm. "I think you should try to find out," he told her. It's important to my dad. My sister learned to fly there, too. And she'll expect to land there when she has a chance to come home."

"Well, I'll go ask. I'll let you and your dad have a good talk." He and his father found a stack of boxes and sat down.

"Is this a girl friend?" Alf asked his son.

"Well, kind of. It was a surprise to run into her again, but the Navy is hiring lots of people, and she got on as an admin aide, like she said. She's actually more of an actress. She's been in plays in Pasadena ever since high school, and I think she's very good. Not a scientist at all, but she doesn't need to be. Don't you think she is beautiful?"

Alf nodded and changed the subject. "What brings you up here this trip?"

"This is kind of the beginning of life up here. They are calling it the Naval Ordnance Test Station, nickname NOTS, and it will be the permanent set of ranges for testing airborne weapons. We've figured out how to launch—well, I can't really say. But I think I'll be here pretty much all the time from now on."

"Really? Will you be living here? Does this mean we'll be seeing more of you?"

"No," Cliff said. "Probably less if anything. They are building quarters for the scientists and the military at the same time, and they're supposed to be pretty good. They need us on hand because we'll be taking every opportunity to use the ranges, and it means not being able to keep a schedule. It's pretty exciting, actually. And I've been meeting some pretty important people."

Monica came back, tucking her hand into Cliff's arm. "Well, Mr. Richardson, I have learned one thing: you don't have to worry about your airstrip. The people planning the base realized that the airstrip is too close to the highway, so they are moving their locations here, and it's a good ten miles from the old air strip. So, your friends can probably continue to use it when they need it."

54

Spring is the best season for people living in the desert. The sun warms the sand and melts the little patches of snow and ice remaining in sheltered canyon corners and under creosote bushes and evergreens. Wildflowers begin to burst out, yellow and white and purple each on their own timetable. The desert tortoises can be seen occasionally, tiptoeing across the hot sand. The ranchers begin to move their animals in the direction of summer pastures, but at a leisurely pace. And school is out, for at least a week and two weekends, so the main street in Independence is occupied by boys on bicycles.

In Spring 1943 it seemed, to the residents of the Owens Valley, as though things might be getting a bit better. Of course, the wartime problems were just as frightening as ever, the rationing of food and gas just as severe. More and more men received notice to report for military service. But, thanks to the sudden appearance of the United States Navy over by dry China Lake, there were more jobs than people.

Len, in his office at the Pine Creek tungsten mine, found himself visited by Navy officers, serious young men dressed in starched khaki uniforms.

"Mr. Reyes, we understand you've been involved with hiring and managing a pretty large workforce here."

"I guess you could say so," Len replied warily. "Just what exactly can I do for you?"

"We need a lot of workers for the construction of our station at China Lake. We need mostly laborers, but we can use all kinds of able-bodied men because we can teach them what we need them to do. We don't seem to be able to find enough local men. We thought you could suggest how to get them."

Len tapped his pencil on his desk thoughtfully. "Where have you been looking?"

"We put out some signs on posts in town, in Independence and in Lone Pine and in Bishop. We put our phone number, for the base, on the sign but nobody has called."

Len sighed. "That's because nobody has a phone, or uses it. And most of the men who can work are either already in the Army or already working, probably at a local mine. I hear that you're not paying all that well, compared with what the mines are paying these days."

The younger officer bristled. "This is a patriotic duty, sir. "

"What they are doing is also patriotic. The tungsten in this mine goes into tanks and guns. The ores from the other mines are also war materiel. Our valley is stretched pretty thin as far as available workers are concerned. Our workers are exempt from the draft so they are very aware that they are helping the war effort.

"But I do have one small idea. There are some Indian reservations. There's one I know of not far from here. There must be others looking for war work. They mostly don't speak English, so they weren't allowed to register for the draft. But they want to serve their country. They're eager to find a way to contribute. I

256

can give you the name and phone number of a contact there, in the Indian Affairs office."

Len later told Alf that the men took the phone number and name with a kind of reluctant politeness. "I know they think we Indians are all strange," he said. "But they could pretend that they appreciate our help."

A week later, the Navaho work force arrived at China Lake: several hundred men in a caravan of buses followed by trucks filled with their clothing, tents and the tools they thought might be needed. The final truck carried a half-dozen horses.

The civilian foreman of the construction crews, impressed but rather baffled at this sight, found the group leader and pointed out the job, the construction of a railroad spur from the main rail line into the new test site. Within an hour, the men had set to work.

They were strong men, and eager to prove themselves. Most of the tools were already familiar to them, and the gear made available by the Navy was admired by all. With no apparent effort, they organized themselves into teams and allocated different jobs. By the end of the day, the first stretch of track had been laid out.

By the end of the week, much of the rail line had been laid out and the first part had been completed. Cement slabs had been poured and set in place at additional locations, and all the construction work was moving along at a brisk pace.

Everybody was pleased and relieved at this unexpected solution to a workforce problem. The construction foreman was praised for his success in instructing the workmen, and the other carpenters were happy to be assigned to something new. It seemed that, for once, everybody was happy.

But at the end of the second week, builders reporting to the work site found their way blocked by a group of men wrapped in blankets, scowling and blocking their way. Something had gone amiss and nobody could figure out what.

"We told them we'd pay them at the end of the week, and it's not the end of the week yet," one officer said. "They can't tell us what the problem is, because they don't speak English."

"How can it be, that they don't speak English? They're American Indians, after all. Americans speak English!" another said.

The foreman was just as confused as everybody else. "They seemed so happy before, just working along like it was the easiest thing for them. Now what?"

Soon all the workmen had gathered around. Construction stopped completely. Before long, the officers who had made the original contract with the Navahos had been located, but they could provide no additional information. Nobody wanted to call Captain Burroughs at the NOTS headquarters building, but it seemed like the next appropriate step.

"I guess I should call that guy at the tungsten mine," one officer said. "Maybe he has some idea. I wonder if he speaks Indian."

Len, reached by phone, agreed to drive into Inyokern and see what he could do. The next two hours were spent unhappily as everybody waited for Len. Nobody wanted to go to work until the problem was resolved. The Navaho men stood silently, still wrapped in their blankets, apparently not bothered by the increasingly hot temperature of late Spring in the desert.

Finally, they could hear the unmuffled engine of the Pine Creek Mine truck trundling down the highway. A dusty Len climbed out, surveyed the scene, and walked to the group of Navahos. He stopped in front of the tallest of them and extended his hand. They shook hands, then the two walked away from the group.

It seemed a long time, but after only about fifteen minutes, Len returned and summoned the construction foreman and his Navy contact. They, too, stepped aside for a conference.

This one took a little longer and included some gestures by the foreman and some head-shaking by the Naval officer.

Returning to the larger group, the foreman announced, "We need to talk to Captain Burroughs. This will take a while. Everybody who wants to be paid for today, go back to work."

With a certain amount of grumbling the group dispersed, leaving Len, the Navaho, the construction foreman, and a visibly worried Naval officer to climb into a jeep and head for the administration hut.

After a little more than an hour they returned. Later, Len, chuckling, told Alf what had happened.

"If I'm the only interpreter they can find, we're all in trouble, I think," he laughed. "People think we all speak the same language, but it's not true. They're just lucky I had a Navaho friend during the year I spent at Indian school. Of course, most of the Navaho I learned was cuss words.

"But we got it done today. What they wanted was to have appropriate housing. They need a sweat lodge."

Alf grinned. "That's it? They can make one in a half day and get on with things. Did you get permission for them?"

Len laughed. "It wasn't easy. At one point, they wanted to look in the military housing books to see what kind of plans were needed. My Navaho friend had to get down in the sand and draw a picture with a stick to show what they need. Fortunately, he's a good draftsman. Didn't take him long to convince the Captain.

After that, it was easy. It should be all ready for them by tomorrow."

And it was.

55

By summer, 1943, life in the Owens Valley had settled into its strange new patterns. At Manzanar, the first high school graduation ceremony had been a big success, partly because of the formal ball which was the highlight of graduation week. Several babies had been born to internees and were admired by all every time they were taken out for a walk. Now that most of the trouble-makers among the internees had been removed to other camps, the former habits of joking and conversations resumed. The gardeners had devised stone-lined paths, had created small ponds filled with water from the irrigation canals and had even stocked them with carp sent by friends from Los Angeles. The vegetable crops were so healthy that potatoes and squashes were shipped by truckloads to other camps.

The Navy, too, was making its presence known. The new Naval Ordnance Test Station in Inyokern was sprouting Quonset huts, roads, a network of air strips at the new Harvey Field, and the beginnings of an entire village of homes and commercial buildings. It was clear that the Navy intended to remain there.

There were, of course, setbacks. The vulnerable guayule plants were not adapting well to the desert climate. The biologists working on the project were hopeful that if they could create a more protective environment, the plants could survive and thrive, but anybody who had watched the Manzanar orchards of the 1920s knew that the combination of freezing winters and dry summer desert winds was just about lethal. A smaller experimental lab was doing better but was not what the government required.

Howard was continuing his babysitting schedule. Knowing how much Henke and Sophie liked challenges, he had unearthed his old collection of chess books and loved creating problems for them to study, and they felt quite grownup.

One summer day, Howard brought out his chessboard and pieces, setting them up on a table on his porch. Then he went to the bakery to find the two children.

He had learned that the same bus that took his mother to work in the morning made several trips each day. Hilde had given her permission for him to take them on a bus ride after the chess class.

The two children were so excited about the bus ride that the chess class was given up for the day. Now they stood at the bus stop. Sophie carried a basket with three jugs of cool water, Henke had his camera, loaded with a new roll of film, and Howard was the tour leader and carried the bag of sandwiches.

They had, of course, taken bus rides before, but this was the first time the children would be on the bus without a parent. Sophie jumped up and down, just once, every few minutes. Henke talked earnestly to Howard about schoolwork, hoping he sounded grown up. When the bus arrived, they climbed on and found a long seat along one side, near the front.

"Please let us off near Manzanar camp," Howard told the driver, who nodded.

They watched as the bus moved from their familiar neighborhood through patches of creosote bushes and scrubby brush. The bus was still new. There were not many stops and few people got on or left. After almost an hour, the bus stopped and the driver indicated that this was their destination.

From the bus stop they climbed on a narrow footpath up into the foothills. Soon Sophie was winded, sitting down every few minutes to catch her breath. She looked around, spotting the occasional lizard, hearing the birds around her.

"I hear voices," she said.

"Oh, come on, Sophie, you're just slowing us down. We're all alone here. Don't you want your picnic?" Henke asked.

"But I hear voices."

Howard took her basket and encouraged her to get moving.

The path twisted, avoiding a rock outcrop. As they passed it, they, too, heard voices. They stopped, then cautiously walked along, looking left and right.

Suddenly, ahead of them the path dipped. They saw a half-dozen men crouched at the side of a stream, each wearing a straw hat and holding a fishing pole. Buckets already held several fish.

"Shhhh!" Howard warned the children. They stood silently, staring. They were close enough to the camp to see the high wire fences, and into the camp where people were walking, hanging laundry, going about their business.

"Isn't that your mom?" Henke whispered, pointing.

"Shhhh. She's a teacher there. Yeah."

They watched two men inside the camp approach the fence, then duck down, lift a corner of the fence, and crawl under. Carrying buckets and fishing poles, they joined their friends.

For perhaps fifteen minutes the children watched the fishermen. Then they left the group and moved on along the path up into the hills. Reaching a level spot shaded by several cottonwood trees, Howard assembled their picnic lunch.

"Howard, if I asked them, would they let me go fish with them?" Sophie asked. "I have my own fishing pole."

"I think we shouldn't bother them," Howard replied. "I think they're not supposed to be there, and I don't want to be the person who gets them in trouble."

Sophie nodded and took another sandwich. "It surely is a pretty river."

56

Barbara tried to keep herself busy. Although she would never admit it, she knew her mother had given her good advice. If she could manage to avoid worrying about Walt and George during the daylight hours, maybe she would even sleep better. And there was nothing she could do to bring them home safely. All she could do was to work hard to bring the war to a quicker conclusion.

So she tried to find herself a job. Everybody was talking about how all the men had either been drafted or had enlisted—at any rate, many of the local men were in uniform. Surely there would be work for her.

But it seemed that nobody needed an aging, overweight, woman who had never worked in an office. She could teach piano lessons, but who needed that? She could drive a car and probably she could even drive the bus, but it didn't seem like something that would help the war effort. Even the vegetables in her garden, although they were eagerly accepted by family and neighbors, seemed like just something that was ordinary.

Finally, she made an appointment to see Ralph Merritt at the Manzanar Camp. She found that she was surprisingly nervous on the morning of her meeting with him, perhaps because she was so unaccustomed to speaking with people she didn't already know well. Tony made her a detailed map to the camp. She started early just in case of getting lost, even though she knew the area down to the tiniest details.

"I am looking for work that I can do to help the war effort," she told Merritt when they were seated in his office. "I find myself worrying too much about Russell's brother. Did you know he is in the Merchant Marine?"

"Oh, yes. Russell has a picture of Walt in his uniform. He keeps it on his desk in his office. What do you hear?"

"We don't hear anything. That's the problem. He is on a ship in the Pacific Ocean, that's all we know, and you know how the Japanese seem to be winning. We heard that a ship like Walt's had been sunk, but even if his ship is hit, we may not hear. We may not ever..."

She stopped and briefly closed her eyes. "Anyway. I want to do something that will be helpful and that will send me to bed at night all tired out. Do you have anything, anything I can do?"

"My dear. I wish I did. But I think it would be too hard for you to work here, surrounded by the Japanese internees. I do have an idea, though. Remember that before Russell came here to work with me, he was working at Pine Creek, for Len Reyes? Well, I was talking to Len a couple of days ago and he said the mines are going to open a new joint office right in Independence? There are issues that they can work on together, like contracts and worker safety and security questions and all. I think they could use somebody sensible, like you, in their office. Would you be interested in that?"

She nodded, he picked up his telephone, and shortly sent her back up the highway to the new office where she would find Len Reyes. Their interview was friendly, quick and quite satisfactory.

"Guess what I'll be doing, Tony?" she asked that night at supper. "I'm going to be working at the new mine office in town. They're setting up a cooperative office to take care of things like hiring and shipping schedules and contracts, like that."

Tony was at a loss for words, but only for a moment. "But. You haven't ever done anything like that. Do you think you can? And will you like that? All those miners all the time? And what about your garden? And how can they cooperate like that? They are competitors, and they hardly want to give up their secrets. Who hired you? What kind of cockamamie scheme is it anyway?"

She laughed.

"Len Reyes—you remember Len? He was looking for somebody to staff this office. It's his idea, so I'm going to trust that he'll make this work. The things we'll be doing are things that aren't very competitive anyway, at least while the war is on.

"And I know I can do it. Remember when I was working in the orchard? I made all those recipes and sent out all those ads and made address books and stuff? It's just the same kind of work."

"But what gave you the idea to suddenly start doing this?"

She looked at him with the expression that he knew well. It was This Is Important.

"Mom did. When she came up, she saw I was fretting about Walt, and she gave me a talking-to. She said I need to find something useful to do. I hated to hear that, but I knew she was right. So, that's what."

Tony gave her a long hug. "That's my girl. I'll help you the best I can. You know I worry about him, too. We need to mention his name and talk about him. Can you? It's very hard for me."

She couldn't speak, but she nodded against his arm. They stood quietly without moving until both could move again

57

"**I** have become a bureaucrat." Ralph Merritt screwed a piece of paper into a crumpled ball and tossed it into a wastebasket already half-filled with scrap paper.

"Is that bad?" Russell asked.

"I think so. It's almost a year since the riot. I don't think I have solved any underlying problems. All I did was use my powers as an administrator to ship some of the trouble makers out of the camp. They'll continue to make trouble wherever they are. We gain but the camps as a whole are no better off. That's how a bureaucrat operates—make the immediate surroundings better and don't care whether any real improvements are made."

"Joyce says people are more calm these days. They're resigned to living here till the war ends, whenever that is."

"Is Joyce any less angry?"

"Not at all. She sees her friends enjoying their second year in college while she marks time here at the camp. Now she's trying to decide if she wants to go to college and law school, or whether she needs to get going on something more direct, because she feels she's wasted almost two years of her life."

"She hasn't wasted a minute of it, from what I can tell. Now it's almost December, 1943. She has made big changes here; she is learning all the time. I know she is reading, because our library budget is largely spent on her selections of materials. Tell her she should keep college as her goal."

"Yeah. Like she would listen to me. She did tell me there is a way she can get to college by going to a school in the Midwest. Is that true?"

"Yes, Russell. It is, and I just found out about it myself. We need to publicize it, and we can also begin to offer jobs to adults in the parts of the country that are away from the West Coast. People who are willing to give up their homes and go to a new location..."

"Like everybody here?"

Merritt sighed. "Yes. Like everybody here.

Barbara took to the work at the new mine office from the very first day. She already knew many of the men working on the cooperative project, and solidified her relationship with them by bringing cookies to the office several times a week. By using tricks such as sweetening her cookies with applesauce instead of sugar she worked around the ration stamps problem; several wives of the mine managers were impressed, and secretly jealous, of the success of her new role.

She found that she could keep the records and make the lists and schedules they needed. Russell would be impressed, she thought. She refused to think about Walt, whose ship was now overdue in port by two weeks.

One morning she was just leaving the post office when she met one of the Independence women she had never liked; a brittle, sarcastic middle-aged woman, wife to an insurance salesman, who announced repeatedly that she hated the Valley. Barbara smiled, as she usually did, playing a little game that she could trick the woman into smiling back. To Barbara's surprise, today it worked.

"Oh, my dear Mrs. Pershing," the woman called. "I'm so sorry about your boys."

Barbara's heart jumped. She clutched the railing on the Post Office steps. "Why, what do you mean?"

The woman's voice seemed louder than usual, as though she hoped to attract the attention of others.

"I haven't seen them in a while, and the last time I saw Russell, he was not in uniform. Every able-bodied man or boy, no matter how useless they might be, should be in uniform these days, don't you think? I wondered if maybe he was sick, or in the hospital or in jail. I know draft dodgers get sent to jail all the time."

"Russell is working for the Federal government," Barbara replied, trying to be as frosty as possible.

"So many are," the woman said, nodding solemnly. "But not everybody is helping the war effort. The post office, for example. Not much of a connection there, I shouldn't think. If he was helping the war effort, I should think he would have a uniform. How about the other one?"

"Walt is in the Merchant Marine. Now if you will excuse me..."

"But tell me, Mrs. Pershing, aren't you embarrassed that nobody in your whole family seems to be in uniform? My Sonny is only nineteen but he wants to get into the Army, except that he has this problem with his foot."

"Good bye now," Barbara said, hurrying on.

Late that afternoon, when she knew Sara had returned home from the Camp, Barbara went to her house and told her about the meeting on the Post Office steps.

"Do you have any of the same problems?" she asked Sara.

"No, but that's because Dana is a girl, and nobody expects women to be military. Howard is still too young, thank the good lord. And Cliff, of course, can't stop telling everybody that he is doing secret exciting work that he can't talk about. Maybe that's what we should do – inform everybody that we are engaged in secret military espionage.

"Oh, Barbara," she went on, "I'm just sick and tired of everything. Even the kids in my classes are just hanging around. They aren't interested in learning anything because why should they? At any moment, they could be picked up and moved someplace else. Or drafted into the Army. Did you know they are drafting some of the young men from the camp into the Army? And sending them to fight in Europe? It's outrageous."

"Sara, I had no idea. I'm so selfish. I came over here hoping you'd find some magic words to make me feel better, but I never worry about you."

"You mustn't worry about me. We are all ok. I'm sure you'll be hearing about Walt's ship soon. I'm sure it's hard for them to make sure the families know about schedules and changes and all. Now tell me, how is your new job?"

58

Russell and Joyce decided that the best Christmas gift they could give to Ralph Merritt would be a list of the accomplishments in Manzanar for 1943. He had seemed discouraged and unsure of himself, a frightening development in a man usually so confident and tireless. They decided to interview people, and have Toyo Miyatake take some photos, and put everything together to give him at Christmas.

"He got rid of the searchlights," Russell began.

"The watchtowers are all still there. And the soldiers with their guns."

"But he tried hard to get them pulled down, or not even begun. And the lights were the worst part and he did that."

"But not until almost right now."

"Joyce, you are still just as angry as you always were."

"I'll tell you why when we finish this list. Now. He had that contest to decorate the front yards. That was genius."

"Yep. He had them make the playground for the littlest children."

"He got rid of the gangsters and most of the bullies. Everybody feels safer."

"He got rid of that man who wanted everything in English."

"He started the Japanese language newspaper."

"He supports the rubber project."

"And making the camouflage netting. Are you writing all of this down, Russ?"

"Yes. He started the student nurse program so the girls who had already begun could keep going."

"He found enough rice and stuff so we now have rice and tofu and shoyu. And no potatoes!"

They continued adding items until their list was several pages long.

"Now, tell me, Joyce, why are you angry today?" Russell asked. "I thought you were feeling more, well, settled."

"See, that is it exactly," Joyce countered. "I don't want to be settled. This is not my home. My home is on top of a little store near Los Angeles. This is the prison where my family was taken. I let myself relax for a while, because there are some really good things happening here. Like the flower arranging classes and the Sunday night concerts—are you writing those down, Russ, because you should."

She continued, "but now I hear that they are letting people leave. I know my family will not want to go, now that they are here. They say they are too old to change again. But I need to leave because I need to go to college and start my own life. Do you see this, Russ?"

"Yes, I do. I was going to talk to you about that. Have you applied to a college?"

"Of course I did. In my past life, before this happened. But I applied to UCLA and now I could never go there. I don't know what to do."

It came out as a wail, so completely unlike Joyce that Russell was shocked. He gathered her against his chest, holding her as she sobbed. Finally, he could feel her taking deep breaths, regaining control of herself.

"I'm sorry."

"Oh, Joyce, don't be sorry. Be angry. It's better when you're angry." They both laughed, a little shakily.

"Aren't you thinking about college, Russ?"

"I never did. I never did enjoy schoolwork. I kind of fell into the office work, first at the mine and then here. I like it because every day is different. If I had to go to school, I would want to learn something special, but right now I'm doing what I like to do."

"Me, I'm much different," Joyce said. "My family always told me that I would go to college. I would study and become a lawyer and be a champion of my people and help them live a better life. My brother wants to be an auto mechanic."

"They are setting up a program here, starting right after New Year I think, but soon anyway. They're letting people go to places that need workers, and there are other categories like college and training."

He paused.

"But I hope you don't go, Joyce. I really hope you will stay here with the camp. And with me."

She gave him a long look, and left the room.

59

Barbara and Tony had not heard from Walt in almost two months. At first, they knew it was foolish to fret, because he was busy and the mail service was uncertain at best. But he had told them he expected to be back in port by the first of November, and it was now past Thanksgiving and there was no news. At the family Thanksgiving dinner, Tony announced that he planned to go to San Pedro and talk to the people in the Merchant Marine office. It was a surprise to hear his plan, because Tony almost never left the Valley.

"This is a special case. This is Walt. I'll let you all know what I find out."

He left very early, driving Alf's big truck. Every family member who had ration stamps for gas gave them to Tony. Alf and Tony had a feeling that Tony might be bringing some of Walt's possessions up to the Valley, but they did not want Barbara to suspect any of that.

By the time he reached the offices of the Merchant Marine in San Pedro he was tired. He thought about Walt and George making the long trip from Owens Valley on their motorcycles and realized that he would have worried about them if he had given it any thought. But they always seemed so happy and confident it never occurred to him.

The officer who met him took him into his office and spoke with great sympathy.

"I have no information for you. We don't have any idea where the ship is, or even if it is still afloat. I realize this is terrible news for you."

Tony concentrated on appearing unsurprised. Surely this pleasant officer didn't need hysterics from a parent.

"Ordinarily, I imagine you keep in touch with your vessels, or at least you know when to expect them," he said. "Walt has always given us fairly accurate ideas about the length of his cruises, even if we don't always know where he goes. But in war time..."

The officer nodded. "Now, in war time, we aren't even allowed to know all of the routes and destinations. Or the schedules. We just guess and put whatever little scraps of information we get together. One of the things that has happened is that a ship is disabled and the crew makes it to shore but we have no way of knowing where they are or how to get them out. Once we get better control of the territory that should change."

"But we have to win the war first," Tony sighed.

"We will though. It's looking better all the time. But until that happens, there are some practical things that you might want to do. For example, Walt and his friend George, as you tell me, have stored their possessions, just like everybody else does. You could pay the current storage, pick up their possessions, and then they can reclaim them when they are able."

Tony nodded.

"We need to leave word here that Walt Pershing and George Taylor can pick up their gear at Walt's parents' house," the officer told a clerk, who began to make notes. "We should also note that we have informed Mr. Pershing that his son is still listed as on active duty. No problems about being absent without leave."

Looking at the piles of packages in Walt's and George's spaces, Tony thought what a small stack of worldly goods those boys have. Of course, they had things with them—clothes, books, George's guitar, Walt's new ukulele which he bought just before he sailed. That's probably more precious than these boxes. The two motorcycles stood in one corner. Tony fetched his truck and, aided by a couple of young mariners, got the motorcycles and boxes loaded.

"He's really a pretty good guy," one of the young helpers said. "He just doesn't know what to say. He gets the run-around from the Navy because they're so careful not to give away any secrets about where any of our ships are. So, when he says he doesn't know, he honest-to-God doesn't know.

"He sees people like you every day. Parents, girlfriends, you name it. They come in and beg for any scrap of information. And sometimes the ships limp home, and you couldn't believe they could get even half way to port, with enormous holes in their side or the superstructure in ruins. But they make it. A lot of the time. So probably your son is ok, just not able to get back here. Don't give up."

They had finished loading. Tony gave them some beer money in thanks and started the long drive back to the Valley. He felt terribly tired, as though he had been carrying the heavy packages all day long, instead of standing by while the strong young men made it look easy. That's what it was, he realized. He and Barbara were getting old.

60

Ever since fourth grade, Howard's thoughts in Spring turned to baseball. He had wanted to be a pitcher, but never could master the fine-tuning involved in getting the ball reliably into the strike zone. He discovered at the beginning of high school that he could be an excellent infielder. He had a good eye and could follow a ball as it arced above him. He could throw straight, right away after catching it, and he was a great sprinter. Since every other boy had designs on being a pitcher, competition for third base was not so intense. He soon owned that position, first in his junior high team, then in high school.

The Spring, 1944, baseball season started with a set of games against other towns nearby in the Owens Valley. Independence High School won all its games in that series, but was faced with the fact that there were not enough schools in the area to offer them competition throughout the end of the school year.

"Coach," Howard asked after one practice, "have you thought about arranging a game with the kids at the Manzanar Camp?"

"The Jap camp?" the coach asked. "I didn't know they knew about baseball."

Howard laughed. "They have baseball games there all the time. The adults and the kids too. They have maybe a half dozen baseball diamonds that they've made. They're all crazy about the game."

"How do you know so much about this?" Coach asked suspiciously.

"My mom teaches high school at the camp. Sometimes she gets me a pass to go to the games. I could get you a pass, too, I think."

The coach thought. "I'll talk to some folks. When's the next game?"

By the time the weekend was over, the coach had arranged for a game against the Manzanar Coyotes, after school the following Tuesday.

The boys clambered aboard their bus, excited about going to a place they had not been before, but as the bus continued down the highway, they became quieter.

"I thought there would be soldiers," one boy said.

"There's watchtowers at least. They say they can turn on those lights at night if they need to, to catch somebody."

"Somebody like Michael, here, sneaking in to meet girls!" somebody called.

"I wouldn't!"

Now they were at the first gate. The driver stopped and opened the bus door. Two uniformed soldiers carrying rifles stepped aboard and quickly checked names on a list. The passengers were completely silent.

"OK, you may pass through."

Now they were at the inner gate. There was no more conversation, but heads were turning as each boy tried to see every inch of the camp grounds.

The athletic fields were at the end of one of the main streets, so to the boys' disappointment they were soon unloading and preparing for the game. To their surprise, the baseball diamond looked as good as the one at their school, and better than the one for the summer baseball series, which needed new paint. Bleachers lined the space along two sides of the diamond, and they were filled with spectators: parents and teenagers clapped and waved as the Independence Broncos trotted onto the field.

"It was a really good game," Howard reported at dinner that night. "They surely can play! And they are getting good coaching, too. You can tell."

"Who won?" his father asked.

"Well, they did. But coach says they have the home field advantage, whatever that is. He has lots of ideas for how we can do better the next game."

61

Sara found a letter from Dana waiting for her one afternoon when she returned from school.

Dear Family,

I think the last time I wrote to you, I told you about how we were towing targets for the gunners on shipboard to learn the new weapons. We also have done other work like that, and I'll have lots to talk about with Cliff when I see him next.

Now I must tell you about an experience that has been very sad—for me and for all of us.

Our friend here, Mary Ann Severson, died almost two weeks ago, in one of our rare accidents. She had been instructing a new pilot, and they were flying in formation with a half dozen others. One of the other planes got too close to Mary Ann's plane and clipped its wing, slicing it right off. She and her student pilot died in the crash.

This was the first fatality in our group. We hadn't thought about what would happen after. But we soon learned that while the Army would provide a casket, the WASP are not entitled to the honor of a military burial because we are not "really" in the Army. It turns out it was one of the many battles our officers have been fighting all along, just like getting us uniforms and medals and actually any kind of recognition. But they didn't tell us, because they didn't want to worry us!

So, it was up to us to take care of Mary Ann. Her family lives in Minnesota and they wanted to bury her there. We took up a collection among all the pilots—WASP and Army—and raised enough money to arrange her passage home. The Army chaplain very unofficially led a short but very moving service. Lots of people, including all of the Army pilots and all of us, came.

I volunteered to accompany her home. Mary Ann and I had roomed together in the very first days, because we were two of the very first women to get here to Sweetwater. I didn't know her very well, but I liked her.

Somebody had to go with the casket. It couldn't just be on the train by itself. It just didn't seem right, her riding all alone like a package.

I packed my dress uniform instead of wearing it, because I didn't want to have to answer questions on the train, and I wanted it to look good in Minnesota, but I wanted to show my respect, so I pinned our badge on the collar of my jacket. A couple of people asked about it, which was nice.

It took us two days and two nights to get to her family's station. It was a tiring trip.

When we got to her station, her whole family was there. The conductor knew what was going on, and he arranged for them to unload the casket as soon as the train stopped. The railroad crew had put it on a rolling cart. He helped me get off early, so that I could be there with her when we met the family.

It was her mother and father, her grandmother, a couple of uncles and her younger brother and sister. They were all crying, although the men were mostly just quiet with tears on their cheeks. Fortunately, we had thought to buy a flag, which I gave to her father. Then I went off to the hotel they had found for me, and went to bed, and slept all the rest of the day.

The funeral was next day, in the local Lutheran church, and it was filled. Lots of people came and said hello and thanked me but I felt awkward about that, because I didn't come to Minnesota for anything except to keep Mary Ann company. I did wear my uniform, so they could see how Mary Ann would have looked.

They buried her in the church cemetery on a hilly spot, very beautiful, under a large old tree, next to the grave of her sister who had died as an infant.

It's the first funeral I ever attended.

Afterwards we all went back to the church hall, where there was just lots and lots of food. They asked me to tell about what she had been doing, so I told them how important her work was and how she taught many men who would be pilots of fighter planes and bombers and transports. I told a couple of stories about her, though I really couldn't remember much—I admit I made up some of them. But they liked them.

Then an uncle drove me to the train station and I went back to Sweetwater.

Love,

Dana

62

Cliff had been involved with Tiny Tim and Holy Moses and was not entirely happy about the military's insistence on naming weapons with what he considered cute names.

"OK, I like some of them," he told his father. "Like Holy Moses—that's a pretty big rocket and it got its name because one of our guys just hollered it out when we saw it make its first run. But that Tiny Tim rocket is just enormous."

Cliff was now a full-time scientist at the growing NOTS installation. Like many of his colleagues, he moved between academic disciplines, following the development of his special project. His experience so far at Caltech taught him that things always changed, so he was prepared for teaching or whatever else they wanted him to do—whatever it was, it would be interesting.

His opportunities to show his father where he worked, however, had become limited, because the projects destined for military use required much tighter security than before.

"I feel as though everybody is doing something secret except for me," Alf mildly complained. "Not that I want anything to do. Just don't tell me anything I shouldn't know."

"Basically, we're doing the same stuff we've always done," Cliff answered, "making things blow up. The only differences are in shapes and sizes and locations."

"You have just described modern science," said Alf.

"It seems so, doesn't it? We had a test not long ago, dropping a bomb from a plane. The test was done on the range, because the usual place was too soft and boggy, and they thought they would have trouble retrieving it after."

"To use it again?" Alf asked, disbelieving.

"Well, maybe, if it was still usable. They don't come cheap, you know. So, they got it all assembled and boy was it big. Big plane, big bomb, big crowd of people to see it happen.

"Plane takes off, flies down the range, discharges the bomb, it sails down and just disappears into the ground! They said afterwards it left a hole that could hold a ten-story building!"

"Must be pretty exciting to see," said Alf, who couldn't find anything else to say.

"But, you know, it's a bomb. A very large brick. Now, rockets are much more interesting. There's so much that goes into making a new rocket. There's all the components, the fuel, the fuze, the warhead, all the design all the way through, and then there's all the details of putting it on the plane without messing up the flying characteristics of that plane, and after that's all done, you have to consider how the pilot is going to aim it and release it and get safely out of there."

"I can see that that would be complex," said Alf, whose head was starting to hurt. "Tell me, how is Monica these days?"

287

"She's fine. She seems to have found a sailor who wants to take her dancing a lot. And she may decide she wants to go to a larger city and have some auditions and stuff. I don't see much of her these days."

He glanced at his watch, preparing to leave for a lab which he could not show his father. Alf took the hint and headed back to Independence.

63

Alf had become accustomed to receiving phone calls with surprising messages. Tuck Watson had calmed down somewhat after learning that the Navy, while interested in his airstrip, was only casually interested in that piece of real estate. Still, he occasionally called just to make sure that there was no impending development that nobody had warned him about.

Today it was Len Reyes, surprising both of them. Len had a deep aversion to the phone and used it only when other methods, like face-to-face meetings or letters, were not possible. This time, however, he was eager to have his friend come to the mine as soon as possible.

"Alf, I had the most amazing idea, and I want to talk to you about it. Maybe we can get rich!"

"We're not the kind of people who get rich, Len. Just forget that. But if it is an idea that will get me away, I'm in. I'll be up there this afternoon."

Alf found it much easier to reach Len's office in Independence rather than going all the way to Pine Creek. He waved to Barbara, busy at her desk in the outer office, then joined Len in his office.

The plan presented by Len was mysterious and exciting. "I get reports from time to time from prospectors," he told Alf. "They'll bring me ore samples—they're mostly weekend rock hounds just messing around, thinking they will strike it rich somehow. This time, the guy brought me some rocks which seem to be rich in scheelite."

"Does he have a good claim? Are you thinking we want to get on it with him?"

"Well, that's part of it, but only part. He also says he has a way to separate out the gangue—the worthless bits that are attached to more valuable ore. He had some samples, like before and after. It was pretty convincing. He's looking for partners because he's just about broke. I think it is probably a trick, a con, but maybe not, and if it is on the level, why not be part of it?"

"I don't know much about your end of the mining business, Len. Do you get proposals like this often, or is this something really unusual?"

"We see a lot of prospectors who think they have found something, but it usually turns out they don't know the first thing about the different minerals they've come across. So, I don't know. The difference here is his idea of processing the minerals."

"What do we know about him?" Alf asked.

"I don't know him. Maybe Barbara does. He talked to her."

Len walked over and called Barbara into the office. She smiled at her brother and drew up a chair, prepared to describe the prospector of interest.

"No, I haven't seen him in town, and he doesn't seem to know anybody here, either. He was asking around for a place to stay. In fact, he is asking a lot of questions in general."

"What's your feeling about him, Barbara?" Len asked.

"Len, on the surface he seems well educated and smart. He's very polite and cordial, not at all rough like so many of the miners and prospectors we see. But I just don't feel right about him. There's something I don't understand. For one thing, I'm not sure he understands all of the chemistry he talks about, and he keeps changing the subject when people ask questions."

Alf nodded. "Let's invite him in and talk to him. I'm curious."

They set a meeting for the following afternoon.

Alf arrived early for the meeting and set up the conference room with papers and pens, water glasses and pitchers. Barbara had established herself at a small table in the corner of the room with plenty of paper and pencils of her own for taking notes.

Soon Len re-appeared with their guest, introduced as Peter Simmons. He was a forty-something man with sunburned skin, dressed in jeans and a patterned shirt and work boots. He carried a small case which he opened and set on the table, explaining it contained the ore samples he had earlier shown Mr. Reyes. Alf and Barbara examined them carefully, as did Len, who indicated that in fact they seemed to be the same rocks.

"Do you have more samples?" Alf asked. "I mean, wherever you gathered these, did you get more at the same time?"

"This sample, you call After," Barbara said. "Of course it looks totally different from the others because you have processed it, but can you tell us how it compared in size with the others before you worked it?"

291

"Of course, to all of your questions. Yes, I have several boxes of these rocks, and I have noted where I found them, and most of them were within a few dozen feet of each other." He had a slight accent, almost unnoticeable, Alf thought.

Simmons continued, "You might think this is surprising, but you know you have some rich veins of tungsten ore in your mountains. If you decide you would like to join with me in developing this mine, I'll be happy to take you there.

"Now, as Mr. Reyes has probably told you, I have developed a process which purifies the ore more quickly and efficiently than anybody else has done. If you decide to join with me, I will show you how I am doing this work.

"In answer to Mrs. Pershing," Simmons concluded, "sometimes you end up with almost nothing once the gangue has been removed. Sometimes you have almost as much as when you started. In the case of this particular rock, much of it washed away during my process. It started somewhat larger than the other rock I show you, and as you see there is relatively little left."

"Thank you Mr. Simmons. Would you please tell us a little about yourself? Your background in geology, your professional credentials, how you happened to come to this particular place to do your prospecting?"

"No."

"I'm sorry?" Len said. "I don't understand."

"I'm not prepared to offer you any information until I see that you and your colleagues are serious about working with me. When we have a working agreement, signed by all concerned, then I will be happy to tell you more. I will leave now. I will return tomorrow at this same time. I anticipate that you will have a decision for me then."

He returned his materials to his sample case and left the room, walking quickly down the street to his waiting car. Len, Alf, and Barbara stood speechless in the conference room.

64

I t just didn't feel right. Len, Alf and Barbara easily agreed on that fact. This man had appeared out of nowhere and seemed to offer the possibility of riches to anybody who would join in business with him. But what would that entail?

"Remember the German and Russian businessmen who came to Pine Creek before the war?" Len said. "I know we all talked about it, because they were so eager, and they had money to burn, and it was tempting to let them buy into our mine. But if we had let them, think how much tungsten and other ores would be on their way to Germany right now? And maybe Russia too, because who trusts Russia?"

"It was your boss, Len, who put a stop to all that, right? He and the FBI told us to keep our mouths shut and send them on their way."

"And they took all that wonderful money with them," Len said mournfully. "Barbara, did Russ ever talk to you about that?"

"Not then, but sometimes when he comes home from Manzanar he'll talk about the mine, how much he loved working there, and how he misses it. He worries, I think, that Len is too trusting and might let spies or enemies know too much. Russ has never been too trusting!"

"I wonder what we owe to our members," Barbara continued. "Back when you had those possible spies, before the war, we didn't have this group of mine managers who are all supposed to work in concert."

"Good point. Maybe he has been approaching them, too. Barbara, have you made any good contacts?"

"I'm in a book club with Martha Goodwin, the wife of the manager of the Great Betsy mine. I'll see whether she has heard anything."

Alf contributed, "I'll check with Sam Norcross on the paper. He can see if there's any gossip."

"I think we are agreed that we'll not sign up for anything with this man until we know more," Len said. "Now I have to go out and do some mine work."

The following day saw the return of Mr. Simmons, who left again immediately upon learning that the Pine Creek group was still considering his proposal. "You're in great danger of losing out," he cautioned. "I have many other fish in the oven."

But they were unable to learn anything new about him. After asking other mine operators they concluded that all had been contacted, because nobody would say anything about the man. The newspaper consulted its files, and Alf asked the Caltech library for a search of any materials related to Peter Simmons, miner, without success.

Len was the first of the three to decide he wanted none of this. When he told Alf and Barbara, they quickly agreed with him and returned to business as usual. But within a few weeks, news began to spread. The Marigold mine had been sold to a mysterious buyer and was closing in order to remodel its processing plant. Then the Great Betsy announced that it would no longer be hiring miners. Finally, work began to enlarge the road to the Marigold mine, using a company from out of town that no one had heard of previously.

"The Great Betsy! Isn't that where your friend's husband works?" Alf asked his sister.

"Yes, and she is just beside herself. Her husband won't tell her anything, except that they will be moving away from the valley. He is upset, she is upset. Apparently, he got an enormous check from the company that bought them, and wants to put it to work to start another business near Los Angeles. She doesn't know what to think."

Len had just entered the office. "I think I may have the missing information," he said slowly. "You know I checked with my own boss, and he advised me to stay clear. Turns out that the FBI is very interested in Mr. Simmons. But Barbara, you are not allowed to mention any of that to your friend. I'm sorry, but do not say a word."

"But." Barbara said. "We're having a book club meeting tomorrow."

"Better get sick," Len advised. "This is serious business."

The next few weeks seemed so ordinary that Simmons was almost forgotten. But one day Len received an angry phone call from one of the other mine managers, accusing him of ruining a possible business opportunity for several mines in the area. At first, he was mystified, but then he remembered Peter Simmons.

"The man was a fraud, just as we had suspected," he told Alf and Barbara. "But he wasn't a simple con man. My boss has been checking with his FBI contact and tells me that Simmons is a

Russian citizen, all but certainly a spy. He was looking for information on our mine managers, so that he could blackmail or threaten them into giving control of their mines to him."

"But they are blaming you."

"Yes, Barbara, they are and if we had gone ahead and signed up with him right away, maybe they still would, but in that case, we would have at least got some money. I think there's a good possibility that your friends may have been able to get out of town and use the Simmons money quite legally, but I don't know, and we may never know."

"It just seems like the world is full of too many things we may never know," she said sadly.

"Yes. Well. We all need to get back to work," Alf said. He just hated it when Barbara became so sad.

65

Manzanar was beginning to empty out. Only a month or so ago, towards the beginning of the desert springtime, people seemed to crowd the streets and common areas in the residential areas. The schools were busy with end-of-year celebrations and graduations, and through the open windows he could hear choirs practicing songs and hymns. The flowers planted in the front yards during last year's garden contest were coming up again, and the rose bushes were filled with buds. (Even though everybody knew the soil had been enriched by the remains of fish illicitly caught beyond the back fence, everybody praised the hard work of the gardeners).

Now that it was becoming clear that the Allies would ultimately win the war, small areas of good sense were beginning to open up. Internees were offered opportunities to move to the Middle West where farms were desperate for labor. Students were being allowed, in an increasing number of cases, to return to college and specialized training. The increased sense of well-being within the camp led to several weddings, delighting participants with parties and opportunities for new clothes.

The residents of Manzanar now needed to begin to consider the rest of their lives. Ralph Merritt, aided by Russell, had started making visits to the blocks of housing in order to meet with small groups of residents and explain that at the end of the war, Manzanar would be closed and torn down. All residents would have to find new homes. Merritt would carefully explain that the government would help them find their new homes, and give them advice on how to get there, and maybe find some way to pay for transportation. At this point, the older people would sometimes weep, and the men would ask how they could get to a new home if they had no money and no job.

It was then Russell's job to be comforting and vague and offer to make lists and write letters and wouldn't it be a good thing to start now, and did anybody have relatives in the middle of the country—or at the very least, somewhere away from the West Coast—who would like to receive a letter from a Manzanar cousin? If Joyce were part of this visiting team, she would suddenly appear with tea, and they would break for refreshments and a chance to calm down. Ralph Merritt would sigh and go outdoors and stand in the sun for a while and look around, and then shake his body like a wet dog does and return to more conversation. Sometimes they visited the same group several times and held several identical conversations.

"Are we getting them placed?" Russell asked one day.

"We're getting closer. I'm not even trying to think about those who have no place to go. Or those who insist upon returning to the place they lived before the war. Because each one of them is a special case."

"What are you going to do, sir?"

Merritt smiled. "I'm going to retire. I'm going to sleep for a month and then go fishing. That's my plan, anyway. And I need to do something special for my wife. She has had lonely times here and she has never complained. So we'll take a family vacation first. What I'll really do, I don't know. What about you?"

"I'd work for you if you had a job for me," Russell answered. "But if you're asleep, then I want to go back to Pine

299

Creek mine and work for Len. If he'll have me. We haven't discussed it."

"And what about Joyce?"

"She has found a school she likes. It's in Arizona, so it's away from the coast, but close enough so that she can visit family. They have a number of Japanese students already. She's working on getting scholarship help now."

"I wondered whether you would try to go with her."

"No. She wants to go by herself and I can't blame her. I think I would be a bad memory for her. But she said she would like it if I came to visit, once she is settled. I'm going to do that. I think. We'll have to see how everything works out. Her parents are still unplaced, I know."

66

Cliff found himself busy day and night, as the Caltech and NOTS teams prepared the final adjustments to the first air-launched rockets. As a graduate student in chemistry, he was primarily interested in the fuel to be used in the launcher, but at this point everybody who could be at the NOTS ranges was here, tightening bolts, raking the sand, stacking supplies, making everything ready for the first test flights of a major new weapon system.

The planes to be used for the tests were already fitted with the rails attached to the underside of their wings. They would carry two rockets for these tests, one under each wing, although the hope was that in the future there would be two per wing. The most exciting part was the fact that these were the enormous Tiny Tim rockets, longer, heavier and with a larger diameter than any previous air-launched rockets developed by NOTS.

First, ground tests were set up on the NOTS ranges. When the scientists were assured that their constructions were successful, they arranged for the real thing: A Tiny Tim rocket would be launched from an airplane in flight. Tiny was heavier, longer and wider than anything they had tried before.

There was no point in trying to keep the launch a secret. By midmorning, Navy and Caltech personnel had gathered near the range in question. Cliff found himself standing next to a pair of Navy officers. Under the hot desert sun, the observers began to tire.

"Guess you like planes, huh?" one of the men said to Cliff.

"I'm with Caltech," he answered proudly. "I'm involved with the chemistry of propellants."

"Wow. I guess that's why you're here, all right. Do you fly?"

"No, but my sister Dana does. In fact, she is a test pilot for the Army. Have you heard about the WASP?"

"Have we! And that's your sister! You should know how important her work is. We both of us had some training in Texas with WASP pilots. Actually, one of them taught me to fly. But I hated it and now I stick to ships. Hard to imagine a ship in the Texas desert, huh?"

"That could have been my sister. She's in Sweetwater."

Both men looked impressed. "Those women pilots do a lot scarier things than we could ever do."

Now the flight test was getting underway. There was a murmur of surprise as the watchers caught sight of the large rocket being loaded onto the underside of the plane's wing.

The pilot made a thorough pre-flight examination of his plane, then climbed in as the observers clapped and cheered for him. He started the engine. Soon the plane started moving slowing forward, gradually gaining speed until it took off and flew higher, now silhouetted against the mountains. The glare of the summer sun made it difficult to keep the plane in view.

The rocket shot out from under the wing.

The plane nosedived into the rocky ground and disappeared.

A small plume of black smoke could be seen against the horizon.

The observers stood transfixed. Small planes took off from the neighboring runway, dashing to the point of the crash.

Then there was nothing to see and nothing to hear. People began slowly to walk away in small groups, speaking quietly to each other.

The man who had been standing next to Cliff found him and put his hand on Cliff's shoulder. "Your sister is a brave woman. When you talk to her, tell her how much we all admire the WASPs."

67

Though the news from the War zones was that the United States and her allies were winning, the Richardsons felt that life was a long way from returning to normal. For one thing, they were scattered.

Charles was in Alaska, doing whatever Charles found to do; Barbara and Alf were working in Independence, both feeling as though they were marking time before resuming their ordinary life. Dana was in Sweetwater, flying planes that would terrify her parents if they had any idea of her activities; Howard was about to finish high school, continuing his secret plan of becoming a famous baseball player someday. Cliff still worked at Caltech but would not talk to his family about his activities. Russell, on the other hand, would not stop talking to anybody he could find. He missed Joyce, he was tired of running pointless errands for people who would soon leave Manzanar, and he could not decide what he wanted to do when Manzanar closed.

Tony was amused to see that the movies now being made in the Alabama Hills and surrounding area had begun to include adventurous films about exotic foreign locations. The old Westerns were losing their allure, he thought, but bringing in camels to the Western desert was going a bit too far. And it was hard to build a set amid the rocks and sand which would appear to be an ocean kingdom with mermaids, even if those mermaids were really beautiful. Every now and then, when Barbara was distressed, he would persuade her to see a new film, because they were so outrageous she just had to laugh.

One day, he was called to the office for a phone call. It was the Merchant Marine officer he had met in San Pedro months before.

"I wish had had better news," the officer said. "But I do have *some* news. Naval intelligence has received a distress signal from your son's ship. Right now, that's all we know, except that the chances of eventually locating the ship and crew seem more promising than they did. As soon as we know more, we'll let you know."

"Thanks. It's definitely better than nothing, as far as I'm concerned. Although I think I won't mention it to my wife."

"That's why we try to call our contacts at their work. We're hoping for the best."

Tony went back to work, still thinking about the phone call. When two hours had passed and he was still sitting in his truck, he decided he needed a person to talk to.

"I couldn't decide who to bother just now," he told Alf over coffee in the little coffee shop in Independence. "I think I should be talking to Russ, not you, but it's too hard. I'm their father and I can't just say I'm heartbroken and I don't know what to do. They have always expected me to be the grownup to them."

"I understand exactly what you are saying," Alf said. "I think you are doing the right thing, though. Russell and Barbara don't need any more anxiety. How is she doing?"

"I think her new job is good for her. She is tired when she comes home, and after we get dinner and the clean-up done, she's off to bed and actually goes to sleep. And I don't hear her whimpering like she'd been doing."

They were silent, thinking about a device that could send a signal into the skies even though the ship could not be found. Finally, Alf stood and prepared to go back to work.

"Call me any time," he said. "middle of the night, any time. Sara says so, too, or she would if she knew we were talking about this."

Tony nodded.

Russell was so busy that he seldom thought about anything except the issue immediately in front of him. The task of re-settling the internees was almost overwhelming. It was a good thing, he thought, that many of them were preparing to leave the camp. That way their problems and concerns could be handled at a more personal level.

There was so much to do: Packing clothing and household goods involved returning some things to the company warehouse; those taking farm jobs for the giant packing company who had hired so many of them would need paperwork, and travel money, and tickets, and maps.

Students going off to college, like Joyce, needed records of their grades and parental permission if they were still young enough. Would Joyce remember him? Would she really like it if he came to visit her? Would she be embarrassed? Would she mind that Russell had never gone to college? Didn't want to? He ran that set of worries back into the place where they rested until he relaxed; then they returned to bedevil him again.

This morning's crisis involved Toyo Miyatake. He had been invited to a university in the Midwest, to work as a Photographer in Residence. He, however, had other plans. He felt his place was with his people, and the growing collection of photographs of life in Manzanar should include some from the times following its closure. This, he reasoned, required him to stay until the very end. It was Russell's job to make sure he and his family would be able to re-settle after the closure of the camp, even if Merritt and the other administrators were no longer around.

And what about the other, more widely-known photographers? Ansel Adams had made many visits and his photos had received positive publicity, which made the government happy, but Adams planned to publish others, and write a message that would paint Manzanar in a much less positive light. Russell planned to ignore that entire subject.

The photos by Dorothea Lange, for example, which were more emotionally meaningful in Russell's opinion, had been captured and hidden away in government archives—would they ever emerge again?

He turned, hearing a knock on his office door. It was Ralph Merritt, in baseball cap and carrying a picnic basket.

"Come on, Russell," he said. "There's a double-header with Independence this afternoon. We've got to leave right now to get good seats."

68

As summer 1944 began to turn to Fall, Cliff found it hard to continue working on the rocket propellants. He kept remembering the plane diving into the desert on its test flight. It seemed like an insoluble problem: Creating new rockets and bombs was necessary in order to win the war, and it seemed even more a clear need because the enemy was so strong and so brutal—any step to help our country defeat this enemy was clearly a patriotic duty. But the new weapons brought with them their own risks and dangers. The immense rocket under the wing of the plane that crashed and the vast amount of powder that was judged necessary for its launch killed that pilot. By now he knew a half dozen men who had died while working on the rocketry projects, and he was sure there would be more.

He found himself considering the older scientists from Caltech who had already been working with rockets for decades, despite lack of both funding and interest from the military. There was something that drove them to keep building models, write equations, combine elements, to drive out into the desert and set up a launcher and send a dozen or twelve dozen rockets into the air and then describe what exactly happened to cause all of them to miss the target. And then do it again. And again.

"I'm not sure I can keep doing this work," he told his father. "Maybe I was wrong to change from geology to chemistry. There is so much evil in chemistry."

"Now just a moment here," Alf answered. "There's nothing either good or evil in chemistry, or in any other course of study. Evil comes from people who use the information to do evil things. So, before you go much farther, consider whether what you are working on is, in fact, evil? Or is it really scary and deadly dangerous?"

"Both, I think. But I knew about the scary part from the first time I started in the lab. I think about the bombs and the rockets, and everything we've been hearing about the war, and the damage they do is immense. When you have weapons like these rockets, you must know that the chance of civilians being killed is almost certain. Although I guess civilians are always getting killed in wars. But fire! And blood! And buildings being just, just disintegrated! And of course, I'm thinking about Walt on his ship."

"How do the rest of the project members feel? Do you talk about it?"

"Not much, but I'll tell you something. The military officers, and especially the pilots, are about the least bloodthirsty men I've ever met. I think it's because they know too much about the damage that can be done."

"You've had that experience before. Is it that you are finding evil in things you hadn't thought about before?"

"Kind of. I mean, I knew we were building weapons. I know their purpose. But seeing that plane just—it didn't just fall to the ground, it *sped* into the ground.

"I suppose there isn't any point in my saying, if you don't make weapons, then somebody else will, and it won't slow things or change things by a minute."

"I was thinking exactly that. I've been doing nothing but thinking about it ever since. And I have decided that what I must do is not quit chemistry, but instead change the kind of work I do."

"Why?"

"Well, they don't talk about it outside the lab, but you can be sure that every instant of that test is being studied. What went wrong? Here is a plane that has been carrying bombs under its wing for a long time. Why did it suddenly mess up the launch? I was really worried for a while, because I worked on the formula for the propellant, and I was so sure that it was appropriate, but what if it was somehow responsible?"

"But wasn't it the plane, and not the rocket?" Alf asked. "I think you said that it looked like it jerked up as the rocket left the wing, and then tipped down."

"Right. And it seems they have decided that two things were responsible. They had used a stronger propellant—more black powder—than they had planned to use, and the plane had been just slightly modified several months before they ever thought of using it in this test, so nobody realized that Tiny Tim was heavier than the plane could handle."

"And they learned all this already?"

"Nobody's stopped to eat or sleep since the accident," Cliff continued, "So I'm changing what I do. From now on I'm going to be on test and quality assurance teams. These are the guys who do exactly that—figure out how to make things not go wrong. It's so important but there's no glory, because if things go right nobody knows anybody was fixing anything. No medals for Cliff, I'm afraid. But I think I'll sleep better."

"And Caltech will not have a problem with this?"

"My professor seems to be actually happy. It's been an interest of his for a long time—probably why I even thought of it at all. Anyway, he says he'll support my change of direction, and I might even get a dissertation topic out of it, because this field is so new."

69

Barbara waited until after supper before telling Tony what she wanted to do. Her work at the mine office was making her more content with herself, because she could see that she was useful to Len's business. She was sleeping better because she was tired at the end of the day. She had acknowledged that there was nothing she could do to find her son: Only the Merchant Marine could do that.

She found Tony sitting in his favorite place on the front porch, and, taking his hand, led him out into their back yard, where the apples on their young tree were just starting to ripen.

"Tony, it's the garage. We need to talk about the garage."

"Well, OK. Just what is it we need to talk about? It's a pretty good garage, I think."

"But you think you are keeping a secret from me. You told me yourself that we have to talk about Walt, and mention his name, and hold him in our thoughts. And you went and stacked his gear in the garage where you thought I wouldn't see it."

"Oh." Tony figured she would find out eventually. He had arranged to arrive back at their house while she was working, and had enlisted Howard's help in unloading the boxes and bags he had brought from San Pedro. Barbara ordinarily never spent much time in the garage, keeping her own garden supplies in the shed he had built for her. But very little escaped Barbara.

"I was just putting things off," he said. "I was waiting till you felt up to dealing with it. I guess that's now, right?"

They stood in the driveway and looked around.

"Yes. We need to talk, anyway." The garage was so full that Tony parked his truck outside. The gradual accumulation of tools, bicycles and scooters and wagons, woodshop projects and cartons of Christmas decorations took up much of the space. The remaining floor space was now occupied by the packages Tony had brought from San Pedro.

They stood in the doorway and looked around.

"Barbara, it's been almost a year. By Thanksgiving it will be just about a year since we heard from Walt and George."

"But we can't move these."

"No. We won't. We are sure they will be back home, sooner or later, and they'll want them. Barbara, I'm going back down again, to talk with the people at the Merchant Marine. Maybe they'll have some idea of somebody else we can check with. Maybe not. Want to come with me?"

The next morning as they were packing a lunch for the road, the telephone rang. Tony answered, with Barbara listening from the doorway.

"Yes, this is Tony. Yes, Walt Pershing. George Taylor. Yes. Oh, my God. Yes. Yes. OK. Any time."

He hung up and started to cry. Tears rolled down his cheeks. Barbara, who had never seen Tony cry, pulled him over to a crate where they both sat down.

"They have located the ship. The Navy is sending a rescue ship. They know that at least some of the crew are alive. That's all they know. But they should know more in a week. Or less."

Barbara was trembling, her hands shaking visibly. She hugged Tony.

"Oh Tony! Let's take that lunch we just packed, and climb in the truck, and go up 9 Mile Canyon and have a picnic and just enjoy this day. I know we don't know whether ....whether... but we will know the answers before long."

70

Russell entered Ralph Merritt's office and threw himself into the visitor's chair.

"If it's not one thing, it's another," he complained. "I'm breaking my back trying to find places for people to move to, and jobs that they know how to do, and people who genuinely want them to come, and what do they say to me?"

Merritt looked up from his stack of papers, and grinned.

"From what you're telling me, I'm going to hear that they don't appreciate your efforts," he said.

"Darn right they don't! You'd think everybody would be crowding around the gate trying to get out. I found this great organization that needs farm labor workers. They can take as many as we can send them, they have housing for them, and there are even already quite a few Japanese-American families. Wouldn't you think this would be perfect? But no!

"Well thank goodness most people are happy, but there are some who don't want to leave Manzanar! They've got all kinds of excuses—it's a new place, will they like it, it's too cold in the winter, how long will it take to get there? Can you believe this?"

315

Merritt sighed. "You have to remember, for the older people in particular, they lived in one place all their lives. Forty, maybe fifty or more years. Suddenly we picked them up and put them down here in this desert. Bad enough, but now we want them to go someplace else and start over again! I think I would feel the same way: just leave me alone, I've moved enough!"

He stood and took his hat from the hat rack by the door.

"OK. I'll go talk to them again. I know the group you're talking about. This will be the fourth conversation. Eventually they will realize that we're not changing our minds."

As Merritt began his impromptu meeting under the cottonwood trees near the barracks, Toyo Miyatake appeared with his camera, and stood snapping away. *I wish Joyce could see this,* Russell thought. *She'd really like it.*

71

It took more than a week. Little bits of news were telephoned to Tony and Barbara. The rescue ship reached the tiny island where the missing ship had gone aground, a large hole in its hull. As the rescue crew reported, most of the crew members were still alive and in reasonably good condition.

The crew had managed to land, tend their wounded and create shelters. They salvaged supplies from the ship, including food and drinking water, and had tried to reach help, but the ocean was so large and the island so small that it had never been mapped or named, and they had no working signal devices.

They were being transported to San Pedro, and from there were sent to hospitals or to their homes, depending upon their condition.

The next few days were tense times for Barbara and Tony. How had Walt and George survived the wreck? Would they recover completely? What kind of memories would they have, and how changed would they be? Would they resent Tony's removal of their possessions from San Pedro? What about George's family, with whom they had never been able to make contact?

One morning, Tony received another phone call from the Merchant Marine. His son was a passenger on a Navy van now on its way to the Owens Valley. They should expect him before noon.

Tony and Barbara flew around the house, making it ready. The small bedroom where George had stayed previously was made up with fresh bedding and flowers on a table by the window. Walt's room was freshened up as well, and his favorite foods were ready in the kitchen. Tony polished the motorcycles till they shone, and dusted off the other packs and boxes in the garage.

Alf sent an urgent message to Dana in Sweetwater telling her the news, and urging her to take some leave to come home for a few days.

Finally, the big blue van pulled up in front of the house. Barbara and Tony reached the gate just as the door opened and Walt, taller and skinnier, with one arm in a sling, climbed out and into his mother's arms. George followed with a large smile, as Barbara included him in her hug. Tony thanked the driver and called greetings to the remaining passengers. The four of them entered the house.

For a short time, everybody talked at once. Walt and George reassured Tony that they appreciated his taking care of their gear and saving them the rental charges in San Pedro. Barbara continually said "You're home, you're home" until it became a kind of undercurrent to the other voices.

Then Walt and George told their story. They had been part of a convoy of freighters headed toward Panama and the Canal when their ship developed problems apparently due to being overloaded.

"It was just wallowing in the water," Walt said, "losing speed gradually, till the rest of the convoy had to move on. We signaled for help and ships were sent, but by the time they reached our expected path, the Japs had found us. We took a torpedo that blew a hole in us just above the water line."

"We were lucky," George continued, "that the initial damage wasn't greater. It allowed us to head toward land. But we didn't realize that what we thought was Central America was actually an island that nobody had known about. It was a small island and had previously been considered part of the Costa Rican mainland. So, I guess we are explorers. Maybe they'll name it after our ship."

"If it ever gets on a map," Walt objected. "Now they're telling us we can't talk about where it is or anything about it. Military secrets. Huh."

Barbara said, "You're home. You're alive. You have come home."

"The other lucky thing," George said, "was that we had time to raid the ship for supplies. We had all pretty much escaped getting hurt, except for Walt here who seems to have messed up his shoulder. So, there were a lot of us to go through the ship and gather food and water and medicines and just about everything that we could move. It kept us going, and actually kept our spirits up pretty much in those early days."

"We managed to put together a kind of camp," Walt went on. "we built shelters from the weather, and were able to keep blankets dry. George and his group set up a kitchen. It turned out that one of the guys had grown up in El Salvador and he knew a lot of the plants, and so we had fresh fruit every now and then."

"Weren't there any other people on the island?" Tony asked.

"If there were, we didn't see any. And to tell you the truth, we didn't look hard. For the first weeks, we thought our signals were getting out, and it would just be a few days, or maybe weeks, till we were spotted. By the time we realized nobody was catching our signals, we decided that if there were any people there, they would have seen us."

"How did they find you?" Tony asked.

"Actually, it was by chance. An Army patrol plane was chasing a possible Japanese ship, and flew above the island. He thought the wreckage he saw was some kind of construction, so he turned and flew over again to check and by that time we had got to the beach and started waving like crazy. All of us."

Barbara had calmed down enough to announce that lunch was ready—sandwich makings were on the table. With relief, the men moved toward the food and lighter conversations.

72

They were all excited to hear the boys were home. Howard ran all the way to Barbara's house after school to see them and hear their story, and to offer to maintain their motorcycles until they wanted them again.

"So are you going back on the ship?" he asked. "And what happened to your arm, Walt?"

"Fell through an open hatch while we were pulling supplies out of our wrecked ship. Hurt like a son-of-a-gun, Howard. Make sure it doesn't ever happen to you!

"And in answer to your question, we're going back to the Merchant Marine in just a few days. They gave us some extra leave time, but they need everybody just now."

Dana had started for home the moment she received her father's message. Thanks to the network of the pilots she worked with at Sweetwater she managed to find space on a military plane heading for a base north of Los Angeles. Even better, she shared a ride from Los Angeles to Independence with a Sweetwater colleague and arrived home, breathless and excited, only hours after Walt and George.

They all settled down to five days of a relaxed life before the three young people were due to return to their duties.

But Dana had an additional job to do before she returned to Texas: a visit to NOTS to inquire about a possible post war job. George had immediately noticed that although she was happy and relieved to see him home and healthy, she was clearly thinking hard about something. It did not take him long to convince her that it was a question that the two of them needed to decide together.

"They're getting ready to shut us down," she told George. "They don't admit it, but there it is. No schedules are being made after the end of this year, the only supplies they are buying are the ones we need immediately. There are no recruits coming in."

"You must feel very sad." George said.

"Actually, I do and I don't. There is something exciting about being forced to choose a new direction. And I'm like my uncle Charles—after I do something for a while, I begin to want something new to do. The only thing is, I should find out if there is work for me closer to home."

She was determined to make her visit to the Naval Ordnance Test Station at China Lake. She made sure that her uniform was spotless and pressed, her lapel pin bright. Her boots, carefully polished, shone.

The officer who greeted her was polite but distant. She could tell he was uncomfortable speaking with a person who was almost, but not quite, a military officer.

"Good afternoon, sir," Dana said. "I think I must be the first WASP pilot you have met."

He acknowledged this, and immediately began to compliment her and her fellow WASPs on their success.

"We have heard from a number of our men how much you ladies have contributed to the delivery of aircraft, and to the training of pilots. It's most remarkable. I'm sure you all will be happy to return to civilian life, now that we are able to find returning male pilots to take over your duties."

He began to describe the offer he was prepared to make, to her and to any other WASP officer who wanted to apply. He told her about how NOTS was testing and delivering air-launched rockets and bombs, how they were experimenting in all aspects of the process from the design of aircraft to the rockets themselves.

"Now as you know the military does not allow women to be pilots. So, you will be looking for other areas in which you can serve. Here at NOTS we have several openings for secretaries..."

Dana held up her hand.

"Sir, I understand your position. But I want you to remember that I am a pilot. I'm certified on all of the military planes now flying. I've instructed your men. For some of them I certified their first solos. I'm sure you can find a way to circumvent the system, so I can put my flying skills and knowledge to the best use for our country." She looked at him hopefully.

The officer cleared his throat. "I wish with all my heart that I could think of a way we could hire you. We need people like you. But my instructions are very clear and the policy regarding women pilots is very specific."

Dana smiled and shook his hand. "Thank you for your time, sir."

Back outside, she told George, "I was all set to make a scene, because I'd heard from the other girls that there's no hope, but I looked at him and saw how embarrassed he was. I think if he had his way he would have taken me on and I could continue to fly those big beautiful planes. But he has no authority and he's afraid for his own career. I just felt so sad for him. He never has a chance to make his own decisions. But now I'm ready, really ready, to sit down with you and figure out what we will do together for the rest of our lives."

73

It wasn't hard to decide to have the 1944 Thanksgiving dinner early. Just about everybody was already home, and Charles was hoping to get to the Owens Valley in time. That would complete the table.

Sara and Barbara shared the kitchen duties, with help from Molly who had to sit down to rest more often than she would have liked but otherwise seemed cheerful. Tony and Alf put together a long table in Tony's back yard, because they were inviting others as well. It was late October, to be sure, so they planned to eat in the middle of the day to catch the sunlight and whatever heat would be there.

The baking began several days beforehand. George made his special dinner rolls, remarking that he was relieved to be able to step right up to the job after so much time away from the kitchen.

Grandma Schmidt offered cookies—big round sugar cookies for people to nibble on while waiting for the turkey.

On the morning of the dinner, everybody was busy and happy, preparing the parts of the dinner they had been assigned. Barbara's kitchen had been stripped of all the furniture that could be moved so that there would be room for people to stand around in groups and to serve themselves from the dishes filling the counters.

The long table under the trees now held several bunches of flowers from everybody's gardens. The day was sunny and warm with a cloudless sky.

"God is smiling on us," Barbara said quietly to her mother.

In the past several months, many of the internees had left the Manzanar camp for jobs or schools elsewhere. The gardens had been somewhat neglected. Now many of the rules restricting civilian access to the camp at Manzanar had been set aside, resulting in a brisk trade in fruits and vegetables from the camp garden. Today's dinner would contain squashes, tomatoes, many different kinds of beans, and some vegetables nobody in the house had ever seen before.

There was turkey, of course. Ralph Merritt and his wife contributed a large ham. There were casseroles of many kinds, often involving potatoes and cheese.

And to finish there were pies and cakes and more of Grandma Schmidt's cookies.

Surveying the astonishing variety of dishes, Barbara said, "We wanted to make sure there would be enough for everybody, because George and Walt reminded us that they have a lot of missed dinners to make up."

Just as they were about to eat they heard a car pull up. In came Russell with Joyce Takahashi, whom Russell insisted on introducing to everybody immediately.

"Thank you, Mrs. Pershing," Joyce said. "I hope I'm not intruding. Russ wanted me to meet all of you."

"Oh, my dear, I'm so glad to meet you!" She made sure Joyce had a full plate and a place to sit next to Russell.

Like all of the Richardson family gatherings, it was a noisy, chatty affair. In addition to Ralph Merritt and his wife, they had been joined by the Crawford family (Sophie would not leave Howard's side and kept bringing him little tidbits to eat, to his embarrassment) and Grandma Schmidt and Len, who had as always brought a special food. This time it was squash pudding and was a great hit.

After everybody had finished dinner, Spence rose and tapped his knife on a glass for quiet.

"We have finished another year, and we seem to be doing about as well as can be expected," he said. "We hope that by next year our country will be at peace. There have been so many changes in our lives, and there will be many more to come. We know too that many of you will be leaving soon to resume your responsibilities, but we have this opportunity to send you off with our love.

"Now," he continued, "we need all of you to tell us what you are planning to do and where you will be going."

He motioned around the table. "For example, Charles!"

To a murmuring of Welcome home Charles, he stood.

"I'm going back to Alaska. That seems to be the place where I do best. I'm still flying on photographic mapping missions, but it still is for the Coast and Geodetic Survey, and I think it is very useful work. I seem to have met a young lady, whom I hope to bring down with me on our next visit. She couldn't come today because she races sled dogs and couldn't leave them."

Barbara shook her head, murmuring, "Charles, Charles."

Ralph Merritt was next. "I'm planning to retire as soon as the camp is shut down, but that will take about a year as I see it. We are finding homes and jobs for most of our clients. Then we will see about removing the last buildings, until all that is left of Manzanar are the little rivers, the gardens, and the baseball diamonds."

"I'll be staying with Mr. Merritt," said Russell, "to help him with the closing. Then I plan to move to Arizona where Joyce will be finishing college and starting law school. She says she has found some places where I can find work I like. And Joyce..."

"I am liking Arizona," she said. "It is my third lifetime. First I was a child in Los Angeles, then I was a prisoner in Mr. Merritt's prison, and now I am a college student. I think Russell will like Arizona but he will also like coming here to visit, and I think I will like that, too."

Walt stood. "Joyce, we're so happy to find somebody who will put up with Russell."

They all clapped.

He continued, "I'm going back to the Merchant Marine. Well, I have to, anyway, because I signed up for the duration, and it's a requirement. But I want this to be my future too. I want to be part of a system that will send a ship out to find me if I get lost!" More laughter. "I'm looking forward to the time when I have command of a ship. It's just the right job for me."

George stood next to his friend. "I'm going back down with Walt, and we're both going to finish our tours with the Merchant Marine. But while I'm doing that, I'm thinking about what Dana and I will want to do together. You know we've been writing letters to each other, ever since my first visit here. We're both happy to have a good partner to make plans with, and that's what we'll be doing."

Dana, blushing, stood and held George's hand. "I have had a great adventure as a pilot. If I could continue, I would. But they won't take women pilots. So, George and I are going to figure out a different idea for what we want to do. I'm thinking a combined bakery and airplane school would be a great idea. Or, there are small air strips all over the country. Maybe one of them needs people to run them, light the runways when necessary, pump gas to visiting pilots, that sort of thing. We're going to be making plans for the next couple of months, till the WASP closes down."

Next to rise was Howard. "Guess what? I just found out today that I've been accepted at *college*! I got the letter this morning! It's a school in Arizona that also has a terrific baseball team. I hope Russell and Joyce don't mind that I'll be close enough to bug them from time to time."

Russell whooped. "I knew you could do it! I just knew it!"

Cliff, on the other side of Dana, leaned over toward Howard. "Good going, little brother!"

"And do you have any special plans, Cliff?" Barbara asked.

"Nothing to speak of. I'm still working for Caltech. And the Navy."

When it became clear that he planned to say no more, the conversation moved on.

Hilde Crawford stood. "I thank you for being so kind to us and to Grandma. Your friendship made it possible for us to stay here, and for Grandma to find out that there were people who actually like her!"

"Once we realized she isn't so fierce," Howard put in.

"What is this, fierce?" Grandma asked.

"Never mind." Hilde continued. "We have renewed our lease on the bakery, so we will be here. If George wants a job, we would be happy to have him, at least part time, while he and Dana make their plans."

"What about you, Len?" Alf asked. "Any changes?"

"I'm giving up the mine works," Len answered. "I've been watching all of the changes, and I realize nothing much has touched me directly. I never meant to live my life like that. So, I'm going to my people. The Paiute and Shoshone need help from those of us who can cope with the white man's world. I've got a job at the tribal office, starting after the holidays."

"We'll miss you, Len," Sara said.

"I'm not that far away, Sara. You'd be surprised. We Paiutes have a long history of being pretty invisible, but you'll be seeing a lot of me."

They began to say their good byes, gathering up leftovers and dishes, making plans for the next day. Alf and Len stood on the front porch. Ralph Merritt and his wife joined them, thanking them again for including them.

"I didn't want to mention it, but I'm so curious," Len told him. "What feelings are you taking away from your time at Manzanar?"

"I'm still sorting them out," Merritt answered. "Frankly, they are so mixed that I give up each time I spend more than a few minutes looking back. I believed then and I believe now that it was a terrible idea, completely un-American, to uproot an entire group of people identified only by their race and imprison them.

"Joyce was right, by the way. It *was* a prison. I agreed to work there because I felt that I would do a better job than many of the other people they might choose. At least I could see them as people, not as enemy aliens.

"We kept them safe. I think many of them would have been in danger if they had stayed in their neighborhoods. But it meant that their entire lives were disrupted."

He held up his hand.

"Here's where I just get stopped. What if I hadn't signed up for the job? What if I had told them, this is not right, it's un-American, I can't be party to it. What then?"

Alf said, "You said it yourself: somebody with a real hate, or somebody not capable enough, might take the job and the result at Manzanar would be ten, a hundred, times worse."

"And that's the best answer I can come up with, myself. But it's not good enough. If we all took the ugly jobs just because we could make them less bad, then we fail our country. It's not only that we made these ten thousand—*ten thousand!* —people suffer, lose their homes, their cars, their jobs. It's that we did it in the name of the government of the United States. It wasn't Ralph Merritt's prison; it was Franklin Roosevelt's prison! For years, maybe decades to come, people will talk about how we were no better than the Axis, rounding up people and putting them behind fences.

"But how could I not take it? I had no way of convincing the President that he was wrong, and I am still not entirely sure, myself. In all the craziness, decisions had to be made in a hurry. We all did the best we could. I guess."

He sighed. "I'll carry that with me for the rest of my life and that's a big disappointment for me. All the things I've tried to do, this was the biggest and I think I shouldn't have done it."

Soon the only guests left were Spence and Molly. Barbara and Tony joined her parents on the porch.

"Every time I see Walt, I feel such a mixture of emotions," Barbara said. "I want him to stay home now. I want to keep him safe. But I know I can't. He has found his best path and we have to respect that. But it is so hard."

Molly squeezed her hand. "But he's alive and reasonably healthy, although I think he is much too skinny. We Richardsons seem to have got through the worst part of the war without too much damage."

Tony added, "We're all here. We are not rich, never made much of a profit from this war, like the people they talk about, these war profiteers. We can say that as a family we more than did our share for the war effort."

"Although nobody will know that," Spence growled. "No medals, no flag in the window, no parades. Not that I ever wanted any of that. But the children should be honored."

"They know what they have done. They'll have such stories to tell their children," Molly said.

"And we will have grandchildren!" Barbara said. "Isn't Joyce just the prettiest thing? Did you see Russell light up every time he looked at her?"

"We're pretty fortunate people, all right. I'm glad we stayed in the valley," Tony said. "Molly, did you know Barbara has started new apple trees from the Manzanar root stock? We'll have a good year, I'm sure.

"Now, who's for ice cream?"

44422989R00193

Made in the USA
San Bernardino, CA
14 January 2017